NIGHT OF THE LIVING PROOF
Neighborlee Book 5

Michelle L. Levigne

www.YeOldeDragonBooks.com

Ye Olde Dragon Books
P.O. Box 30802
Middleburg Hts., OH 44130

www.YeOldeDragonBooks.com

2OldeDragons@gmail.com

Copyright © 2020 by Michelle L. Levigne
ISBN 13: 978-1-952345-10-4

Published in the United States of America
Publication Date: January 1, 2021

Cover Art Copyright by Ye Olde Dragon Books 2020

Welcome to Neighborlee, Ohio.

Where? Somewhere on the North Coast of Ohio, south of Cleveland, right off I-71, north of Medina, in the heart of Cuyahoga County.

What is it? That's a little harder to explain.

Neighborlee is a place you need to experience.

The most important thing you need to understand: Neighborlee is *magic*. Some people say the town is alive. It exists to protect the weird and wonderful (and sometimes a little bit scary) from the cold, practical, material world.

More important, Neighborlee protects the outside world from the weird and wonderful that come to visit … and sometimes come to stay.

First stop: Divine's Emporium, a four-story Victorian house sitting on a hill overlooking the Metroparks. Whatever you really need, you can find at Divine's. Even if you don't know what you're looking for when you walk in the door. The shop is often bigger inside than it is outside. Angela is the proprietor. Please stay on the first floor. You don't want to find out what is hidden and locked safely away upstairs. Like Aslan, Angela is good, but that doesn't mean she's safe. And neither are the secrets and wonders and doorways to other worlds that she protects … and keeps securely locked.

Come in and explore. Meet the people who help Angela guard Neighborlee. Share their adventures of magic and wonder, danger and sacrifice. You never know who or what you'll run into as you walk the streets and listen to the stories of their lives.

Chapter One

I spoke too soon.

Yes, getting the DVD from our missing parents raised spirits for my brothers, Harry and Pete, and for me. Despite the fact Charlie and Rainbow Zephyr were still missing somewhere near the Bermuda Triangle, I anticipated a great Christmas after all. We crowded into my office and put the disk into my computer and skimmed the document files to see what they had sent us.

"Way too much to sift through." Harry grinned and stepped back from looking over my shoulder at my computer screen. "It's Christmas Eve, after all."

"Don't even say it," I said, cutting off Pete when he batted those unfairly long eyelashes at me. I could see in his eyes what he was going to suggest.

"Say what?" My littlest brother got up from where he knelt next to my wheelchair and gave me an innocent look that hadn't worked in years. Not since he grew taller than me. Then he frowned. "Lanie, you feeling okay?" He gestured at my neck.

Not a good distraction tactic. Still, I didn't say what I wanted to say: if we didn't go to the Christmas Eve service, our parents would know, no matter where they were. The words caught in my throat, because the next logical thing to say was that they would find a way back to us, just to scold us for missing that tradition.

We wanted them to come back. Ordinarily, I would want Harry or Pete to respond that if skipping church would bring our parents back, then yes, definitely, let's skip church. But it wouldn't be funny. There's nothing worse than a tried-and-true family joke going flat and turning nauseating. So I kept quiet.

"You're scratching a lot." Harry caught hold of my hand.

I was surprised to find my hand on my neck, and my skin was hot. He was right, I had to admit. I had been so busy with my catchup Christmas baking all day, I didn't notice until now that I had been scratching my neck. How long? Hours now?

"Lanie … you've got hives." He rested his fingers on the side of my neck where it met my shoulder, on the right side.

"I don't get hives," I said, and brushed his hand away. As soon as I said it, the itchy sensation multiplied.

"You've got them now. Go look in the mirror."

"Hives mean allergies, and I don't have allergies. Just like I don't get colds. It's about all the superhero invulnerability God saw fit to give me." I returned Harry's glare for a few seconds, then finally gave in and wheeled down the hall to the bathroom.

I hate it when my brothers are right about stupid things like that. I had a red, thumb-sized blotch on my neck. A few smaller blotches spread out from it, just big enough I couldn't cover the whole area with my hand.

From there, the day went downhill fast.

We had no calamine lotion and no allergy medicine of any kind. Granted, I had never needed it, being a semi-pseudo-superhero with some immunity to colds and allergies, but my brothers did, and they were living with me. I knew I had bought an entire shopping cart's worth of cold and allergy medicine, but not a bottle or pill remained in the house.

Harry ran up to the grocery store to find something for me while I dug through the kitchen cupboards, looking for some of Angela's miracle-working teas. Something to cleanse my blood and ease the itching. Nothing seemed appropriate. I called Felicity to see if she had anything in her medicine cabinet, but she had already left for Christmas Eve dinner with Jake. I called Angela, thinking I could catch Harry while he was out and ask him to swing by Divine's Emporium and pick it up for me. Angela's phone was busy, for the first time since I had ever known her.

A text from London, asking for a face-to-face, sent me to my office. When an Artificial Intelligence makes contact, it's generally wise to respond ASAP. When I opened the communication link she had installed on my computer, static filled the screen for a few seconds. Her face, so much like Doni Halliday's, took a few seconds to resolve.

"Hi, Lanie," she said, and even her voice was full of static. "I'm trying to find Kurt. Do you know where he is?"

London should have been able to just contact him through his phone, or at least activate the GPS in his phone, and track him.

"Why do you need him?" I asked, while my brain scattered in several directions, trying to figure out why a computer-based intelligence couldn't find him, with all the resources of the World Wide Web.

"There are all sorts of power fluctuations at Eden, and the experimental security system he installed is—" For a second, the screen froze.

I had a momentary vision of some vicious hacker finally finding a way to erase London Holiday and her AI boyfriend, Sherwood. Athena Longfellow had shared with me over the summer one of her lingering fears: any damage to London and Sherwood would somehow have real, physical effects on the people who had served as their templates, her cousin Doni Halliday and Doni's boyfriend, Cosmo.

"Found him. I should have realized the fluctuations were blocking anything within the boundaries of Eden." London smiled. "Sorry for scaring you."

"But?"

London was enough like Doni, I could read emotions in the pale blue eyes on the computer screen. She had ideas she didn't like.

"During the whole mess with those boys, we were picking up some reverberations, energy fluctuations throughout the town. We've been busy the last week or two, tracking the anomalies in the power grid. Sherwood thinks they aren't actually in the power grid but ..." London shrugged and gave a thumbs-down gesture.

Pointing down, under the foundations of Neighborlee. To the interdimensional entity we referred to as the snake?

"So whatever or whoever was behind them attacking me, those people are still around?"

"We don't know. Except that everything seems focused on Eden and the ground under the building. It's making the CO_2 detectors go off, and the smoke detectors. The security system and the heating go out, and the ventilation system tries to generate tornadoes. If I didn't think Gina would have a heart attack, I'd pop up on her screen and tell her not to worry, we're keeping watch." London shrugged, and that somber flatness of her mouth softened, hinting at a mischievous glint.

She was right. With all the stress preparing to drop on Gina, the day after Christmas, she didn't need the mind-blowing strain of accepting that the social media personality London Holiday was the first real electronic sentience. Better to let Gina get through all the craziness of the New Year's Eve blow-out party at Eden, crash and recover, before dropping that little revelation on her. If ever.

"Kurt's trying to contact us." The screen flashed and London vanished.

Okay, I did not need those worries. The itching tripled in intensity. I tried calling Angela again. She sounded a little distracted, and I hesitated to ask her who was on the phone before. She asked me if I could contact London or Sherwood. The energy defending Divine's was flickering and she couldn't get her computer to work, to contact them.

"They're both kind of busy. Something's happening at Eden, and underneath it." I gave her most of my conversation with London. "What do you need them to do?"

"I was just on the phone with Bethany. She was supposed to be home by now for Christmas, but her plane was grounded halfway back. She's alone in the Denver airport, and I hoped one of them could access the security cameras and check up on her. I hope I'm being silly, but … well, Bethany has very good instincts and she feels like somebody is watching her."

"Maybe somebody recognized her from those snack cake commercials?"

That got a little chuckle from her. I promised I would send a message to London, and finally remembered why I had called: tea for my hives.

"You don't get hives," Angela said, all humor leaving her voice. She promised she would have several remedies for me, waiting for Harry to pick up. She warned me I would be sleepy if I used both the salve and the tea.

I itched and dozed my way through Christmas Eve. I had no taste for the traditional nibbling goodies. We didn't go to church, and so we didn't go to the Longfellows' house to spend the evening with Ford, Charlotte and their son, Jinx. Athena and Doni had plans to spend Christmas Eve with their boyfriends' families, and then Wallace and Cosmo would spend the day with the Longfellows. Kurt was supposed to come over Christmas day, one of our traditions, but he was at Eden tracking down power fluctuations and equipment malfunctions until past midnight, and had to go back in the morning.

I woke up late Christmas day with a splitting headache. Along with the hives that kept spreading, despite Angela's tea, my joints ached. I spent most of Christmas day sprawled on the sofa, sipping tea and dozing. The boys got to gorge on all the goodies: shrimp, cheese ball and crackers, smokies in barbecue sauce, wings, egg rolls. My stomach did backflips just thinking about the food I was missing. Felicity and Jake elected to have a quiet, romantic Christmas day at her place, rather than joining us. I didn't blame them. I made a bet with myself she would get a ring for Christmas.

My big mistake was combining Angela's salve and tea with antihistamines. I spent the day in a haze, broken at irregular intervals by strange dreams that kept jerking me up out of sleep, trying to fly away from something nasty. My strongest impression through all those twisting, looping, slimy dreams was of something trying to drill or melt or pound its way through a shield around Eden. Sometimes it turned into the Wishing Ball, and Divine's Emporium was inside it.

Friday morning, I woke up before dawn with the worst dream yet. In it, Bethany and Athena were having a sleepover at Divine's, like they used to do when they were little. The house filled with shadows that reached out tentacles from the walls and tried to grab both girls. That frightened me, because Bethany had made it home for Christmas just before midnight. She and her father, Ben, had spent Christmas day with Angela, who was Bethany's godmother. I was worried because we had kept her ignorant of her heritage as the daughter of a guardian. Stephanie had died defending Neighborlee from the snake trying make our town its doorway to invade Earth. We had honored her wishes that Bethany not become a guardian. What if the snake or whatever that ugly, persistent enemy really was, had made Bethany a target *because* she was ignorant and untrained?

Yeah, right, like Divine's Emporium wasn't the safest place in the entire town, if the snake attacked?

Yet Athena and Doni had been sleeping over at Divine's when the snake attacked them. Athena had stepped through a wall into another dimension, tricked into thinking Doni was in danger. There were weak spots, even at Divine's. Stephanie's death and my broken back proved the energy defending our town was weakening. Continually fading on us.

I slathered more salve on my hives, waited until it was nearly dry, got dressed, and headed for Divine's Emporium. My dreams likely meant I had been eavesdropping on the enemy's intentions. The guardians needed to consult with Angela. Felicity had sensed something was wrong, and she was awake and dressed and ready to go when I came outside. She met me at my Jeep. I wanted so much to hear how her Christmas with Jake went. The fact that she wasn't shimmering with excitement meant she didn't get that engagement ring. Instead, she made me tell her about my dreams.

Kurt's truck was sitting in the lot next to Divine's when we arrived. I pulled up and parked at the curb in front of the gate, behind a now-familiar sedan with a discrete military sticker in the window. A powdered sugar snow was falling as I slid out of the driver's seat and braced myself on the door. My head throbbed when I prepared to pull my wheelchair out of the car with telekinesis. I couldn't do it with my arms because I still ached in all my joints. Felicity told me to wait, and she came around to take care of it for me.

While she unfolded my chair, I got that shivery-creepy feeling down my back that I always equated with someone nasty watching me. I looked around, but the snow thickened and I couldn't see anyone on the sidewalk on either side of the street. For the first time, I was not glad there were empty lots next to Divine's and across the street. The lights from the nearest houses looked miles away. The big olive-and-gold Victorian house looked a little creepy in the growing haze of snow.

Kurt and Col. Hayward came out to meet us. The Colonel took charge of pushing my chair and Kurt walked around my Jeep twice, scanning it with one of his gizmos. I didn't want to know what he was looking for, any more than I wanted to know why he thought he should scan for something nasty.

"You don't have allergies," Hayward said, once we were all inside. He was still behind me, and I turned enough to see him frowning at the back of my neck.

"Now I do," I said. Then I saw Angela standing in the doorway of the main room. She looked like she hadn't slept, and she had her peacock shawl wrapped around her, over her usual blue handkerchief print dress. "I've had invasion dreams. All day yesterday. The snake is moving."

"The defenses of the town are ..." Angela shrugged and took a deep breath. Exhaled. "Wobbling is the closest description. Fluctuating, strong and weak, badly enough to cause discord with the music of the shop's defenses. It was heavy Christmas Eve, faded during the day, then resumed once Ben and Bethany left. I spent most of the night bringing everything back into tune." She held out a hand to me. "Franklin and I have been discussing your problem."

Kurt was heading down the hall ahead of me, and he glanced back, cocked an eyebrow, met my gaze, then shifted to Hayward, who was still behind me. My brain was working slower than normal before I caught on. So that was Hayward's first name. Franklin Hayward. Since he was also a Lost Kid, I wondered who had found him and where, and the reasons for naming him.

My woolgathering got me to the main room of the shop. Angela had assembled a little operating room, with tweezers and antiseptic, witch hazel, a pot of her herbal salve, and a few doctor's instruments, including a scalpel. It all waited on a thick white cloth on the little bistro table where we usually sat to drink chai and discuss guardian matters. I was in no shape to either force my unsteady legs to get me up the stairs, or work with Kurt to fly me up there. Just the thought of using my telekinesis made my head throb again.

"Whoever took the Parker boy was prepared," Hayward said, once everyone had taken seats and Angela started washing my neck before examining it. "They were ready for failure. If as you speculated the three boys broke free of their handlers, maybe they were closing in. They could have witnessed the takedown on Tuesday. One telling factor in the report I got, which was more extensive than the one your friend, Stanzer got ..." He glanced at Angela, who was standing behind me.

"What?" I said, trying not to snap, when the look he gave her was full of communication. I very much hated feeling I had been made a little kid again who needed to be protected.

"Parker was itching and had red patches on his neck. Those false military walked in with their paperwork and took custody of him before the doctor arrived to examine him."

"False military?" Kurt said. "You're sure?"

"I have contacts in all the branches. Those people who took the boy were not military, no matter how secretive."

"So you're safe," I said. "Nobody will turn you in, reveal what you're doing here."

"We can only hope," Hayward said with a slight nod and a weary, thin smile.

"I think you're right." Angela rested two fingers on the right side of my neck. "There's something in Lanie's neck, and the hives are an allergic reaction, resisting the invader."

"They shot me with what … a tracker?" My neck burned where she touched me. Hopefully just psychosomatic.

"I'm thinking drugs. Reinforcing their mind control on the boys," Hayward said. "The question is if they intentionally shot you, or you got in the way when they were shooting Parker."

"Can you get it out?"

There was blood and Angela had to use of that scalpel, after much digging with those tweezers with needle-fine tips. She used something to numb my neck, but I felt a tingling-humming down in my bones, the longer she probed. I would have been more comfortable if Felicity hadn't been holding my hand. She squeezed harder, the longer it took to get the dart out. That and her little flinches made me want to scream and punch someone.

The worst part was having to wait to hear what Angela and Kurt had done all Christmas day. I would have appreciated some distraction, but Angela needed to concentrate.

What she pulled from my neck was as long as the first joint of my pinkie, thinner than a hair, with a brief greenish glint, reflecting the light, as she turned it. Hayward put it in one of the wooden boxes Angela used to store things on the fourth floor.

"Ah, I'm sorry." An unfamiliar voice came from the hallway.

A shimmering kind of sound, more felt along my skin than heard, accompanied the creaky-silvery voice. I nearly jerked, as Angela pressed a thick gauze pad cold with salve over the hole she had dug in my neck. From the corner of my eye I saw a skinny old man with a halo of white hair around his pink bald head, wearing a dark purple jogging suit. He leaned into the doorway, blinking his huge green eyes and giving us all a sheepish grin.

"I received your call for assistance after some delay, my

dear." He stepped into the room. He had an enormous doctor's bag, also in dark purple. "Is there anything I can do? I must apologize for arriving too late to handle the dirty work for you."

"Thank you, Doctor." Angela pressed tape over the gauze, fixing the pad into place, then patted my shoulder. "I would appreciate a more experienced eye. I hope you won't take it the wrong way, but I do pray this doesn't fall under your expertise."

"Not at all, not at all." He stepped over behind me. Cool, thin fingers touched my neck, but didn't peel up the gauze.

A silvery kind of song spun through my blood — the only way I can describe the sensation. It washed away the dregs of the itching. The throbbing in my sinuses turned into a tickling sensation, then vanished.

"You'll be glad to know you didn't need my help dealing with the consequences," the doctor said after a few moments. He sniffed loudly. "Ah, I see Delphinia has graced you with some of her miraculous salve. You're in good hands, young lady. Very wise, coming to Angela in matters of poison."

"Poison?" Kurt yelped.

I turned to face them all. Angela was giving the doctor a scolding look. Col. Hayward's concern became a scowl, and I felt a moment of fear for whoever got the full blast of that anger. Then I felt good, because he was angry for me.

"How do you know it's poison?"

"Oh, not to kill. No, to debilitate." The doctor stopped, mouth open as if about to say something else. He narrowed his eyes at me, then held out both hands to me, palms up. "Indulge me?"

I hesitated, then glanced at Angela. She frowned at the doctor, but she glanced at me and nodded. I put my hands in his. Again, that singing feeling. The numb patches in my legs and my back woke up to tingles that burned for a few seconds, then faded entirely. I felt like I could walk up the stairs to Angela's apartment without holding onto the railing.

That sporadic sense of being whole, of my legs being reliable, had been missing since fall. When the doctor asked how I felt now, I told him that.

"All right, you want to fill the rest of us in?" Kurt said.

Sometimes I really loved it when he slid into his protective big brother role.

"Angela's theory is correct. Something has been slowly draining the defensive energy enclosing the town and supporting the wellbeing of its defenders. The same parasite, if you will permit such a crude term—the same parasite also taints the energy that remains."

"Meaning Lanie should have been healed, but the taint is having the opposite effect?" Hayward said.

It struck me as odd, a violation of some unspoken natural laws, that this stern military man understood what I suspected came under the heading of magic.

"So if we can get rid of the parasite and stop it poisoning the energy ..." Felicity's eyes narrowed. She tipped her head to one side, studying me. "Eventually she could walk again, and fly again?"

"Such a determination would require intensive study from those who are more qualified, with centuries more experience than I possess," the doctor said. "But yes, in theory. Here's the frightening aspect. I sense some inimical intelligence attached to the poison. If it was left in place long enough, it would eventually have overcome the natural defenses of heart and soul and mind, establishing a foothold for some very nasty invaders. And the smell, the taste of that power ..." He sighed, and his eyes got big, sad, like he might tear up in a moment. "I am sorry, my dear, but it is another face of the ancient malevolence."

Angela let out a soft, slow, deep breath and settled into the chair facing mine. A shaky little smile twisted her mouth.

"You know, I'm almost relieved to know that."

"One enemy instead of several?" Hayward said.

"Exactly."

"Okay." I probably shouldn't have been speaking what leaped into my head, but my brain felt clear for the first time in more than a day. "So the creeps who sent Jay and the other guys after me are the same ones who have been sucking out the energy that defends Neighborlee? And maybe they're the same creeps who are causing my dreams? So maybe these guys are working with the snake?"

"No." The doctor shook his head, just twice, the movement sharp enough to make his fuzzy hair whip around. "That ancient enemy is an entirely different song and aroma. What attacked you, my dear young guardian, is entirely of terrestrial origins." He sighed and seemed to deflate about two sizes. "However ..."

"It's trying to contact the snake hiding underneath Neighborlee, isn't it?" Felicity said, nearly on a whisper. She offered a weak little smile, and Kurt slid an arm around her shoulders. "I really hate it when I remember dreams I forgot. There's a big, ugly ... thing, trying to make contact, like Morse code, and someone heard it."

That morning we started referring to the snake as Big Ugly. The new label reduced the squirming feeling and the mental image of *Dune* sandworms bursting up from the floor, with buzz saws for teeth.

My phone rang. Harry had just gotten back from an early morning delivery and worried as soon as he saw my Jeep missing. By the time I assured him and Pete that I was fine and at Divine's, the doctor had made his farewells. Funny, but I didn't hear the door open and close. I didn't hear it open when he arrived, either.

We all trooped upstairs, and I found out I was wrong again. By the fifth step, my legs went wobbly. I hauled myself up, gripping the bannister, and Kurt linked arms with me to steady me. We settled into Angela's apartment. Felicity helped her throw together a late breakfast for all of us while Kurt reported on his Christmas day. London and Sherwood had traveled Eden's electrical system, analyzing all the points affected by the power fluctuations. Kurt followed them with some sensor equipment he cobbled together and kept altering and refining. Their work would have been complicated by the everyday traffic if Eden hadn't been closed for Christmas. Every time an alarm went off, Kurt could get there to investigate without having to work around people or explain what he was doing.

However, the lack of people added to the mystery, because there was no one to blame for nasty tricks. Pieces of equipment seemed to vanish from the system, then reappear. No indication how sensors and power feeds had disconnected and then reconnected. Everything calmed down about mid-afternoon, but Kurt and the two AI's stayed on patrol, circling the building, bouncing ideas back and forth, recording the energy patterns, until late afternoon.

"Even though everything is quiet now, once Gina opens the

doors and all those kids on Christmas break pour in, all those minds and all that energy could trigger something." Kurt rubbed his eyes with the heels of his hands. "London and Sherwood are on watch. They'll alert me if anything weird resumes. Still, they can't do much except be an advance warning system. Once we're done here, I'm going out on patrol. Drive around town for a while, try to figure out if maybe whatever was attacking Eden moved on or it's catching its breath before another attack."

Bottom line: Neighborlee was essentially the patch to reinforce the weak spot where multiple dimensions touched. Divine's Emporium was essentially a gate or doorway, to establish some control over the opening. The energy of the doorway acted like a beacon for nasty things like the snake. We were overdue for another attempt to break through. Last time, we had been lucky. Athena Longfellow and Doni Halliday had awakened to their destinies as guardians, inherited from their grandfather, Ford. We needed reinforcements to train up to join us, even though none of us would have wished such a weight to land on the girls, who were in middle school and high school at the time.

The snake or something else trying to break through had taken advantage of Athena's computer genius and some weird, otherworldly technology she had found at Divine's Emporium. London Holiday had been born from that merging of technology and magic, and we were still reaping the benefits.

We had to consider ourselves lucky that the newest members of the guardians were Ford Longfellow's granddaughters. The feud between the Grandstones and Longfellows protected the girls from being recruited by our town's self-proclaimed royalty. We had learned some depressing bits of Neighborlee history in the last few weeks. Not only was the first Grandstone a Lost Kid, but he and his descendants had been wooing other Lost Kids to the dark side through the decades, destroying their potential as guardians. Kurt and Felicity and I had grown up with the current generation of Grandstones. Our school days feuds conditioned us to resist any attempts to recruit us as Grandstone minions.

"London and Sherwood," Hayward murmured. He had an odd, crooked little smile, and shook his head slowly. "I still find the whole story and situation hard to believe."

"That's saying something, considering all we've seen and

done over the years," Angela said with a chuckle.

"How can they defend against the snake? That's what I find hard to wrap my mind around. Magic and technology don't mix. Or they shouldn't."

"I don't really care, as long as it works," Kurt said. "They can sense this energy attacking the town. It's moving constantly, but most of the assaults, the waves, are directed at Eden."

"Wait a second," Felicity said. "How much do you know about London and the whole thing with Doni and Athena and her computer class? It hasn't even been a year."

"Angela keeps me apprised of our up-and-coming young warriors," Hayward said, with a sideways glance at Angela.

"Just how long have you been keeping tabs on her?" slipped out of my mouth before I really thought. Just a hunch. There were reams of communication in that momentary glance they shared. I really hated that sense of being relegated to the kiddie table while the adults had the truly interesting conversation.

Hayward chuckled, but he didn't meet my gaze. "Long enough to be proud of her. And tempted sometimes to shake her until she learns to be a little more careful."

"As careful as you and Portia were, when you were her age?" Angela murmured. She gave him a sideways look and I swear, for a second there, I thought Hayward might blush.

I let the subject drop, feeling queasy as that hunch hinted maybe I didn't want to know how exactly Hayward knew Athena's mother. Both of them had grown up in Neighborlee, although I thought Hayward was five or ten years older than Portia Longfellow.

"Please continue." Hayward nodded to Kurt. "There are some errands I need to complete before I leave town, to ensure our mutual adversaries don't connect us."

Kurt related how London and Sherwood grew more adept at sensing the build-up of energies, alerting him, so he could refine his prototype sensor. Eventually, the physical alarm systems at Eden stopped going off, and the intensity of the energy spikes or enemy probes or whatever they were dialed back. Kurt soon managed to arrive at the target spot before the attack happened.

"It was like my being there kind of slapped a patch on the fabric," Kurt said. "What Stephanie used to do, but I didn't consciously do anything. London and Sherwood said they were trying something, mending with energy, but they couldn't guarantee they did any good."

"You did some good," Angela said, gazing down into her half-empty cup. "I could feel it. Just being physically there helped reweave the damaged spots. The snake was looking for weak spots, to escape the place where it languishes, caught between worlds ..." She glanced up, her gaze meeting ours. "At least, that is the image I carry in my head. I could be wrong."

Hayward snorted and when she looked at him, he winked at her. That little bit of skepticism and teasing seemed to put more oxygen back into the room. I certainly felt better.

"Why Eden?" Felicity said. "Should we cancel New Year's? All the people gathered for the New Year's lock-in, all that energy, the emotions, collected in one spot. It would be a good target. Is there some magic in the turning from one year to another?"

"So much of what happens in our strange little town is predicated on the power of belief." Angela slowly put down her cup and reached to rest her hand on Felicity's wrist. "People believe strange things will happen at Halloween, so they do. People believe bizarre things are possible on Senior Prank Night, and lo and behold, they accomplish feats they wouldn't even dream of trying the rest of the year. We *make* magic happen, because we *believe* it will. So yes, if as the doctor theorizes, something is trying to contact our enemy, New Year's could provide energy enough to break the barrier, unlock the door."

"So ..." Kurt shrugged. "How do we cancel the lock-in?"

"You don't," Hayward said. "All your effort yesterday drained the—" He grinned, a little fierce. "Big Ugly. It drained energy that thing needs to try to break free. I'll be outside, keeping watch, waiting for whoever took the Parker boy to act. You'll be inside. We're warned, and that gives us the advantage." His eyes narrowed. "The other two boys will be targets. They could have been power sources for the effort, and Parker was the focus, the sighting mechanism. They both have Lost Boys in their ancestry."

"I will talk to their parents, if you want to take charge of removing them from danger," Angela said.

"But where can you take them so they'll be safe?" Kurt said.

"I have some ideas ..." Hayward took a deep breath, and his

gaze seemed to focus a thousand miles away. "I was almost taken by someone, when I was sixteen. Another boy in my cottage was twelve and waking up to his talent. He could do light shows, fracturing the light around him. I felt it when he used his gift. We were just starting to develop a partnership between us, with me offering advice and doing research." A raw little chuckle escaped him. "Like what the three of you did with the comic books. I wish I had thought of them, when I was your age. Anyway … someone came out of nowhere and tried to snatch him as we were walking home from school. I fought them. They took me because I was making noise, drawing attention. The next thing I knew, there were two old men blocking the road out of town and they …"

He shrugged and leaned back and rubbed at his face. Hayward suddenly looked exhausted.

"I don't know what those two old men did, but they rescued us. They told me there was a war coming. The other boy had no choice, but I did. I could come with them, or I could go back to the orphanage and pursue my plans for the military when I graduated. Kind of startled me that they knew, because I had only talked to a recruiter, hadn't told anyone. Not even Mrs. Silvestri."

"Bet she knew anyway," Felicity said softly. "Bet she knew before you did."

"Probably," he said, with a brief grin. "I chose the life I knew, but those two old men found a way to send me messages every once in a while. Warnings when they thought the other men, their rivals, spent too much time around Neighborlee. They've helped me defend our town through the years, warning when their rivals were interested in people and might endanger them."

"Those warnings are why Portia and Lenore Longfellow both chose to make lives outside Neighborlee," Angela said. "Both of them had no real abilities beyond brilliant minds and sensitivity to things and events most people never noticed."

I almost asked if she meant the winkies, but that would just cause a detour in the explanation. I hadn't mentioned the winkies to Felicity or Kurt. Too much else going on lately.

"They chose to move outside the energy and shield, to make themselves less sensitive, less prone to strange reactions that would gain the wrong kind of attention. To protect their family."

"But Portia left Athena here …" I caught a very distinct flinch from Hayward. "She knew Athena could be a guardian and have gifts? She left her here, where she would be safe?"

"Guardians are called upon to make many sacrifices for our town."

"Gee, and all these years I thought she was kind of ditzy, one of those brilliant people who can't handle reality." I watched Hayward as I spoke. He didn't react to my criticizing Portia, which kind of killed the hazy suspicion growing in my head. "Does Athena know? Do Ford and Charlotte know?"

"Yes, and someday Athena will know and understand," Angela said with a sigh.

"So we were right all along?" Kurt said. "Two groups of people watching us and taking kids. Are the two old men the good guys?" He let out a bitter bark of laughter when Hayward just shrugged. "Yeah, kind of childish, wanting clear labels. Good guys and bad guys."

"If it's the rivals attacking the town, then yeah, the old men are the good guys," Felicity said.

"How can we be sure who sent those boys after you?" Hayward said. "Here's something to think about. Whoever was pulling the strings, they have high and powerful connections. According to my sources, all three boys were withdrawn from the military more than a year ago." His expression turned wintry when we reacted to that bit of news.

Chapter Two

"But Stanzer's sources said Toby just got out, and the other two guys are still in," Kurt said. "Okay, yeah, his sources are good but yours are better."

"Perhaps. For all we know, the two old men have been feeding me information to use me, to create an opening through Neighborlee's defenses." He got up and went to the couch where he had dropped his heavy brown overcoat. "Speaking of information." He pulled a thick manila envelope out of an inside pocket and stood a moment, turning it over in his hands.

"I was able to dig up a little more information on what was going on while your parents were making their preparations. Unusual storm readings. Electro-magnetic fields and meteorological activity off the charts." He offered a flat-lipped little smile that barely affected his lips, let alone his eyes. "I helped them gather up storm data from the last thirty or forty years." He held out the envelope to me. "I can only dig so far. The less I remind the higher-ups I'm a friend of your parents, the better my access to information when it really counts."

"True." I took the envelope and really looked at him.

Why was he here, in Neighborlee, the day after Christmas? Didn't he have anyone? He had mentioned a dead wife, back when he asked us to rescue Pete, after his parents were killed. I assumed they never had any children, since he said he was Pete's only living relative. What would he have done for Christmas, if he hadn't been looking out for us?

He hadn't come in uniform, meaning he was here as a friend, under the military's radar. Hayward risked his own career to shelter us from inquisition. Would I be putting him more at risk by telling him about the DVD Mum and Pop had sent? We hadn't really looked through it yet. What if we needed outside, scientific help, to understand the things our folks entrusted to us?

"I can hear the gears churning," Hayward said, as he settled back in his chair.

"I wouldn't worry until we start smelling burning oil," I said, and got a snort of laughter. I decided. "Mum and Pop sent a DVD with a whole bunch of data. It came Christmas Eve. We haven't started digging yet. Maybe something here will help," I added, tapping the envelope.

"Make multiple copies and hide the original."

"Why?"

"Just in case you didn't convince Parker's puppet masters you weren't a mutant, and someone decides to search your house. You won't lose anything important."

"Do you want a copy? You can follow me home and I'll burn one for you."

"Thank you, Lanie, but the more in the dark you keep me about certain matters, the less pressure on me, when it comes to my duties. I'm glad you trust me, but just knowing the DVD exists might be pushing it. Don't tell me anything, show me anything, until you're desperate for help."

"That bad, huh?"

"Actually, that's the good news." The infuriating stone-face winked at me. "Don't contact me if you find out something. Wait for me to contact you, when it's safe."

"Got it. Thanks." I swallowed hard and wondered if it was safe to call Pastor Rocky and ask the prayer chain to get started passing the word about Mum and Pop again.

"Charlie and Rainbow Zephyr have the kind of luck you only see in the movies. I wouldn't worry about them too much."

"They're my parents. Of course I'm going to worry."

"Something would be wrong if you didn't. I'm just saying, don't get an ulcer or lose any sleep. They'll turn up one day, and everything will go back to normal." A snort of laughter escaped him. "As normal as anything ever is in Neighborlee."

I shivered. Until that moment, I had been rather calm about Mum and Pop, sure that whatever had happened, they had landed on their feet and they would come home with new, weird stories to tell.

Now, for some reason I couldn't pinpoint, I was scared for my folks.

Hayward drained his cup and set it down. "If I'm going to get those boys out of harm's way, I need to get moving. False paperwork to arrange, and defenses to set up. I will be back in time to stand guard outside the town." He touched the brim of a non-existent hat in salute to Angela as he got to his feet. She chuckled softly, the sound ending in a sigh. He snatched up his coat from her couch. We were all quiet until he pulled the door closed behind him.

"Well, despite feeling as if we have been talking all day, the business day has just begun." Angela smiled around the circle at us. "Tomorrow night, after I close up, we'll have dinner and share whatever we learn between now and then, all right?"

I laughed, when Felicity and I were in my Jeep less than twenty minutes later. None of us asked what Angela wanted us to learn. We didn't really need to ask. We were to do like we always did as guardians: keep our eyes and ears open, think hard, and find what wasn't normal. The problem was, "normal" for Neighborlee wasn't exactly equal with "normal" in the rest of the world.

Since I was feeling almost normal myself, I took Felicity home and turned around and headed to the office. There was our shortened, rearranged newspaper schedule to deal with next week, thanks to the holiday landing on a delivery day two weeks in a row.

~~~~~

There ought to be a law against a workday landing between Christmas and the weekend. I knew what waited for me. The half-awake feeling of the day after a holiday at the newspaper office. Everyone straggling in, fighting the don't-I-get-a-holiday-too pokiness of the computers. The computers at our office made me believe in animism—inorganic objects having sentience. For instance, in college, my adviser celebrated the first snowfall of the season throwing snowballs at the window of the Humanities dean … until one snowball broke it. When we had a freeze two days later, the only pipes on the entire Willis-Brooks College campus that froze and broke were in his office. Animism.

My brain still churned over our breakfast conference, the poisoned dart in my neck, and the adrenaline rush of having had my life threatened. I could have claimed some invalid status, either physical or emotional. But no, I had responsibility branded into my genetic structure by my parents. Which was weird, considering what hippies they were.
~~~~~

So with heavy heart and slushy gloves, I pushed my chair through the sludge filling the parking lot and up the ramp to the office door. And nearly got brained by the door when Daniel pushed it open just as I was reaching for the handle.

Yes, I had finally gotten into the habit of calling him Daniel instead of the Evil Overlord. Honestly, how could I hate a fellow Trekker who was a not-so-secret-anymore fan of my comedy?

"What are you doing here?" I nearly forgot to grab at my wheels to keep from sliding backwards down the ramp.

Having the new owner show up before the office was officially open for business was odd enough to be suspicious.

"Good morning, Daniel. Did you have a nice Christmas? Yes, thanks, how was yours, Lanie?" He gave me that crooked grin too similar to my brothers' when they were hiding something.

I echoed him obediently, which got a chuckle from him, and wheeled into the building. I paused and wobbled my chair from side to side (getting a wide-eyed look of shock and admiration from Daniel) to knock the sludge off the wheels, onto the entryway mat.

"So what are you doing here? Hiding from something?" I had to ask.

"What makes you say that?" he asked just a little too quickly.

Guilt. Sure sign of it.

"You don't have to be here. You don't need to be here. Especially on a Friday, when there's probably tons of work to do at your own office. Therefore, unusual circumstances." I led the way up the ramp to the level where my desk sat. The *Tattler* office occupied all four units in a row of buildings, with the common walls knocked out years ago. I maneuvered as I always did through the detritus from yesterday's delivery crises. No chance of seeing his face when I made my Sherlockian deductions. Which might have been a mercy stroke for him.

"Maybe I want to see how the newest member of the company is doing, as we get ready to step into a new year?" His usual confident, pleasant expression was back on his nicely square-cut face when I turned around. I had to wonder if I mistrusted him more because he was good-looking than because he took away my beloved sports beat and stuck me with the lovelorn advice column, *Talk to Terry*.

"Well, I know you're not fishing for an invitation to the next Trek party, because you have Mandy's email and phone, so you can ask her."

"I have just about everybody's email and phone." He grinned triumphantly as he settled down at Franny's desk, which faced mine. Nice of him not to sit on my desk and look down on me. That was a power move I always resented. Sometimes I considered ramming people's ankles with the footrests of my chair in response.

"Besides, the ship isn't having a New Year's party."

"So that means you're free?"

Ah ha! We finally touched on the reason for his visit.

"I'm very expensive, and don't you forget it," I shot back.

That got raised eyebrows, then a more relaxed grin as he sat back in Franny's chair. It conveniently tried to collapse into the full recline position, which it was not constructed to do.

While he struggled to get upright again and put Franny's three sweaters back in place on the back of the chair, I fought with the paralyzing realization of the implications of his question. He wasn't asking me to go out with him for New Year's, was he? Why in the world would he do that?

"I'm busy. Working," I said, when he was sitting upright and gazing hopefully at me again.

"Great. New material?"

"Not sure yet."

"Umm, hate to tell you, but New Year's Eve is only five days away. So where are you performing?"

"Eden." It was no good keeping it a secret from him, since it was in yesterday's newspaper. "It's the annual overnight lock-in."

"Lock-in? Like, no one gets out for the entire night? And no one gets in, once the doors are locked?"

The excitement in his voice made me suspicious. I was tempted to reach across the desk and grab his hand, to try to pick up any images in his mind for clues into his reasons and thoughts. However, no way did I want to hold hands with the ex-Evil Overlord. My only option was to ask or guess.

"What do you need an excuse not to do?"

"Not exactly do, but see." Daniel shrugged and put his elbows on the desk and rested his chin in his hands. That made it hard for him to talk, but he managed. "How many times do you have to tell someone you don't want to spend time with them before they stop insisting that you're being silly and immature, and you were meant for each other?"

"Sounds fair to me."

"What's that supposed to mean?" That crease between his eyebrows got so deep, it threatened to bisect his nose. It struck me as kind of endearing, even cute. Panic shot through me a moment later.

"You never took the hint when you were chasing me around town."

"Yeah, but I'm not a bloodsucking gold-digger with a Mata Hari complex."

"Oh, a *female* stalker." I had a hard time smothering laughter, but I tried, just out of a sense of pity.

"Save me. If we're friends at all, give me a good excuse not to be available."

"Just tell her you're not free. You don't have to give her an excuse."

"My mother needs an excuse."

"Your mother is playing matchmaker?"

"Never. She's just having a hard time walking the line between convincing Mata's parents that their daughter is delusional, no relationship exists between us, and starting a war in social media that will probably send the stock of our corporation into the basement. These people play hardball. They've got this attitude that they're entitled to have anything they want. If that means marrying into the corporation, then their darling daughter and I don't have any choice."

A surge of nausea went through me so strongly, I had probably turned green for a few seconds, at least. The way he was talking about the bride-to-be's family sounded like the Grandstone clan. Reggie had publicly embarrassed himself last spring, insisting he and Doni Halliday were sweethearts. Until it finally got through his egotistical rock skull that his elusive bride was less than half his age. It was the Grandstone tactic to marry into power and wealth if they couldn't lie or sue or intimidate to get what they wanted.

"Are you okay?" Daniel asked.

Maybe I *had* turned green, and it wasn't just my imagination?

I reflected back on the few times I had thought how he and Sylvia Grandstone were perfect for each other. Before I got to know him. Maybe I had imagined Sylvia around town the last few weeks because I was being so mean to Daniel? A guilty conscience making me hallucinate? I scrambled to get my brain back on track.

"So your mother is trying to deflect things and having a hard time? Don't suppose you've thought about living in a castle with a really deep moat, stocked with piranha?"

That got a sickly grin from him.

"The really sad and kind of ironic part is that until this mess started, Mom was starting to put the 'when are you going to make me a grandmother?' pressure on me."

"So, what's this mail order bride like?"

He glared at me. Then he must have seen the idiocy of the whole situation, because he kind of deflated and slumped more in his chair and grinned back at me.

"She showed up on *Christmas Eve*, at my folks' place in Cincinnati, claiming she must have missed my last phone call to discuss our 'itinerary,'" he said, making air quotes. "All apologetic about coming so late, since she was so sure I had something wonderful planned for us to do. I went into panic mode when Mom gave me this deer-in-the-headlights look. Especially since we had been talking about some hinted threats from the future in-laws, if their darling little girl's feelings got hurt." Daniel sighed and rubbed his face, then raked his fingers through his hair. "All I could come up with for an excuse was taking over the *Tattler*. Really busy, ignoring everything, keeping my schedule open for emergencies. It was kind of weird how she didn't react when I said *Tattler*, because she's from around here."

I must have made a sound. Trying to hold back the need to heave. My inner alarm of impending doom was so loud I couldn't think clearly for a moment or two. Daniel gave me that worried look, like maybe I had turned green again.

"She was all sweet and forgiving and said she understood, and she would keep New Year's free for us. I managed to sound halfway coherent and told her she was mistaken. I never called her, never emailed her, never made any plans for the holidays, and I already had plans for New Year's."

"Doing what?" I asked, feeling a little sorry for him. Now I suspected something of what he faced, the intimidation and the guilt factors being piled on him during that confrontation. All this despite my very sore brain refusing to accept the horrified conclusions trying to solidify out in the light of day.

"Exactly what she said. I told her it was business-related, so she'd be bored, and we were still making arrangements."

"Wimp."

That got a grin from him. I thought maybe I had done my good deed for the day, helping him fight through the terror trying to smother him. If my still-nebulous suspicions were right.

"Have mercy?"

"Do I get to dump the *Terry* column and take back my sports beat?" I burst out laughing at the look of utter panic on his face. "I guess that's a no. You know something? You make a pretty pathetic Evil Overlord."

"A what?"

"That's what I called you when you swept into the office back in November and rearranged everything on us." I had to explain, since I had let that slip. What was wrong with me? Besides the fact that I actually liked fraternizing with the enemy?

"I'm not evil. I swear."

"Gotta admit, you're okay. For a rich guy. Even human," I added, when that pitiful, begging look came back to his face. "The sign-up is at Eden."

"You are saving my life."

"Mata Hari must be pretty bad, huh?"

"You know how in *Buffy*, the vampires are always so gorgeous and fun, then right before they sink their teeth into you, they turn really ugly? Lanie? Are you okay? You look like you're going to be sick."

"Close." No way was I going to admit we had something else in common. With my luck, he'd invite himself to the annual *Buffy* marathon with Felicity, Mandy, and a few other girls from the ship. I made a mental note to tell them not to tell the Evil Overlord.

"Maybe you should go home. Can you work from home? Can I give you a ride?"

"Aren't you supposed to butter me up before I give you what

you want?" *I should have called in sick.*

"You are my best friend."

"No, I'm your commodore who doesn't want to lose my new communications officer by having you move to Singapore to get away from Mata Hari. How did you ever get linked up with her, that she thought you two were a couple?"

"It started when we were kids. Granddad rented a house here in town one summer." He leaned back, frowning at me.

"What? What did I do?"

"You probably know her. I think she's your age."

"Oh … man …" I fought down another surge of nausea. "Sylvia Grandstone?" I tried to laugh when he nodded. Maybe I hadn't been hallucinating, catching glimpses of Sylvia? "My condolences. I grew up with her. She did the town a big favor when she ran off to Hollywood and hasn't looked back since."

"Warning, she's back in town, gunning for a June wedding."

"I have some friends in the military who can probably get you into Witness Protection."

Daniel's grin looked a little more normal.

"So what were you saying about running into her when you were …" My head throbbed, like when I had tried to catch Harry before he fell through the ceiling in that old building in England. "That was you. That summer, when this rich family rented my folks' farmhouse when they were out of the country, and the Grandstones chased them all over town, trying to glom onto … That was you," I finished weakly, as some other memories slammed into me.

At the top was hearing how Grandfather Sheridan had climbed into a suspicious dark van to confront the two men driving it. Col. Hayward's words about two groups of people spying on the Lost Kids, just a few hours ago, slammed into my brain. Was Daniel's grandfather trying to drive those men away from Neighborlee or having a conference with his allies?

"Yeah." He shrugged. "Did we meet at all? I don't remember …" He gestured at my wheelchair.

"This is a pretty recent occurrence." I patted my wheel as I scrambled for something to say, so I wouldn't blurt my suspicious thoughts. Somehow, now did not seem like the right time to ask if anybody in Daniel's family had any semi-pseudo-superhero powers. "How did you get the courage to come back to Ohio, after that traumatic experience?"

Daniel laughed, and I was even more sure I had done my good deed for the day.

"She never brought up the local connection until she ran me down here. Now it's all hometown memories and childhood sweethearts and destiny." He shuddered.

"I haven't been following her career —"

"What career?"

"Uh huh. Probably why she's following family tradition and trying to rope in a rich husband. That's what Grandstone women do. Marry rich and marry often, and add their deceased or divorced husbands' assets to the family coffers. Or coffin, as the case may be."

Daniel laughed at that, but the thoughtful light in his eyes showed he had taken the warning in the lame joke.

"If I were you, I'd tell everybody I'm heading out of town for a week of meetings. Considering how well Grandstones can find out what they want to know, I'd leave an itinerary at your office that any traitors in the ranks can pass on to her, and then take off. Tell them you're driving to Chicago. No plane tickets to lie about. Hopefully she'll follow you there. By the time she finds out you're not there, she won't make it back for New Year's."

"Voice of experience?"

"Only if you count dealing with Ferengi, Romulans, and Klingons, and some Goa'ould on the side."

That got a real chuckle from him. I guess escaping a fate worse than death will put a man in a good mood.

"So, Wednesday night. Do I need to dress up?" he asked. For a few seconds, I had no idea what he was talking about.

"Bring clothes you can get sweaty and sit on the floor in. Have you ever played Murder?"

"No. Sounds like fun."

"It's kind of like Hide'n'Seek, played in the dark, in an obstacle course. But the seeker tries to tag people as dead while everyone else tries to identify who he or she is. It's a blast."

Well, fear and loathing for Sylvia Grandstone made something else the Evil Overlord and I had in common. If I could protect him from her machinations, maybe that did make me a superhero after all.

~~~~~

Mum and Pop raised me right—meaning even though I had a good excuse to go home, I stayed to do all the work I normally would, to prepare for a holiday-messed-up production schedule the next week. I also couldn't afford to take Friday off because I was committed (maybe I needed to be committed) to only work half of Wednesday to help set up at Eden.

My head was still full of the breakfast conference and sliding into an after-a-very-late-lunch coma when Sylvia Grandstone swept through the door at 2:15. She paused (posed) on the sloppy wet, salt-crusted carpet.

I immediately felt sympathy for Mildred, who had guard duty at the receptionist desk. The old-fashioned wrought-iron garden fencing that divided the reception area from the rest of the office didn't do much good corralling unwelcome guests. They could either step over it or simply lift the latch and walk in. Hence, we needed Mildred to yell at people. And tackle them, when necessary.

Then again, I really didn't need to feel sorry for Mildred. She could handle the appearance of the Anti-Christ without blinking. Sylvia Grandstone wouldn't intimidate her.

So I sat back and waited for the floorshow to begin.

"Could you tell me, is Daniel Sheridan available?" Sylvia purred.

Was I in a parallel reality? Sylvia Grandstone, *asking* instead of demanding? Polite to a plebeian who worked for a living?

"Since he isn't here, I have no way of knowing." Mildred said after the requisite three seconds to look the intruder over from head to toe. She raised one eyebrow higher than Spock ever managed, until it almost disappeared underneath her wig. In honor of the holidays, it had been crimson with a green ribbon and gold earrings since Thanksgiving. Starting after New Year's, if Mildred followed her usual pattern, it would be silvery-white.

"Not here?" Sylvia's face crinkled with disappointment. "But his secretary said he came here."

"I can call and ask, but since he's the big boss, he's not answerable to us." Mildred gave her that flat, cool, don't-even-try-to-take-your-bad-day-out-on-me-not-giving-you-the-satisfaction
~~~~~

smile. The one that seemed pleasant, yet convinced troublemakers to leave the office without getting what they wanted.

Sylvia, being a typical Grandstone, didn't even flinch.

"Well, that's what I was told. How about if I settle down and wait for him to show up?"

"Suit yourself." Mildred gestured at the seating area, safely contained within the wrought iron courtyard.

Unfortunately, Conrad believed in comfortable waiting rooms. After twenty years working for his father and now being the boss, he still hadn't caught on to a vital principle: at a newspaper, the people we wanted to talk to, we took to our desk area. The people we didn't want to deal with, we left in the waiting area. It was *supposed* to be as unwelcoming as possible. These chairs weren't the chintzy office warehouse specials that creaked and swayed and pinched everyone who sat in them. No, these were chairs with decent cushions, made of wood that had survived a thousand unwelcome guests. And of course, they made unwanted guests so comfortable, they were able to wait until we gave in and talked to them.

I was just hacked enough to yank mentally on Sylvia's crimson hooded cape, as she hung it on the coat tree. It fell down into the slop that had fallen off everyone's boots and melted and overflowed the mat. The cloak fell with a swoosh of musk-scented air so strong I could smell it all the way over at my desk, in another section of the building.

Sylvia let out a little shriek and leaped to snatch it up before it made a bundle on the floor. No more than the hem got wet. She hung it up again. I yanked it down. Another inch got wet before she gave up and took it with her to the waiting area. It was just as well. Using my telekinesis after all I had gone through since Tuesday afternoon made my head throb.

"I doubt he's coming," I said, and pushed my wheelchair over to the top of the ramp down to the next level. "He doesn't come out here very often. He probably won't be back until next month. Next year, if you think about it."

"And how would you know?" Sylvia's eyebrow raised. Not as high as Mildred's. I could see the creases where her latest Botox treatment was wearing off. That cheered me greatly.

"I talked with him. He's driving to Chicago for a series of

meetings, and might have to cancel his New Year's plans. Depends on how the meetings go."

That was a lie, but I was a guardian and Daniel was part of Neighborlee now. Besides, by the time Sylvia followed him to Chicago and realized she didn't just miss him but he was never there, it would be the new year. The witching hour would pass. Kind of like breaking the spell if the prince didn't get trapped by the witch before midnight.

"I know you…" She slithered up to the gate and actually stopped. Maybe there was something to the fable of cold iron stopping evil forces?

"You're slipping, Sylvia. When you graduated from Neighborlee High, you swore you'd never admit you had ever lived here, much less knew anybody who lived here."

"I don't remember any cripples going to Neighborlee High." Her upper lip curled as she looked over my wheels.

Oh, did I want her mouth to freeze in that position!

"Lanie Zephyr. We were in the same class."

"The track star?" A few seconds of shock had her mouth hanging open as she looked me over, and I realized she really saw me. How often did that happen with Sylvia Grandstone? She only noticed women she could use or who got in her way.

I was definitely in the latter category, even though Sylvia didn't know that.

"What happened to you?" She shoved the gate without bothering to fight with the latch, and the traitorous chunk of rusty metal swung open without a creak.

"Lanie is a local hero. She got her back broken when she saved a boy's life," Mildred said. "You haven't told me who you are yet." She raised her eyebrow again, this time directed at me, a clear request for information.

"Mildred, this is Sylvia Grandstone. You know the Grandstones."

"Oh. Nice to meet you. Gotta fill the fax machine." She stretched her mouth in a stiff smile, nodded to Sylvia, and turned to walk to the next unit, with the fax machines, copy machines, scanners, and file servers for the entire office.

"Local hero, huh?" Sylvia tipped her head to one side. "So, you spoke to my Danny today?"

"Danny? The Evil Overlord?" I snorted and popped a wheelie before heading down the ramp. I figured I had to head Sylvia off before she decided to search the office.

"Evil Overlord?" For a moment, real amusement glittered in her eyes. "Why do you call him that?"

"He came in here, took over the newspaper, rearranged everybody and everything, and took my sports beat away from me. You can bet your ..." I almost said 'padded bra' or 'rhinestones,' but pointing out all the fakes that made up Sylvia Grandstone wasn't a recommended method for staying alive.

"Bottom dollar," I finished after only a slight hesitation, "he is not one of my favorite people."

Not yet, anyway. But the more I learned about Daniel Sheridan, the more I liked him, despite my resolve not to. How could I hate a guy who was willing to take over the dreaded job of communications officer for a Star Trek club of over eighty people? I didn't want it, that was for sure.

"Oh. Pity," she said with a smirk. "He's really a lot of fun. But you don't exactly run in his circle, do you?"

"Former athletes?" I pivoted back on my wheels and waggled my footrests at her.

"That wasn't what I was thinking. Well, it was nice catching up on old times, but I really do have to run."

My first thought was: *Not in those stilts you call shoes*. It was a miracle she got across the parking lot and up the steps to the door, with those pointy toes and six-inch high-stiletto heels. Sylvia forced another Botox-straining smile, swirled her cloak around her shoulders, and slithered out of the office.

I wheeled over to the front window and watched her, waiting until she got in her car. A candy apple red Lexus with rental stickers, parked in the handicapped spot next to my Jeep, of course. Um, excuse me? The handicapped parking spot is for *physical* handicaps, not mental or emotional. After Sylvia's car had vanished from sight, I pulled out my cell phone and punched in Daniel's cell number. He didn't answer. Maybe he turned off his phone to avoid her calls? I had to leave a message, which honestly, I preferred.

"Mata Hari was here. Someone at your office told her you were coming here. I told her you were on your way to Chicago. Is your camouflage plan in effect?"

"You're a good girl, Lanie," Mildred said, appearing magically from the no-man's land of office machines.

"Doing my part to protect my fellow man."

~~~~~

In between several more walk-throughs of Eden, Kurt spent the whole day patrolling the town. He was on the alert for some hint of energy at work to show him where Big Ugly might be trying to break through. He got to my house in time for dessert that evening. I suspected something was wrong, because usually his timing to join us for dinner was spot-on. He banged once on the door and came in. I wondered sometimes what he would do if we ever locked the kitchen door when we were at home. He most likely would use his talent to "persuade" the lock to unlock for him, without even thinking about it, much less breaking a sweat.

Pete and Harry took care of serving warm peach pie and ice cream while Kurt related some of the odd dreams he had been having that now felt like warning or eavesdropping dreams. We had to bring my brothers up to date on all the discoveries. I had told them about the envelope Hayward brought, while Pete and Harry were cooking dinner.

"The thing is, nothing is concrete or clear," Kurt said. "Just this nagging sensation of something lurking in the mists. You know, like those really bad, old movies where they didn't have the budget for special effects, just lots of dry ice fog?

"I wouldn't be afraid," he said after a few seconds, "except that there's nothing around me. I can't get hold of anything to fight with. Something is crawling after me. I don't have anything to smash it with, and there's no metal, no energy to pull something together and turn it into a machine to throw at it. I'm completely helpless. Useless," he added with a wry grin, finally looking up to meet our gazes.

I was scared, right then and there. Give Kurt a few pieces of metal, some electricity, he could do things that would rival all those miracles the Professor used to do with bamboo and coconuts on *Gilligan's Island*.

"Okay, so we've been warned." Felicity scraped up some filling. "Once we can see it, I bet it's not a threat at all."

"Remember that episode of *Buffy*, where this monster was
~~~~~

trying to climb out through this magic diagram and infect the world with fear? But when this ugly, spiny thing full of teeth finally arrived, it was only about three inches tall." I snickered. "Somebody got ticked and stomped on it."

"We gotta find it before we can stomp on it." She grinned at me. "If only the world was as easy to save and understand as Buffy's world."

"So, like that makes Neighborlee the Hellmouth?" Kurt sighed and slouched. "You two are a bad influence. I never even watched that show, and I know what you're talking about."

"Not the Hellmouth. Not a doorway into demon territory," I said. "But definitely a doorway into otherness, weirdness."

"So it always comes back to doorways into other dimensions of reality?" Pete said.

"Comes back to?" Then I knew why he said that.

When I got home from work, we had opened a few documents on Mum and Pop's DVD. It was jammed with photos and documents and diagrams. One theory they wanted to investigate was the idea of doorways from other realities, parallel universes, opening up around the world.

The idea of doorways into other dimensions existing in Neighborlee wasn't anything new. Thinking there were other towns like Neighborlee that needed to be kept guarded against invading otherness, wasn't new either. Thinking my parents had vanished because they were investigating that ... made me feel tired and weak and older than was good for me.

Chapter Three

"As long as these doorways stop interfering with the wiring at Eden, I'm fine with them," Kurt said. "Live and let live." He glared at Pete, who gave him a wide-eyed, innocent look that didn't fool anyone.

Just a few seconds later, he hummed a few notes from the Bond theme, *Live and Let Die*. At least, that was what I thought he was trying to hum. He only came close to the right notes, and that was being generous.

Talking about Kurt's dreams triggered more memories for Felicity. That bothered all of us, that she had dreamed but forgot as soon as she woke up. We compared the fragments she and Kurt remembered to my bad dreams. It was like they had dreamed shattered bits from my dreams, which just confirmed, yeah, Big Ugly (gotta love that name) was gearing up for something.

Or maybe the most recent attempt, triggering alarms at Eden, had drained that energy?

We could only hope. But hoping didn't mean we relaxed and let down our guard. We went over those dreams even after we finished eating and loaded the dishwasher. The more cohesive the picture from the dreams, the better our chances of success.

"More power fluctuations today. Not as severe, though. The presence of people in the building muted things. Hiram got frustrated enough to call for help. Illuminating Company and utility services. But it helped, too." Kurt got up to help himself to the pot of tea I started on Fridays and kept replenishing through the weekend. It was a tradition Mum and Pop had started. Something that had to be done, or the universe would start unraveling.

"And?" Felicity prompted.

"I'm pretty sure now the fluctuations aren't *in* Eden. The impact on the electrical systems was like aftershocks. Hard to locate accurately. Sometimes around it, in the air. Sometimes underneath." He paused in pouring in cream to meet our gazes and nod, punctuation to what he had just said. "Something is warping power. Sections of the wiring are blinking out at odd intervals, like they've got breakers attached to them that take them out of the loop for no reason at all." He sat back down and swirled his cup around a few times before sipping. "I kept thinking about what that doctor friend of Angela's said, about the source being terrestrial. People or things here on Earth, rather than ..." He flicked his fingers skyward. He wasn't talking about the attic, or even outer space.

"So ... maybe the nasties want to stop the party at Eden?" Felicity offered after a long period of thoughtful silence.

"That might be better than the idea they want the party to go on as scheduled," I said. "Change your mind? Coming after all?"

"Jake wants a romantic evening." Felicity shrugged. "He has a big security job Downtown from now until Wednesday morning. He plans to sleep all day, and wants just the two of us together, bring in the new year quietly." She smiled. A moment later it faded. "But if you think there's going to be trouble, then I need to be—"

"Between the two of us, and Angela, and Ford, we'll be fine," Kurt hurried to say. "The two of you deserve ... well ... if you think it's time to have the talk with him, I approve. Not that my opinion means anything."

"It means a lot." Her voice cracked with surprise.

I was surprised, too, but there were tears trying to force their way out. Kurt liked Jake, but he was like big brothers everywhere, positive that no one was good enough for Felicity or me. For him to give his permission for Felicity to have the talk with Jake, easing into revealing her as a semi-pseudo-superhero, that was a major milestone. And a nice Christmas present.

~~~~~

That night, I dreamed of the Spindelmutter building. I floated through the building, following a slender woman with long, wheat-colored hair, as she walked around, measuring walls and checking out the few display cases left behind by the last tenant. I was so excited I nearly yanked myself out of the dream. Finally, a glimpse of the future spa owner.

Or maybe not. Maybe it was just a dream-dream, not a vision of the future. She turned semi-transparent and flew up through the second floor to the dusty, dark apartment on the top floor. I
~~~~~

followed her. Before I could figure out what was going on, she zipped up to the dusty skylight and pressed her transparent hands against the glass. For a second, I caught a glimpse of green-blue eyes and a small mouth in the reflection.

That mouth flattened into a hard, angry line as her face faded out entirely. She vanished. Then the next moment I got yanked up through the skylight and zipped across the countryside, to the back road along the edge of the Metroparks where Darbyville met Neighborlee.

Hayward's car sat nose-down in a ditch, right where two park roads intersected. Steam spiraled up from the crumpled front end. All the doors were open. Figures in dull gray HAZMAT suits swarmed it. They had air tanks and bulky headgear covering their faces, and looked like escapees from a movie about an outbreak of Ebola. Some were pumping a greenish-gray gas from what looked like old-fashioned bug spray pumpers, while others dragged Toby Malone, Steve Muldoon and Col. Hayward out of the car.

The woman from the Spindelmutter building turned semi-transparent right in front of me. She grabbed Toby and Steve each by an arm and shot up in the air. All three turned invisible as the boys' feet left the ground. The men who had been dragging them away, toward a dark van, fell and staggered around, spinning and suddenly arching up in the air. The men struggling with Hayward suddenly jolted backwards away from him, and they started doing the same strange dance. Hayward collapsed onto the gravel road.

For a few seconds, I swore I saw a woman with silver streaks in her hair, dressed in a rainbow-streaked jogging suit. But there were at least a dozen of her, running circles around all the men in their HAZMAT suits, kicking them and knocking them down. A few times she left a trail of sparks, like the air was too heavy and combusted when it resisted her passage.

I jolted awake, reaching for my cell phone, sweating and hovering about a foot above my covers. While it was nice I had gotten back some of my kinda-sorta flying ability, now was not a good time. I called Gordon and prayed I remembered right, and he was on duty that night. He had been telling me all the trades he had made, so he could have New Year's Eve and all New Year's day free, to spend with Mandy.

"Whoa, slow down," Gordon said, as I blurted what I considered the most important details: the location and the fact the boys had just been kidnapped. "We just got a report about a ruckus on that park road. It's down a ravine, and in the winter the people on the park road above it can see down into the road. I mean, we *just* got the report. How'd you know?"

"Gordon, don't ask questions you don't want to hear the answers to, okay? Just get there. The Colonel is a friend of my folks, and the boys could be kidnapped by the same creeps who were brainwashing them."

"Already got teams from the park service, Darbyville and us on the way there, down all the roads. No way they can get out of there without going through a lot of swamp. We'll catch them." Gordon hung up. He was a stickler for not talking and driving at the same time.

They found Hayward's car. They found the big black van — stolen two days before — and a lot of footprints, heading into the swamp. No sign of the guys in the HAZMAT suits or Hayward, Toby, or Steve.

Before Chief Tanner came over the next morning to talk about the incident, I had enough time to get over to Divine's and have a conference with Angela and Ford. Bethany, Athena and Doni were running around in the clothes rooms, putting together costumes for a drama fraternity party at WBC on Sunday. It was good to see the girls having fun and relaxing.

So when Chief Tanner came to my house just before lunch, I had my story prepared. It helped that I had already told Gordon Col. Hayward was a friend of my folks. I wasn't lying when I said he was involved because of the attack on me, and he had taken the boys into custody to protect them. The only lie I told was that I had been on the phone with Hayward when the attack occurred.

I didn't like lying to Chief Tanner. He was a friend of my folks. He held my hand that awful night at the quarries when I broke my back. He put up with a lot of weirdness in town, when we needed to go to the authorities in the course of our duties as guardians. That lie put me into a bad mood for the next several hours. And my nose started running and my throat felt sore. Great — now I was getting a stupid cold, after I thought I had completely recovered from whatever that dart inflicted on me.

Fortunately, Felicity was the only one in the house as I grumbled and indulged in way too much homemade fudge and braced myself to work on my next *Talk to Terry* question. Harry and Pete were at a meeting for the games committee for the New Year's Eve overnighter.

"It's the constitutional right of all superheroes to have invulnerability as part of their superpowers." I clunked my mug down on the counter as I waited for the electric kettle to come to a boil so I could make more of Angela's miracle-working tea.

"Somehow, I don't really think we count as superheroes," Felicity said.

"Why not?" I responded, instead of retorting that yes, we were superheroes. Just semi-pseudo-superheroes, but that still counted. Didn't it?

"We don't have outfits. I admit, I'd look good in spandex." Her smile looked a little strained as she smoothed her hands over her disgustingly perfect figure. "But I'd much rather have those tough leather outfits from the X-men movies, thanks very much." She looked over her shoulder at me and smirked, but she didn't turn around fast enough. I saw how that smirk seemed to just fall off her face.

"What's wrong?"

"Kurt's right. It's time for the talk."

"Hey … if Jake really loves you—"

"Oh, I know he loves me, and once he gets over the shock— heck, Jake has seen enough weird stuff, between his security jobs and seeing me kill electronics with just a temper tantrum …" She tapped her spoon on the side of her mug as she stepped up next to me and stared at the kettle. "It's just that I can't control things. The other night, we were kissing. In his car. Getting to that point where it's just about perfect, slow kissing, just holding each other, quiet … and it seemed like I was inside his head." She sighed and reached for the tin of cinnamon vanilla tea. "I wondered if that was another weirdness that came along with my zapping talent."

"I don't know. Mum and Pop sure seem to read each other's minds all the time, and they're ordinary mortals."

"You think." She winced. "Kinda wish we were sure your folks were intergalactic freaks like us, just so we'd be more sure they'll get out of whatever jam they're in."

I said a quick, silent prayer along the lines of, *I trust You, God. Please take care of them, okay?*

"Jake is perfect for you. He'll take the truth behind your zapping power in stride. And I bet he decides you'd be a perfect addition to the security team."

"I doubt it." She brushed her hair out of her face. Today it was ginger streaked with mahogany and silky straight. "The thing is, I got so startled, I blipped." A snort escaped her and mischief glimmered in her eyes. "The radio came to life, his police scanner came on at chop-and-liquify volume, and that big portable spotlight he keeps in the back seat lit up."

I slapped both hands over my mouth to stop the laughter, but it didn't do any good. We giggled and snorted until tears filled our eyes. We could always get over our "mutant blues," as Kurt sometimes referred to our situation, by laughing about something. The day we couldn't find some humor in the utter weirdness that surrounded our lives, that was the day we'd turn ourselves in to the government spooks with the underground laboratories.

Once we got hot water into our mugs and our different brews were steeping, we got down to work. Felicity still hadn't sent out her Christmas cards, and she refused to waste the Christmas stamps she had bought. She had come over with all her paraphernalia as soon as my brothers left, to spread out in the hallway leading to my office and keep me company while I tortured myself with the next *Terry* column.

She didn't take over the kitchen table because she didn't feel like carrying on a conversation, yelling down the hall while I worked. She needed to see who she was talking to, even if I was turned in profile to her.

Dear Terry:

I know all the psycho-babble about dreams are our brains downloading all the events of the day into our subconscious. I know we work out our problems in our dreams. Most of the time it's just a tangle, and I'm fine with that.

But what if your dreams seem to be warning you, but the warning doesn't make sense?

See, there's this girl. We've been neighbors our whole lives. We never really talked except for helping each other with homework or yardwork. But now we're in college and carpooling and talking. She's got a brain and she really likes me. And when her ditzy friends tease her about me being her boyfriend, she blushes and stammers instead of denying it.

That's a good sign, right? So I asked her the other day, what she thought about us. And she's like, 'Oh, I don't know how a guy like you could ever be interested in a girl like me.' That's so crazy. I was the wimpy kid Grandpop always talked about, in those ads in the back of the comic books. All I had were my brains until high school, when I got into basketball.

But she really likes me now. So, okay, we're perfect together. But I've been having these dreams that are like all last year's horror films in one. The only one I remember clearly is where she's this humongous spider and she wrapped me up and sucked the juice out of me and then chewed on my head.

So do I listen to those dreams and run for my life?

Depressed in Dayton

~~

Dear Depressed:
First of all … you haven't been watching some B movie with mutant spiders from outer space and eating radioactive Mexican food before you go to bed, have you? That could explain some of the weird images.

I do know that psych class stuff about dreams and your subconscious speaking to you, but what has this girl done to make you think she's a bloodsucker?

If she hasn't done or said anything, maybe someone is trying to ruin what could be the start of something great. Anyone jealous, trying to get between you two?

My advice: TALK TO THE CHICK!

Unless you're Spider-man with spider-sense to get you out of jams, the only way to be sure of anything is to talk to people. Learn to communicate. Don't depend on your dreams. You can go to twenty different psychotherapists and get twenty-five different interpretations.

Talk and build a real relationship. She might be flattered that you're anxious about things. She might laugh. You won't know until you talk. So talk.
Happy New Year,

Terry

~~~~

Harry and Pete came home in mid-argument and laughing. Pete kept saying "No," and "You're nuts," and Harry kept saying "Yeah," and "It's the only way" and "You gotta or you're dead meat!"

Then Harry threw a handful of papers down on the table. I guessed from the way Pete dove for the papers, Harry had taken them from him and was part of what they were arguing about. Not surprisingly, the paper was all artwork. Pete had probably been scribbling all through the meeting.

"What's with the anthropomorphic trees?" Felicity said, snatching a paper heavy with ink out from under Pete's fingertips.

"Antho—what?" Pete slammed up against Harry.

"Trees looking like people." She tossed me a page with a pine tree in an "angry" stance, stick arms, down-slanting eyebrows, mouthful of sharp teeth, pinecone fists jammed into its hips.

"We're studying cults in youth group." He sidestepped Harry and dove, snatching the picture from my fingers and managing to get half the other sheets back into his grasp.

"What does that have to do with trees?"

"Truman was at the meeting, talking with some of the older guys about a fake cult the youth group made up for fun, about ten, fifteen years ago," Harry said.

"Church of the Blue Spruce," I said, the words yanked out of my mouth before I could stop myself.

"What do you know?" Felicity pulled a chair out from the table, turned it around, and straddled it, resting her arms on the back of the chair. "Spill. Now."

"I want to know about the trees, first," I said, to buy some time while I waited for memory to slide back into place. In point of fact, the Church of the Blue Spruce had started when I was in college. Back before the big growth spurt in our church. Truman, now the teacher for the high school and college-age classes, was one of the ringleaders.

"He said something about the holy scriptures of the Blue Spruce lost in his files, and he'd bring them to class. And I started thinking a book needs a cover, right?" Pete shrugged. "So ... you don't have a copy of the Blue Spruce Bible, do you?"
~~~~

"*Book of Seedlings*," I corrected him, remembering the giddy afternoons a bunch of us spent scribbling and twisting scriptures, without the assistance or interference of drugs. The strongest stuff any of us had in our systems was cola and chocolate.

"Kind of thought you were one of the guilty parties," Harry said. "Pete was sketching all through the meeting."

Pete waved the sketches under my nose. "Want to blow Truman's mind and have a printed book to hand him tomorrow? I figured we could go the whole cult track he was talking about. Secret revelation and writing scriptures and schisms and even put him on trial for heresy at the end. The whole works."

"What kind of a church do you guys go to?" Felicity said, laughing.

"We already put Pastor Rocky on trial." I snickered when Pete's grin fell off his face. "Everything's recorded. Somewhere."

I knew where the incriminating evidence was. I kept everything from that really insane, fun year when we were studying different cults. One of our goals was to sift out the truth from the poison, to find out how much various cults borrowed from the Bible, and how much the new prophet could warp God's truth before people started asking questions.

It started as a joke. Our teacher, Ford Longfellow, had pointed out the window of our classroom and said he could come in and tell us God had spoken to him through the blue spruce tree sitting there. Nobody could deny it had happened, they could only say they hadn't heard. That was how a lot of cults got started, especially the ones with roots in Christianity. Claiming an angel had spoken directly and privately to one person. That justified adding to the Bible and throwing out whatever contradicted the "new revelation."

The next week, some joker, who still remained nameless, wrote a letter on official Church of the Blue Spruce stationery, gently scolding Brother and Prophet Longfellow for speaking so lightly of divine revelation. The letter finished with a quote from the *Book of Seedlings*, chapter 7, verse 12, promising the faithful would have their roots planted in streams of living water.

A bunch of us couldn't resist the challenge. If there was a chapter 7 and a verse 12, there had to be a whole lot of other verses. So one snowy afternoon with a whole lot of caffeine and chocolate and chips in our systems (and, to be honest, a really boring OSU vs Michigan game on TV), we created scriptures.

WOOD CHIPS
Scattered translations from:
THE BOOK OF SEEDLINGS
The Holy Scriptures of the First Church of the Blue Spruce
The Next D-Generation

From Chapter 1:
1 The Grand Pew-bah, the Prophet, has climbed high among the branches of the family tree.

2 And lo, a vision has been granted to him, to edify the splintered masses. That all may again take root and grow in peat moss and truth.

10 Though he may be high in the tree, remember that he is a sap, as are we all. Let not the crown of his leafy head be lifted too high, lest in the hurricane of truth he be snapped and deprived of the sap of life.

From Chapter 3:
2 And the command came, to pass the commandmints through the splintered masses, though it be painful as the holy kidney stone, though they be mocked like bleached blondes on Saturday night.

3 (And the holy commandmints are beneficial to the seedlings and aged oaks, for they are sugar-free and 99.45689748927867477% pure.)

4 By the mercy of the Most High and Leafy, to the ten commandmints are added these four suggestions.

5 Thou mayest, should you decide to accept this mission (none of these words, of course, are being accepted by the built-in dictionary of the prophet's secretary – editorial note), never worry, but be happy.

6 Thou mayest, when coming down from the top of the Terminal Tower, use the stairs instead of the window of the most glorious view.

7 (There is some philosophical discussion among theologians and horticulturalists whether the view is really all that glorious. Also discussed by the interpreters of this text is why the tower is terminal.)

8 Thou mayest cease from roller skating in a buffalo herd.

9 (There is further philosophical discussion – five miles further – as to why the chewing gum loses its flavor on the bedpost every night.)

10 Thou mayest, as the spirit moves thee, have a bottle in front of thee rather than a frontal lobotomy.

From Chapter 5:
*7 That you might grow lush and green in the land, these paradigms
are presented to you (by Ford, who has a better idea):*
8 One of life's great warning signs is the phrase "Blind date"
9 Why is a man who has vowed celibacy called "Father"?

"That's utterly wretched," Felicity said, muffling giggles.

"Yeah, but I noticed you laughed," Harry said.

"I can see where Lanie's comedy routine came from. The
lobotomy thing has been in some of her routines."

"It's also borrowed from someone else," I said.

"Why do you want to print the Blue Spruce scriptures?"

"We're all divided up into study teams. Each group has to
take a cult or do some research on the practices of cults and how
they get started and all that," Pete said. "I figure, my team can
start their own cult as our study project."

"Cheating." Felicity crossed her eyes at him when he glared
at her.

"Especially since Truman knows about the Blue Spruce
books," I added.

"We wouldn't use your stuff, except to launch our own stuff.
Add to what you guys wrote. Maybe branch out and make our
own breakaway cult," Pete said.

"Ha. Branch out." Harry held onto a cheesy grin for about
five seconds, then his face fell into neutral lines. "Funny—not."

~~~~~

Sunday, we went to Divine's after church for a war council.
Kurt helped me float up to Angela's apartment on the second
floor so we could be comfortable. Harry and Pete went out for
lunch with the Blue Spruce Phase 2 team. I was glad to have them
separate, a little bit, from the burden of the guardians.

Gordon met us to report on what had been found out from
the crime scene. Basically, nothing. The van had been wiped clean,
even sprayed to clean any fragments of evidence, such as DNA
and fingerprints. These guys who took Hayward and the boys
were hardcore.

Gordon and several park rangers followed the footprints into
the swamp. They were shallow enough in the mixed mud and
crusted slush to indicate nobody was carrying anyone. Either the
~~~~~

prisoners had recovered from the gas that knocked them out and walked, or that woman from my dream really had turned invisible and flown away with them. I certainly wasn't going to tell Gordon that part. Yes, he was a Trekker, more open to believing the near-impossible than anyone else in the Neighborlee police force, but that was probably pushing him farther than I could risk going. Not without losing his friendship and his trust, and maybe giving him a nervous breakdown.

We had people at church praying for Hayward and the boys. It wasn't enough. The police were searching. We couldn't contact the military because Hayward wasn't officially here. Besides, we didn't know who to contact without checking Mum and Pop's files. Which were still in the hands of the military. Still, we needed to do something. We did all we could and hoped some of it would overlap and make a difference.

Athena and Wallace joined us, but they stayed in the book room downstairs, waiting until Gordon left. Most of their report was listing what they had done and where they had looked, and all the places that didn't yield any information that would help in the search for my folks.

"We had to back out of a few places where Sherwood's tin can program set off alarms," Wallace said. He wrinkled up his nose at Athena when she sighed at his wording.

A moment later her exasperated look turned to a crooked little grin and a spark in her eyes, silent communication that had nothing to do with telepathy. Kids in love were cute. I was glad for her, but dang, she made me feel old. I was thirteen when she was born and now she was in college, running a computer program design and rescue business and getting ready to graduate early. Where did the years go?

"Do we want to know what the tin cans are?" Kurt said.

"An advance warning system to let us know we're about to set off intruder alert programs. Sherwood and London are both pretty busy monitoring the energy protecting the town," Athena added. "They're kind of jazzed, knowing that even though they're computer-based, they can touch magic energy."

"Uh, excuse me, but didn't magic kind of help them get born?" Felicity interjected.

We had to laugh at that. It was just easier to think of the two

AI's as science fiction constructs, rather than crossing the line into fantasy. We were glad to have them on our side.

A few things Athena and Wallace had found added to the mounting evidence that my folks' disappearance might be linked into the problem we had been gradually dealing with all our lives: the mystery of the Lost Kids, the ones who vanished, who took them, what they wanted, and where they were now.

Kurt frowned and held up a hand, signaling us to silence in the middle of a discussion of where our computer detectives could look next. He tipped his head to the side, eyes half-closed. That listening look meant he was trying to locate someone using their semi-pseudo-superhero powers.

Problem: all the semi-pseudo-superheroes we knew of were in the room.

Angela stood and faced toward her front door. I was convinced in that moment she could see through walls, ceiling, floor and display racks to the front porch. She gasped softly. Before she could do more than say, "Kurt," he was up and running, out of her apartment, down the stairs, thudding hard enough to make the house vibrate.

Athena frowned and looked in the same direction.

"What?" Wallace said, and reached for her hand.

"That's weird. I got a flash …" She shook her head.

"Of what?" Angela headed for her kitchen.

"Every once in a while, I see this man in my dreams. Just for a second or two, like he just pops in to check on me. He smiles at me and looks kind of sad. Sometimes I swear I see him around town, but …" Another shake of her head. "For a second, I got the same feeling I get in those dreams."

"What does he look like?" I asked, exchanging a look with Angela. Where I sat, I could see into her kitchen. She had filled the electric kettle and was reaching for a cannister of the tea blends she created for different healing or soothing needs.

"He's kind of got a craggy face, and nice eyes, and a scar along his jaw." She traced the line.

"Hayward?" I got a shiver. That idea I had been trying to ignore, so I wouldn't scare it away until it got solid, took another step closer to clarity. Felicity hurried to follow Kurt. Wallace followed her without having to be asked. I approved of him more and more for Athena every time I saw him. For a moment, I wondered what Portia would think of him for her daughter.

That was weird. I hadn't thought of Portia Longfellow in years, not even to feel a niggle of resentment toward her, so flighty she would have a test tube baby, then after a year decide she wasn't a good mother, and leave that baby for her parents to raise. Ford and Charlotte said she wrote regularly. She and Athena seemed to be friendly, and I had never heard Athena say anything negative about her mother. Of course, I almost never heard Athena mention her mother.

By the time the water was hot enough to pour into the teapot, Kurt and Wallace had helped Hayward get up the stairs. He looked rumpled, pale, and wobbly. I could have sworn a puff of greenish-gray smoke lifted off him when he dropped down into the couch closest to the table. A whiff of a chalky odor made my nose itch, then it was gone. Angela hurried over to cup his face in her hands and gaze into his eyes for a moment. She bent down and kissed his forehead, then stepped back into the kitchen.

"I don't know if even you will believe me," Hayward said, after looking at all of us gathered around him.

His gaze lingered a few seconds longer on Athena than on the rest of us. I didn't want to wonder why.

"Guys in HAZMAT suits ran your car off the road, gassed you, and tried to take the boys, but a blonde woman with blue-green eyes, who can turn invisible, rescued you and flew away with you?" I offered. Hoped.

The alternative was that the kidnappers had let him go on purpose. Maybe to follow him to Divine's? Maybe to track down the rest of us, get proof we really were freaks, as Toby Malone had shrieked at me just a week or so ago?

Hayward stared at me for a few seconds. His face got even paler. The dirt smearing his left cheek and the left side of his nose got darker by contrast. Then he grinned, took a deep breath, tipped his head back against the couch and laughed.

"You know what's really sad?" he said, after Angela had returned with the teapot and tossed him a wet cloth and towel. He paused to scrub his face. "That's all I remember. Blonde hair and blue-green eyes and the boys fading away. Then I stumbled up onto the porch and here I am."

"At least the bad guys didn't get the boys," Felicity offered.

"We don't know who the bad guys are." Kurt glanced at Athena and Wallace, who were smart enough not to even try to look like they weren't dying of curiosity.

"Has Ford ever told you about Lost Kids who get claimed by people and just vanish from the orphanage?" I asked, turning to them. "The Cliff Notes version is that we think there are two groups who watch for kids like us to start showing off talents. Then they swoop in with paperwork to take them away. Creeps and semi-nice guys. We think the creeps were after me at Christmas. And hopefully, the nice ones are the ones who rescued Toby and Steve and the Colonel."

"Hopefully," he muttered.

"Wallace, I keep some spare clothes for Franklin in the guest room," Angela said. "Would you dig out something so he can clean up?"

"Yeah, I'm kind of ripe," Hayward said. "How long have I been gone?"

"They grabbed you Friday night. Lanie saw it in a dream and set off the alert, and there was enough ruckus the people on the cliff above the road called the cops," Kurt said. "It's Sunday."

"With friends like these, who needs enemies?" He raked his hands through his hair and seemed to deflate a little more.

Then his gaze landed on Athena, who studied him, her head tipped to the left. Her frown of concentration reminded me of when she was four and insisted she could read the bedtime storybook to me, when I was babysitting her.

"Hi, Athena. It's nice to finally … talk to you."

"You were there," she said, her frown smoothing out a little. "When we were rescuing Doni's stuff from the Hallidays. You were watching. And I saw you a couple times when I was little, walking home from school. And you've been on campus." She shrugged. "I figured you were a friend of Jinx, because I saw you talking to him a couple times. How do you know me? You're another Lost Kid, you said?"

"More accurately …" Hayward sighed and thanked Angela with a nod as she handed him an oversized mug of a deep golden, spicy-scented tea.

It smelled like the mix that would revive him, ease muscular aches, and start cleansing toxins from his blood. Probably when she touched him, she could tell he was still suffering the effects from the gas the rivals, as he had referred to them, had used on him. I wondered if the gas had put the blank in his memory, or the blonde woman who turned invisible had done it.

"More accurately, I'm a friend of your mother. Portia has been very helpful in research and investigations relating to protecting Neighborlee."

"Yeah?" The momentary brightness in Athena's eyes told me a lot. She wanted to be proud of her mother.

"I promised her whenever I stopped in Neighborlee on business, with either Angela or the Zephyrs, I would check on you. If I didn't think I would be accused of being a child molester, I would have taken pictures," he added, with a shrug. "She's very proud of the amazing young woman you have become."

Something in his gaze turned painful, and he looked down at his mug and took a sip.

"How long have you known my mom?"

"Since … well, I've always been aware of her, all of Ford's children, because of our connection through Angela and Divine's." Another flick of his gaze, and he tipped up the mug like he wanted to drain it.

Or maybe hide behind it?

That elusive idea was about to leap into the light of day and clobber me, and I couldn't look away, like some people can't look away from horrific traffic accidents.

"Gee, if she knew somebody like you, how come she still went the test tube baby route with me?" Athena laughed as she said it, but her voice cracked a little.

Hayward choked and spilled tea into his lap.

Chapter Four

An image flashed into my head of Portia holding a wriggling bundle of blanket, sitting in that big green easy chair in the Longfellows' living room. Hayward stood over her, looking as terrified as I could never imagine him, but also hungry, and holding his arms out. He took the blanket and cuddled it, and the wriggling stopped. He got the most fatuous look on his face and gently poked into the opening in the blanket with one finger. Even though I couldn't hear anything in that brief vision, I was pretty sure he was talking baby-talk. To baby Athena.

"No ..." I whispered.

Wallace stepped out of the guestroom with jeans and a flannel shirt and something white, probably underwear and socks. Hayward set down the mug fast enough to slop tea on the table. He choked out an apology, nearly yanked the clothes from Wallace, and fled into the bathroom.

"Angela ..." Athena looked like she couldn't breathe for a few seconds. Wallace hurried over and dropped into the seat next to her and wrapped his arm around her.

"Yes," Angela said. "And yes, your grandparents know. And yes, they approved of the whole idea. And yes, you were a test tube baby, your mother did not sleep around and your father did not break his promise to his wife."

She absently blotted up the spilled tea with a napkin and reached to cup Athena's cheek.

"You were planned and wanted and prayed for, the daughter and granddaughter of guardians. The irony is that we knew the moment Portia was pregnant, because gifts that had been hidden all her life woke up. She was like Kurt, sensing active gifts. For her it was a brightening of the air, a mixture of sound and light. She could also touch the sick and diagnose what was wrong." She sighed and sat down and caught up both of Athena's hands.

"Unfortunately, the awakening of her gifts seemed to draw attention to her. The rivals, as Franklin refers to them, set up camp on the outskirts of town. We theorized that they could sense a gift awakening. To protect you both, she went away. And she has stayed away, to protect you."

"Imagine how vulnerable a baby would be and how valuable you would be to the rivals," I said, thinking aloud as the idea crystalized. "They would figure the child of someone with power had to have powers herself someday. If Portia stayed away, they wouldn't connect you with her."

"Essentially," Angela said, nodding. She gave me a grateful look and that kind of scared me. Since when was she afraid to reveal facts and unpleasant details?

I understood almost before the question was clear in my head. Athena had grown up with Bethany. They were as much Angela's daughters as any Lost Kids. She had watched over them, and now that Bethany was in Hollywood, stumbling up pretty steep, rickety steps to stardom, all Angela had left was Athena.

Even more, I understood why Angela agreed with Stephanie's wishes that Bethany not learn her heritage. If the magic in Ben Miller's blood combined with her heritage from Stephanie, and woke up someday, Bethany would be even more valuable to the rivals than Athena.

For the first time in my life, I was grateful that Kurt and Felicity and I hadn't been noticed and snatched by either the rivals or the two old men. Why had I grumbled all these years, feeling like I was rejected because I was only semi-pseudo-super, instead of a full-fledged superhero? Like the blonde woman with the green-blue eyes who could fly and turn invisible …

A tiny snort escaped me, quickly muffled, as I wondered if she had the invulnerability part of the superhero package.

"So …" Athena looked around the room. "So Mom isn't half as flaky as I thought. She's kind of a hero. I mean I never yelled at her about dumping me on Gram and Granddad, but she has to know I'm …"

"So write to her and tell her you just met your dad," Wallace said. "Tell her you think she's great. Heck, why can't you go visit her on Mother's Day this year?" He looked up. "Unless getting together will send up the Bat Signal or something like that?"

That got a sputtering little laugh from Athena. Probably his intention. Yeah, I utterly approved of Wallace for her.

"Your mother is very smart. I liked her, when I was a kid," I offered. "But yeah, I thought she was a ditz. One of those people who was so smart she didn't have a real strong grasp of reality. But would it really be safe to tell her in a letter or on the phone that Athena knows the truth now? With all the spying the rivals or whoever is doing, all the sucking of our energy defenses, everything in the last few weeks … what if they can read our emails? You don't want to give away info like that. Not at a time like this."

"So I can't even tell Bethany," Athena murmured.

"Why not?" Felicity asked.

"Because Bethany had to leave early to go back for some dubbing emergency for the studio," Angela said. "The girls were hoping to spend New Year's together. You'll just have to go out to Hollywood for the movie premiere and wait to share the news."

"Hey, Cosmo would go nuts," Wallace said, gripping her shoulder and shaking her a little. "All the clothes and glitz and giving the paparazzi a hard time."

That got a little stronger smile from her.

"What's he like?" Athena tipped her head toward the bathroom, where the water had stopped running.

"He's a guardian. He asks me about you every time he comes through town to confer. And it might nearly give him a heart attack if you called him Dad," Angela added with a tiny smirk. That got an answering snort from Athena.

"Just not out where people can hear and start asking questions," Kurt said. "Sorry, but we do have to be careful."

"Yeah," Athena said. "Careful. But what's he like?"

The door creaked and the bathroom light flashed out into the short hallway, then vanished. A few seconds later, Hayward came down the hall in his clean clothes and stocking feet. He had his ordinary, military posture, no creeping or hunched shoulders. Very clearly, this was a survival mechanism.

"I've played out several different scenarios for this day, this revelation." Hayward came to a stop in the opening where the short hall met the living room/dining room. "Most of them had you angry with me. I hope we can be friends, at least."

"Do you want to be a father to me?"

That stopped him, with a widening of his eyes and his mouth moving a few times, but no sound able to escape.

"Hey, can I have a vote here? Finding out my girlfriend has a soldier hero-type guy for a father this late in the game? That's kind of scary," Wallace said. "Am I going to get hauled into an interrogation room like on NCIS? And asked about our dates? And if my intentions are honorable?"

Everybody at least grinned. Athena sighed and rolled her eyes and leaned into Wallace. Hayward let out a few crackling chuckles.

"I'm sure compared to what Ford and Jinx put you through, I'd be a pussycat in comparison," he said.

"They don't have to say anything," Athena said. "It's just understood. Wallace is a gentleman. A lunatic, but a gentleman."

"That's good," Hayward said, "because I do have some friends among SEALs and Black Ops who owe me favors."

The chime-buzz that broke in that moment startled all of us and kind of killed the atmosphere that was starting to relax. Angela frowned and again glanced toward the front door. I didn't even think she had a doorbell for the shop. Anyone she wanted to come in, the door would open automatically for them. Granted, no one would be so rude as to come to Divine's Emporium on a Sunday, or after the shop closed up for the night. There were hours posted on the gate at the sidewalk, as well as next to the front door. So who had rung that doorbell I didn't even think existed?

The winkies swirled up through the floor and around Angela. Felicity and Kurt reacted, but Hayward, Athena and Wallace didn't. Interesting. An indication of just how sensitive they were?

"They're … not happy," Felicity said.

I had to agree. Those tiny sparks of light seemed more red than any other color. I couldn't be sure, because they swarmed down and through the floor again.

"Who's not happy?" Athena said.

"Her early warning system." Hayward gave me, Felicity and Kurt a considering glance. "What just happened?"

"We're being invaded." A smirk twisted one side of Angela's mouth. "At least, they think they're going to invade. Just in case the situation has changed … We need to rearrange the setting. Kurt, help Lanie downstairs. We need to look like we're just relaxing with cookies and tea. Wallace and Franklin, you were never here."

Felicity and Athena hurried down the stairs. Kurt supported me and we hobbled down, holding onto the railing, to where my wheelchair waited. By the time we got into the main room, Felicity and Athena had the little bistro table set up for five. It certainly looked like we had been snacking and relaxing for a while.

Meanwhile, Angela went to the front door and made a production of unlocking several loud, stubborn locks I didn't even know were there. Maybe they didn't appear until someone showed up who wasn't welcome. Like an allergic reaction.

Sylvia Grandstone stood on the porch of Divine's. She wore that false little smile all Grandstones used when they played at being gracious and forgiving despite the abuse (they believed) everyone inflicted on them. Usually they would claim they had just discovered a building or piece of property in Neighborlee had been stolen from them, and now they were reluctantly taking back what was theirs.

Honestly, were the Grandstones going to try to claim yet again that Divine's Emporium belonged to them? Every time a Grandstone went against Divine's, it ended badly for them, in terms of public humiliation and enormous legal bills. Everyone was sure Reggie had become a lawyer just because it was so hard for the family to keep lawyers on retainer. Of course, everyone had been utterly stunned that he managed to graduate from law school and pass the bar in the first place.

As a side note, it was pretty much public knowledge that Carr, Cooper and Crenshaw allowed Reggie to be a junior member of the firm to keep an eye on him and cut down on trouble for Neighborlee. The sad truth was, he could have been a great lawyer if he wasn't such an arrogant slimebag with delusions of godhood.

"Oh, hey, I was right," Sylvia chirped, looking past Angela to me at the end of the hall. "I saw your Jeep out front. Could we talk, just for a second? It's pretty important. Not the fate of the universe, of course," she added, with a giggle that should have sounded charming. Should have. There was a subliminal sour undertone to the chimes that made the hairs stand up on my arms. "But you know, where matters of the heart are concerned, all's fair in love and war. Or whatever."

"Love?" Athena whispered. She and Kurt and Felicity were standing just around the corner, out of sight.

"She's trying to snag Lanie's boss," Kurt said.

I wheeled to the door. Angela stepped aside, so Sylvia could have stepped in if she wanted. My right hand slipped on my wheel. What was she doing? A favorite trick of the Grandstones, when they were schmoozing for fun and profit, or trying to intimidate people, was to step up and invade personal space. Especially in doorways. Usually the victim took a step back in unconscious defensive reaction. Another step forward, another defensive step back, and soon the Grandstones were inside. Once they were inside, it was hard to get them out. Kind of like when cockroaches invaded a house, but cockroaches could have learned a thing or two from the Grandstones.

"What do you need?" I approached the front door. Again, my hand slipped on my wheel as the winkies came out of the walls and floor and spun around me, flashing neon shades of red and yellow. Definitely warning.

Funny, but just for a second the chill air sliding past Sylvia, into the shop, had a whiff of the same chalky smell that I caught on Col. Hayward. I took a second sniff as I glided to a stop with my foot pedals just inside the threshold. Now all I caught was an expensive-smelling, heavily musky perfume coming off her.

"Have you seen my Danny?"

"Umm, when you were at the paper, Matilda told you he was out, and I told you he was heading for a conference out of town. Did you check with the corporate offices?"

"I did, but it's the funniest thing. He left town so fast, and the business trip came together so last-minute, and some people had contradictory details." Sylvia giggled and wrinkled up her nose.

She probably thought she was being adorable.

In what universe?

"He plays games like that with me, usually when he's about to get all romantic. So I'm thinking he's preparing a big surprise for me."

"Then if you care for him at all," Angela said slowly, sounding like a lion purring, getting ready to pounce, "don't snoop and ruin the surprise."

Sylvia blinked and she went pale enough I could tell where

her makeup stopped, and guess how thick it was. For just a second there, I could have sworn I saw the outlines of bruises under that makeup, on her cheek and around her left eye.

"I'm just positive that he's in town. I stopped by his condo, but it's the craziest thing, there's a for sale sign and I was thinking … well, I told him about the most incredible house over on Guilderstein. You can tell me, your old school chum, especially since you seem to be buddy-buddy with my Danny." She fluttered her eyelashes.

Maybe it was my imagination, but I could have sworn I saw a flash of light on fangs in her mouth. But no Grandstone would ever have fangs. They spent thousands on ensuring every physical detail would be perfect. Too bad they never spent that much money on mental health and removing the grease on their grasp of reality.

"Me?" I snorted. "Buddy-buddy with the Evil Emperor? Hardly."

"Really? Then you didn't invite him to your Christmas party?" If Sylvia's eyes got any wider with mock innocence, they were going to pop right out of her head.

"What Christmas party?"

That chill digging ice picks into my back wasn't from the icy, perfume-heavy air sliding through the open door and swirling down the hall. Although, the smell was giving me a sinus headache. How had Sylvia found out Daniel went to our Trek Christmas party? I know he didn't tell anyone, and no one in our Trek club would be caught dead talking to a Grandstone or their minions about club business. Daniel had been welcomed to our ship with open arms, so that meant everyone would defend him. Especially if they found out a Grandstone was trying to sink her matrimonial claws into him.

I made a mental note to send out an email asking everyone to close ranks and defend our new communications officer.

Sylvia's lips flattened. She likely knew I was lying, but figured she couldn't call me on it without revealing she had sources.

"I heard he bought the town paper just so he could get hold of you, make you write for him."

"What delusional idiot told you that?" I laughed. I hoped it sounded genuine. It was a stupid idea, but I *had* accused him of that, when he admitted he was a big fan of my comedy.

Note to myself: Call Daniel as soon as Sylvia slithered away and tell him to check the staff at the main office. Someone was either weak enough to be intimidated into betraying him, or had a grudge and was willing to betray him for profit. Or there was a Grandstone spy in the ranks. Considering what I now knew about the long-term plans for a Grandstone-Sheridan merger, that was entirely believable.

"Delusional?" Sylvia's eyes narrowed and I glimpsed the fury she had unleashed in childhood. I moved back from the door.

That wasn't me. Something pulled me back. Winkies covered my chair, making the wheels turn.

Sylvia, being a well-trained Grandstone, stepped forward to take advantage of my retreat. Her fury turned into a triumphant smirk. Her foot crossed the threshold.

A swarm of winkies, at least a hundred strong, spun around her on volcanic red alert. A stink like burned hair and rotting meat replaced the musky perfume. Sylvia waved her arms around her head, batting the winkies away, but from the confusion in her eyes I knew she didn't see them. She only felt them. With a shriek that turned into a wail, she fled backwards, off the porch. The distinct *crack* of her stiletto boot heel snapping off echoed in the falling snow silence of the street.

Angela rested a hand on my shoulder. We watched Sylvia stumble down the walk, bang into the closed gate, kick it open, and nearly go to her knees before she reached that red sports car. Funny, but the shade seemed more poisoned apple red than candy apple now. I kept my gaze on her until her car roar-screeched into life and she pulled away.

A soft sob escaped Angela and she stepped past me, to go to her knees on the porch. Tiny wisps of smoke wavered, traveling upward from the scorched black dots of winkies littering the dusting of snow. She scooped up a handful. They evaporated, with a scent like sandalwood driving away Sylvia's stink.

"I'm sorry," I said, and thought about going to my knees to help her scoop up the winkies. Even as I reached to lock the brakes on my chair, the last black dots in the snow faded away.

"No Grandstone has come so close to trying to step into my

shop in decades," Angela murmured. "Is this another sign of the defenses weakening … or have they found powerful allies?"

"How did they get inside all the other times in the past, when they tried to claim this place was theirs?" Athena asked.

By now, she, Felicity and Kurt were only a few steps behind us. They had probably been drawn by Sylvia's shrieks. Wallace and Hayward stood at the foot of the stairs, watching us.

"They always sent their minions," Angela said. "It was a sad day when Thomas Grandstone could no longer see the winkies. I think he blamed me, and refused to believe when I told him that his own change of heart made him blind. Soon after, he wasn't able to step through the door. I had such hopes, when Sylvia showed up here." She sighed, took a deep breath, and finally raised her gaze from her hand, which held only the last few bits of melting snow.

"So … they were guardians, once upon a time?" Felicity murmured.

"No. They never made that commitment. The first Grandstone had such potential, and he always saw it as a sign he was meant to rule, rather than serve. I think the malevolence waiting in the darkness between worlds managed to make itself heard because Thomas was hungry and angry enough to listen."

"We need to look more closely at the outsiders who have been lurking at our borders," Hayward said. "I hope our theories are right, and there are two groups. If one has allied with the Grandstones … well, the other wants to at least be more friendly to us." He held out a wrinkled business envelope. "This was tucked inside my coat. I found it when I was washing up."

The others headed back to the main room to settle down to talk. I made that quick call to warn Daniel. Again, I went to voicemail. Only after I hung up did I wonder if Sylvia's connections and spies had the ability to tap voicemails. Had I just given away everything, revealed our lies, and confirmed Daniel was still in town, hiding from her? Wouldn't it have been funny if he had indeed manufactured a business trip to Chicago, knowing Sylvia would think he was lying and stay here in town?

The note inside the envelope was short and simple, and mystifying. Plain paper, printed, not handwritten, no smells, no watermarks, and I refrained from suggesting Hayward dust for fingerprints. Chances were good he wouldn't find any. Besides, who could he ask for help without raising questions that would just cause more problems?

The time has come to stop working against each other. We believe we are on the same side. Truce? We have some crises to deal with and will make contact when the situation has quieted. Be assured two of the three boys are safe, and we are working on the safety of the third.

We didn't talk for much longer. There wasn't much more to be said, after sharing all the information we had gathered, our theories, and agreeing to keep in contact. Hayward accepted a ride from Wallace and Athena, to wherever he needed to go. He didn't tell and we didn't ask. I hoped the ride wouldn't be uncomfortable for him and Athena, and Wallace's presence would help bridge the whole situation.

Felicity and I went home in silence. Since Jake was busy with that job that would take him until Wednesday morning, we agreed on a movie marathon. While she was at her place, checking on her dogs, I made a quick call to the church to get a "booster" from the prayer chain. Pastor Rocky was there. Usually he didn't answer the phone on Sundays, but he did listen to the incoming messages, just in case. This time, though, he picked up the phone before it went to the answering machine. He laughed as soon as I said Athena was going through some rough times and needed prayers.

"I know what happened. Angela called me, and I just got off the phone with Charlotte. I suppose Franklin will be calling me soon, so maybe we should keep this short."

It was a good thing I wasn't drinking anything, or I probably would have spit it all over myself.

"You know about the Colonel?"

"Lanie …" His chuckle was more of a sigh. "You forget, I'm a Lost Boy, too. Franklin was a few years behind me. He came to me for counsel after one of the boys we were protecting from the town bullies was snatched. We've been allied in looking after our town for longer than I care to remember."

"Gee, what a coincidence."

"Nothing is a coincidence. Not with our Lord, and not when

it comes to the strange and wonderful things that make Neighborlee what it is. I may not have extra gifts like you and your gang, but I play my part."

"Yeah, you keep us sane and you make sure we don't drift to the dark side."

That made him laugh. We chatted a minute or two longer, updating him on the hunt for my folks, and the whole situation with the three boys. Our church had been praying for them as soon as we knew about the kidnapping on the park road. I didn't think it was my place to talk about the note left in Hayward's jacket, even when Pastor Rocky offered that if the Colonel was returned unharmed, maybe Toby and Steve were all right too.

As all right as they could be, kept away from their families, maybe not knowing where they were or why they had been taken. I hung up and settled in to try to relax and get my mind off things. There was some comfort in knowing everybody in our church would soon be praying about all the new developments, even if they didn't know the details.

<center>~~~~~</center>

Monday at the *Neighborlee Tattler* was the usual jam and crush in reaction to a holiday on a delivery day, with our advertising schedule moved around. I didn't hear from Daniel, which didn't mean anything. He didn't report to me, did he? I did wonder a few times if the lack of calls for help was a good sign, or bad. I had a vision of a dark cave full of webbing, Sylvia dressed up like the Black Widow from that really campy Batman show, and a little voice shrieking, "Help me! Help me!" from inside a tiny blob of webbing. Yeah, I know I mixed old black-and-white movies with LOTR and 60s TV.

On a positive note, Sylvia didn't slither into the office, looking for an update on "my Danny." I sensed if she had found him, she would have come to gloat for a few seconds, at least. Maybe the confrontation with Angela and the winkies had frightened her.

My phone played the opening chords of *Where is My Hairbrush?* While I love VeggieTales, it freaked me out a little, because I hadn't loaded that song into my phone. Either it was malfunctioning, or someone had gotten into it.

I turned it over and a cartoon version of Cosmo's face grinned at me. Not Cosmo, but his computer-copy, Sherwood. He stuck his finger in his ear and my screen flashed to an image of my earbuds. Well, duh, it took me a second or two, but I pulled them out and plugged them in.

"What's up, binary boy?"

"We need you to go meet with Stanzer. All your phones and Angela's, and the rest of the gang's phones are being tapped. They don't know we're talking because I'm going through the wireless, not the phone lines," he said.

"Who?"

"We don't know. But they're watching Bethany, too, so London is busy setting traps. Stanzer has friends that let him go invisible, so he met with Angela and now they need to get you in on the plan."

"Why would they watch Bethany?" I felt sick for a second, then I just got mad. I grabbed my coat and gave a mental push to get away from my desk. "If you two can't track down who, and Athena and her gang can't do it from their side of the computer screen ..." I took a few deep breaths. "Okay, heading out to meet Stanzer."

I glided down the ramp to the reception area, heading for the door outside.

"Fresh air," I told Matilda and didn't care if she saw or not when I mentally yanked the door open and glided out, still in the process of putting on my coat.

Maybe it was Sherwood's warning just putting the idea in my head. I still felt people watching me as I wheeled across the partially cleared parking lot to the sidewalk, and headed up the few blocks to Stanzer's building.

As I rolled, very slowly, and tried not to look like I was watching for people watching me, Sherwood filled me in on what had kept him and London so busy. They were having fun learning about the energy protecting Neighborlee. The poor guy seemed to feel guilty that they were having fun. He warned me they were trying to figure out how to transfer power from their electronic realm, to try to boost Neighborlee's defenses. That sounded good to me. The downside was that until they were sure the power would stay, they might be tied up, unable to help track things leading up to and during, and maybe after New Year's Eve.

"Neither of us like the idea of our originals being at Eden, if the enemy is going to try something," Sherwood admitted. "At the same time, being at ground zero if something happens might just be the safest place."

I almost asked who he meant by "originals," but I remembered in time. Doni and Cosmo had been recorded with a strange video camera Athena found at Divine's Emporium, and those recordings formed the core, the seed, that resulted in London and Sherwood.

"So, what do you know about Athena's father?" he asked while I was still rolling different ideas around in my head. It was a good thing I was sitting down, otherwise I might have skidded.

"He's a guardian, so that makes him one of the good guys. He's a friend of my parents, and he's stood between us and the Feds or Area 51. You weren't eavesdropping, were you?"

"London has a link with Doni, and Doni is worried about Athena. We helped her shield her emails, so she could talk with her mother. We don't want to spy on her or anything, so ... we figured you care about Athena, so if you say he's safe, then we won't go all pit bull on him."

I had to laugh.

"I like him. He cares about people, but I don't know how close he'll let himself get to Athena. My brother Pete is family to his late wife, but he couldn't take Pete when his parents died. To protect him. He asked my folks to take him. He'll be good to Athena."

"That's good. Thanks. London will be happy."

I looked around and found myself across the street from the paper-covered windows of the Spindelmutter building. That itchy feeling of being watched dug onto my back. The paper was still covering the big display windows. No sign of life.

That feeling of nasty eyes stayed steady, and I wondered if it would grow stronger if I headed toward Divine's. We had concluded that my getting hit with that dart had been an accident. Jay Parker's master had been aiming at him, not me. No one had come by the house, no one had followed up, ready to take me into custody as soon as I succumbed to the drug.

I turned a corner and saw Stanzer coming from the other end of the block. That bluish haze in the air beside him was probably one of the Hounds of Hamin, not quite phased into our reality or dimension or whatever the proper term was. Sherwood kept talking, explaining how they had detected the wire taps, figured out how to block them, and the plan for Stanzer to meet me.

"Interference. Somebody let the dogs out," he said, interrupting himself. I was about to ask what he meant when static came through my ear buds. "Can you see Stanzer?" When I said yes, he said good-bye.

"How come they can't protect Angela?" I said, pointing at the haze, when Stanzer was maybe five sidewalk blocks away.

He halfway stumbled, glanced at the haze, then grinned and shook his head. The haze coalesced into a big, black, wolfish thing that stood tall enough its head was even with Stanzer's, all shimmering with blue electricity. He stopped with maybe a foot of space between his shins and my foot pedals and gestured for me to hold still. The Hound walked around us three times, then faded out again.

"Okay, we're clear. We had to wait until no one was watching before the Hound could shield us. We're kind of out of phase. No one can see us or hear us unless we move."

"That's cool, but kind of useless for sneaking or spy work or anything. And is that your answer why the Hounds can't protect Angela?"

"They're assigned to me, and to the rest of the Hunt. They'll protect our friends if they're with us, but that's about the extent of it. Anyway, Angela has some friends of her own, with some nice tricks, and we're setting up a trap mixed with a shell game."

"I could feel someone watching. This whole thing is an attack on Angela? Or is it someone new, taking advantage of the weakness from the drain of all the weirdness lately?"

"We probably won't know until after the battle is over and we analyze the damage." Stanzer shrugged. "Here's the thing. We agree the attack will be either on Divine's or Eden. We won't be sure of the target until the attack starts. She's going to appear to stay at Divine's, to encourage the attack to happen at Eden."

"Appear? How is she going to get to Eden to help with the defense? Dig a tunnel out? Find some of the old tunnels they used with the Underground Railroad? The quarries stopped where they did," I said, gesturing toward the cliffs and slopes where Neighborlee ended and the Metroparks and quarries began, "because the rock changes right here, from pretty stubborn granite to the sandstone that made the Willis family rich."

Yeah, I had written enough history articles or taught enough on the history of Neighborlee, I could give a mini history lesson at the drop of a hat.

"Tunnel, yes." Stanzer grinned. "You met Wilfred and Philomena the last time they were in town, didn't you?"

I nodded. A shiver went up my back that was really uncomfortable, because I had worked up quite a sweat.

"Don't even ask about the physics or the power drain. I don't want to know. The Hounds aren't against it, but they don't like to go near the shop with me when Will and Phil are visiting. I think it has something to do with the subliminal music they give off. Makes the Hounds itchy. Basically, they're going to create a tunnel and collapse the distance between Divine's and Eden, putting each of them inside the other, so Angela can technically be at Eden without leaving Divine's."

"Okay. We're talking …" I had to laugh. "I'm not sure exactly what we're talking about. But the Wood Between the Worlds is real, and a stable is capable of containing something bigger than the universe?"

It took a second for Stanzer to catch the Narnian references. Then he grinned and nodded.

The basic plan was that we would all stay away from Angela and let the watchers think she was sick and would be alone. She had already hung a sign on the gate, temporarily closing the shop due to a bout with the flu. Her usual visitors would be busy setting up for the New Year's Eve overnighter lock-in. She would appear abandoned. Hopefully the watchers would think so, and not look too closely.

The thought of someone being able to spy on Angela, when she should have been safe inside Divine's, made me itchy.

~~~~~

I went to Eden after work, to help with some of the setup Monday night. My timing was perfect, as I drove north, past the town hall and city service complex, skirting the road looking down into the quarries and Metroparks. The light had faded to about halfway between afternoon and sunset. Gina, the director of all the insanity taking place at Eden in just two days, pulled into
~~~~~

the parking lot ahead of me. She parked at the edge of the sidewalk in front of the main doors into the lobby. I pulled up behind her instead of taking the handicapped parking spot another twenty feet down the drive. Her little compact car looked crammed full of boxes and blue plastic bags, meaning she had been shopping for the party. Again. Yet. Still.

By the time I got my chair out of the back seat of my Jeep and slid up the ramp to Gina's car, she had come back from her first trip inside. I held out my arms. She laughed and grinned her thanks and piled some boxes on my lap. More than a few times, I had volunteered my services as a rolling shopping cart—and the use of my handicapped parking card—when she ran errands for the community center. She hit the automatic door pad with her hip and let me wheel through first.

The wind had picked up speed and dropped about twenty degrees in temperature by the time we came out for the last trip. We were both shivering as we slid up the sidewalk to the front door again. A light layer of frost covered the fronts of our coats, from our breath congealing in the icy air.

"We might just have the whole town camping out in here with us New Year's Eve, if the power goes out like it did in the blizzard of '72." Gina gasped a little as she set her armload of bags on the table in the middle of the supply room just past the office.

Eden used to be a factory and had its own generator for power and a heating system that could convert between several different fuel sources. I laughed at a new thought and muffled it into a snort. Gina demanded to know what was so funny about a blizzard blacking out the town. She threatened not to take the heavy box of plastic tablecloths off my lap until I confessed.

Chapter Five

"You know the phrase 'a cold day in Hell'? Well, guess what witchy twit blew back into town?" I waited, but she just gave me a weary shake of her head. "She vowed it'd be a cold day in Hell, or something close to that, before she came back to Neighborlee. Come to think of it, she waited a day or two for someone to beg her to reconsider, but nobody did."

"I don't know who you're talking about."

"Sylvia Grandstone."

"Wait, there's another one? How did I luck out that I haven't met her yet?"

I had to laugh, because I just remembered that Gina hadn't grown up in Neighborlee. When I explained she was Reggie and Freddie's cousin, Gina made a "gag me" motion. Then she rescued my legs by finally heaving the box off my lap and onto the table. Considering there were fifty tables to cover for the party, that was a lot of plastic.

I swore her to secrecy and filled her in on the newest phase in Sylvia's quest to become queen of the universe, while we hauled more supplies around the building. Gina had met Daniel at the club Christmas party, and she liked him. We discussed plans to help him vanish if Sylvia showed up, while we carted some of the supplies brought on previous trips to the different rooms that would need them for setup. Anything to stay indoors for a while and warm up.

"Someone ought to drop a house—" Gina's voice out in the hallway cut off with an odd ringing sound.

The hairs stood up on my arm, which was difficult, under thermal underwear, a sweater, and my coat. I dropped my two boxes of punch mix on the steel counter of the kitchen, turned around, and went back out into the hall. Gina had been right behind me, carrying bags full of cheese balls and logs for the appetizer table. I held my breath and listened, but couldn't hear any footsteps or the sound of something rolling if she had passed out from exhaustion and dropped her grocery bags. Come to think of it, there had been no crash, either. The building was so quiet, I could hear the voices of the decoration team in the main gym, as they assembled the centerpieces.

"—right on top of the whole family, and put them out of our misery," Gina said, and came up the hall from behind me.

But ... I was facing the direction she *should have been* coming from. That ringing seemed to bounce off the walls, just for a second, and this time the hairs on my arms tried to burrow back into the skin. Not a pleasant sensation.

Gina stopped short and stared at me. She looked a little pale, and beads of sweat appeared on her forehead. The thermostat was turned down because there were no activities this evening. That was why we still wore our coats while we put the supplies away. She shouldn't have been sweating.

"What just happened?" She looked up and down the hallway, shaking her head. "Oh, heck, if we're getting another gas leak, now of all times." She stomped into the kitchen, tossed the cheese into the industrial-size stainless steel refrigerator that sat closest to the door, and stomped back out and down the hall to her office.

I didn't think a gas leak could adequately explain how Gina started down the hall from one direction and ended up coming from the other direction. Granted, that could be considered a normal occurrence in Neighborlee, but still ... I sniffed a few times, but I couldn't smell anything. Of course, that wouldn't have meant much, considering how my nose had started to run like a faucet once I was out of the cold air.

When I got home, I called Kurt and told him about the change of direction. He had spent four hours at Eden that morning, checking over everything to make sure the energy fluctuations had done no damage.

"Maybe Gina is a skipper, like Jay," he suggested. "Only she doesn't know it."

"Gina was born in Hadley. I've met enough relatives who fight over who she looks like, she can't be one of us. And she isn't a descendant of a Lost Kid, like Athena and Doni."

"Ah. Yeah. That kind of ruins that theory." He sighed. "Well, just what I wanted. Another mystery. We've barely recovered from the last one."

It was on the tip of my tongue to suggest we go over to

Divine's and talk to Angela. We would have to leave it at phone calls, with London or Sherwood running interference with the listeners, until her fake quarantine had ended. I told Kurt what Stanzer had told me, and suggested the two of them confer, since Stanzer was more of an expert on interdimensional travel than anyone in Neighborlee. Except Angela. And her two friends, Will and Phil. They did have those pointed ears I had glimpsed when they last visited a few years ago.

The problem with Angela pretending to be sick, to trick her watchers into thinking she wouldn't be at the party at New Year's, was that I couldn't raid the vintage clothing room for something glitzy to wear for my comedy performance at the party. Our enemies were certainly putting a crimp in our lives. The tally against them grew larger every day.

~~~~~

Monday night I had one of those odd dreams of darkness and crawly things and teeth. Like Felicity's last dreams. Was I influenced by her words, or was my subconscious unloading things I had picked up during the day?

The big question, when I woke up in the middle of the night and made notes on my dream, was whether taking those psychology classes in college had been a benefit or a handicap. Kind of like the medical student who diagnosed himself with every incurable disease in the world.

I really wished Mum and Pop were around, so I could bounce my ideas off them.

Please God, I prayed after I turned off the light. *Please take care of them wherever they are, and bring them home soon? And if they can't come home, keep us all safe if something weird is building up to happen?*

~~~~~

Despite my dreams and the weirdness on Monday, I went to work in a much better mood Tuesday. Daniel left a message on my answering machine at work. He had gotten into Chicago at nearly midnight, Ohio time, and he didn't want to wake me.

Huh? We weren't that good of friends, were we, that he thought he had to check in with me? And why was he in Chicago? Was he honestly running from Sylvia? Or maybe he just wanted to leave a trail to bolster the story? Just how scared was he? Well, actually … he was being pretty sensible. I had grown up with

Sylvia, and if I was a guy and she had her sights set on me, I'd be trying to book a ride to outer space.

I tried to wrap my brain around the whole problem, feeling sorry for Daniel, and listened to the phones ringing for paper delivery problems.

Come to think of it, the phones weren't ringing as much as they should have been. Factor in winter and holiday breaks, and the usual handful of paperboys who seemed to think since they weren't going to school, they didn't have to work, either. We should have had at least three lines ringing at any one time. I rolled down the ramp to Matilda's area and listened with her. She was one-quarter of the way through the novel she brought with her to read between phone calls and lunatic visitors. The loony quotient always went up during the winter. Cold weather drove them indoors instead of killing them off like germs and roaches, according to Conrad. Usually by ten in the morning, on a paper delivery day, she was only a chapter or two through her book. The number of read pages was a better barometer of calls and problems than anything else.

"Quiet morning, huh?" she said, when I slid up to her desk.

"Yeah, should we be worried?"

"People don't seem to much care about their paper when they're gearing up for New Year's, I guess. It's not like there are any garage sales they're terrified of missing." Her grin stretched her cheeks so wide it got her multi-colored jingle bell earrings swinging and chiming. I wondered how she managed to answer the phone with those humongous bobbles hanging from her ears, but knew better than to ask.

I wheeled over across Matilda's area and down the ramp into the circulation department's domain. The building was built on a slope and each section of the row of connected units sat at least two feet lower than the unit before it. Perry and Felipe were at their desks, feet up, wet socks drying and their soaked boots sitting on the old-fashioned hot air registers. They chatted and drank coffee, munched on donuts, and looked entirely too relaxed for this time of the morning, on a paper delivery day. After all, they were one-third of the circulation department.

"Easy morning, guys?"

"Yeah. Freaky. No wind after midnight, so no papers blew

away. No snow, no sleet, so we didn't have to replace any papers. A lot of kids didn't get their Christmas presents from customers last week, so they're all eager to make a good impression and get nice presents when they collect today," Perry said. "That's my theory, anyway. It's what I did when I was delivering for the *Tattler* when I was a kid."

Well, at least we had a theory for why it was so uncharacteristically quiet. I debated the offer of a donut (blueberry fry cake, one of my favorites) and decided to decline. I still had to hit one of the shops in town to find a snazzy outfit. Something with sparkles, maybe. Every time I thought about buying new clothes, I worried about my figure. Despite my sedentary life, my superhero metabolism still worked in my favor. Most of the time. I did have a slight case of what Conrad called writer's rump. Like tennis elbow, but "inflammation" caused by *lack* of motion.

My cell phone played the main titles theme from *Star Trek: The Motion Picture*, as I started up the ramp from the reception area into my section of the office. That meant anyone from my Trek club could be calling. They wouldn't call on paper day unless there was an emergency. Sighing, I put on a burst of speed and risked a mental snatch, pulling the cell phone out of my purse and into my hand from about fifteen feet away. The bad thing about using my telekinesis to bring things to me was that objects gained velocity the longer they traveled. That cell phone smacked into my palm hard enough to make a loud crack. As long as it didn't crack the bones in my hand, that was fine. I looked around the office to make sure no one had seen as I answered.

"Lanie, do you remember helping me bring in the rental canister of helium for the balloons last night?" Gina said.

"Oh, yeah. We joked about wishing it was light enough to float itself through the door. Why are you asking?" My mind flashed back to that skip through time and space that she made the night before, and something slimy did a dive down my spine.

"Do you remember where we put it?"

"Your office. You made a comment about not trusting the Rooney boys. You put it in your closet and locked the door."

"That's what I thought. I asked Gordon to take the canister into custody when he stopped in this morning, but when I unlocked my office and the closet, it was missing." She sighed. "Along with the Rooney boys."

"How do you know? That they're missing, I mean."

"Gordon is looking for them. Their mother said they didn't come back from delivering their papers this morning. They planned on hitting the sledding hill to try out their new sled, and then they were going out to collect for the paper. The sled is still in the garage."

"I'll ask the circulation guys if they heard about any problems. I think Perry has the boys on his route," I offered. Gina thanked me and hung up. I got down the ramps and across the two office sections in record time.

The Rooneys were generally good kids, but full of mischief. They were either going to be genius inventors when they grew up, or explorers. They liked to experiment with anything they could get their hands on, and couldn't seem to comprehend the idea that other people weren't as interested in their projects and wouldn't be happy to donate spare parts, bicycles, old cars, or wheelchairs, to the search for the latest fantastical gizmo. Kurt was keeping his eye on them, but for now he was staying at a safe distance so no one could accuse him of encouraging them.

"Nope, no complaints about their streets at all," Perry said, when I asked. He frowned, thought for a few seconds, then got up and reached for his boots. "I know their route. Used to be mine. Maybe I better help look."

Felipe went along with him, and I called Gina to tell Gordon, if he was still there, that Perry was coming to help. She reported that the helium canister had showed up, in the middle of the service hallway behind the gym. We hadn't gone down that hallway last night. It was on the other side of the building.

All right, so I slightly slandered the Rooney boys by suggesting they had picked the lock and got into Gina's office. Granted, something they *had* managed to do before. When they realized how heavy the canister was, they left it behind. Just a theory, but it was a logical theory, and Gina accepted it with some relief. After I hung up with her, I called Kurt and left a message. Someone had to keep track of any sudden bursts of unusual weirdness. Odd occurrences were part of the air and soil and water here in Neighborlee, but that didn't mean we could just ignore when the freaky quotient went on the rise.

It was kind of like that old *I Love Lucy* sketch, where Fred said Lucy was acting strange, and Ricky asked: Strange for Lucy, or strange for normal people?

~~~~~

Kurt called just after I returned from lunch and reached my desk. He was on his way over to Eden, and he would do a new walk-through to feel for energy surges, to figure out what happened with the helium tank. He had been called about a problem with the heating system. According to Hiram, head of maintenance, the circuit panel from the main HVAC system was completely missing.

"If it is," I said, "the only way you'll get it fixed and stay fixed is if you stand there and keep your hands on the thing until the replacement parts come."

"No way," Kurt said, sounding tired. "I'm not bringing the new year in standing in the furnace room of a haunted factory."

"Eden isn't haunted."

"You got a better explanation for all the weird malfunctions that fix themselves most of the time?"

Unfortunately, I didn't.

While I was talking with Kurt, Gordon came into the office to update me. He was officially off duty but had permission from Chief Tanner to stay in uniform and use his patrol car, in the effort to look for the Rooney boys. After all the weird things happening in town, two clever, troublemaking kids like Matt and Mike just vanishing couldn't be taken lightly. It just wasn't natural to have so much silence where they were concerned.

"Turns out their mother had something that had to go over to Eden, and the boys took it without telling her. Probably an excuse to get into the office, since they knew Gina ordered the helium. We found footprints leading up to the back door, and no footprints leaving. Near as we can tell, they're still inside the building." Gordon shrugged. "I'm betting they're inside some of the old machinery in the area that was closed off years ago. They just can't hear anybody calling them, and happier than they have any right to be considering the trouble they're causing. Probably a mess, too."

"Might want to be doubly alert, if you go over to Eden to
~~~~~

follow up on that theory. Kurt got called over there again. Equipment is malfunctioning or just disappearing. Be careful, okay?"

"You got it." Gordon snorted. "Wouldn't be surprised if stuff is missing because the boys are building another one of their monster machines, with no idea what they're making."

We could only hope. That explanation was safe.

~~~~~

Kurt was waiting when I got home. He looked grubby and hacked and tired. Felicity wasn't home and her dogs were inside the house. After what had happened before Christmas, she didn't like leaving them outside if she wouldn't be back until after dark.

"Something freaky going on at Eden," Kurt said, sauntering up to my Jeep as I slid out of the driver's seat. He reached in and pulled out my chair for me. "Know what the freakiest thing is? Besides a dozen people thinking they've seen that Grandstone twitch skulking around every corner—"

"Why can't she stick to how she was in high school, refusing to go near Eden because the town stole it from her family?"

He grinned wearily and shook his head. "No, the really freaky part is everybody convincing themselves nothing freaky is going on, it's just pranks and old equipment and gas leaks."

"What's going on is so unbelievable, even for Neighborlee, they don't want to believe?" I settled into my chair and tossed him the house keys so he could open the door ahead of me.

"Okay," I said, once I was at the top of the ramp and sliding into the warmth of the house. "What wasn't so freaky, when it should have been?"

"The circuit box *was* missing. A great big circular hole in the casing. Hiram went back three times to check it after he called me and called the board of directors. If someone's stealing antique equipment, we wanted to get on the trail right away and maybe catch them. There can't be that much of a market for stuff that old. Anyway ..." Kurt sank down into his usual chair at the table. I held up the bag of chocolate cinnamon espresso I kept on hand for emergencies and he nodded. "When I showed up with my camera and everything we needed to start working on the problem and document the damage ... well, it was all there again. And the air kind of stung, the closer you got to the HVAC unit. I didn't hear
~~~~~

that ringing you talked about, but the stinging faded after a little while."

"Hiram doesn't drink, doesn't do drugs, and doesn't hallucinate. So you think the circuit board *was* gone." I finished filling the coffee pot reservoir. "You think you were feeling the energy from it coming back?"

"Or at least becoming visible again. Who knows what was happening? But it's not just stuff vanishing anymore. The gas company called. Wanted to know what happened to the man they sent out, to look for the gas leak. He missed two call-ins. Gina thought he left, after he didn't find anything. We went out back and found his van still sitting there. We found him, passed out in the girls' locker room."

"Why do I have the creepy feeling the Rooney boys are part of this?"

"As suspects or victims?"

"Considering their track record, maybe both?"

"We found them while we were looking for the gas man. Inside the old coal bin, and no idea how they got there. They claim they brought their mother's trays of cookies for the party, and they were looking for Gina to tell her they put them in the kitchen. Next thing they knew, they were in the coal bin. Get this: their watches were more than an hour-and-a-half behind."

"How far behind was the repairman's watch?" I guessed from the gleam in Kurt's eye, he wanted me to ask.

"Almost two hours. How do you explain that away with a gas leak?"

"Wish it was real, for one thing, so we could legitimately shut down Eden." I wrapped my arms around myself and shivered, cold on the inside despite the warm kitchen.

"Yeah, well, he already looked, no leak, so that option is out." Kurt shook his head and got up, his movements tight and jerky like they got when he was frustrated and wanted to pound a balky machine into submission. He snatched a mug, pulled the carafe out of the machine with the other hand, and spilled coffee in from the half-filled carafe.

"We have to consider something we've never done before."

"There are a lot of things we haven't tried yet. I've always wanted to blow up something big. If Eden isn't there tomorrow, they can't hold the party." He bared his teeth at me in a nasty grin. I knew he was joking and tired and in a bad mood.

"No, I mean confiding in someone with authority."

"We already have Stanzer involved. How can we go higher than Angela?" Kurt lifted the mug to his mouth and drank it scalding hot. I winced with sympathetic burns on my tongue. "What use are his critters, anyway? We can't have him walking patrol outside Divine's and at the party at the same time. Although … what's happening at Eden might be more up their alley."

"I mean someone who can get the police ready, just in case something big and nasty happens."

"Gordon is the only cop I would trust not to throw a net over us and haul us off to Area 51. The thing is, despite everything he's gone through with us, this might finally send his creep-o-meter over the edge. What if he believes us, and turns on us? Do we kill him?" He laughed when he said it, but the laughter didn't touch his eyes.

Kurt stayed for dinner. We filled Pete and Harry in on what was happening at Eden. I might have been looking after them while our parents were out of town, but I knew Mum and Pop had told the guys to look out for me, too. Besides, they had more time to read all the new SF books and magazines and watch Discovery and Smithsonian Channel while I was at work. They might have more or different ideas than we did.

"You think tesseracts are real, maybe?" Pete finally said. He grinned triumphantly when I had to stop and think what he was referring to. We had the choice of the tesseracts as explained in the Madeline L'Engle books, or the blue cube in the Marvel movies.

"Don't you have to activate them?" Kurt said, when we explained the premise of the book. "Nobody here is activating them. Are they? Maybe that's what's been sucking the energy around town, but why focus on Eden?"

"What do we really know about tesseracts, if they even really exist?" I said. "It's not like we can call any of the authors of the books or scripts, and ask for the scientific basis of what they wrote. Who knows?"

"Stanzer might be the closest thing we have to an expert," Harry said. "His guard dogs are kind of like living tesseracts. You think? What if just being here in Neighborlee so long has made something happen, warping the fabric of space and time?"

We all went silent after that hypothesis. It was a good one, and bad, if he was right. What if the Hounds just showing up every once in a while made something warp? Kind of like that episode of *Lois and Clark*, when Luthor made it look like every time Superman used his powers, he affected the weather.

Finally, Kurt stuffed the last bite of pizza into his mouth, washed it down with the last of the coffee, and stood up, reaching for his coat.

"I think I'll go have a talk with Stanzer before I head home," he said. "I'll let you know when I come by Eden tomorrow whatever we figure out or decide."

"If Eden is still there tomorrow." Pete tried to smile, to make it a joke, but my troublemaker brother looked worried.

~~~~~

My original plans for Wednesday were to have a leisurely breakfast, spend some time at Divine's looking for some glitzy performance clothes, and head to Eden around lunchtime to help with the setup for the party. Most of that got changed on me. I couldn't go to Divine's while Angela was pretending to be sick, and "leisurely morning" usually translated as sleeping in to 8 or 9. I was awake before dawn, unable to sleep, too restless to stay in bed. I was puttering around the kitchen, playing with the idea of a blow-out fancy breakfast.

A light came in on Felicity's place. I was considering calling her to find out if she was as restless as me, when someone knocked on the back door. Before I could even turn my chair to face the door, it opened. In walked Will and Phil.

They were glowing. As in wrapped up in shimmering streaks to rival the Aurora Borealis. Felicity was with them and she looked a little starry-eyed.

"Test run," Will said, and held out a hand to me, beckoning.

I should have asked questions, because I had a lot of theories about those two, with their elegantly pointed ears and the fact they never seemed to change or age, despite seeing them come visit every three or four years ever since I was in elementary school. However, I just grabbed my coat and headed for the door.

A swirling tunnel, maybe eight feet long, filled with the same
~~~~~

shimmering aurora that covered Will and Phil, was anchored to the frame of my back door. The other end was anchored to the back door of Divine's Emporium. Felicity and I went through. By the time I turned around to thank Will and Phil, and ask a couple dozen questions, they just vanished. And the tunnel with them.

"Well, that worked out very nicely," Angela said, from the doorway into the back hallway. "I have the curtains closed, so no one will guess anybody is here, but do hurry if you can. I'll have breakfast waiting when you've picked out your outfit and your taxi should be back in about an hour." With a wink for us she turned and hurried down the hall.

"Okay, that was cool," Felicity said. "I honestly thought I might get airsick or vertigo or something."

She stepped back to let me wheel out of the back room, a combination mudroom and unpacking area for shipments or boxes Angela brought from the cellars. We hurried, because it was just plain dumb to make Angela wait when she was making breakfast for us.

The magic of Divine's worked for me once again. After only ten minutes of searching the racks, I found exactly what I was hoping for. A sparkly, dark royal blue top, with poufy sleeves, and matching lace at the cuffs. I loved it at first sight. Best of all, it didn't have a waistline and it hung long, covering up my lap, and was split up the sides so it didn't create those ugly, unavoidable wrinkles that came from sitting all the time.

Divine's Emporium had a tendency to do that. Whatever we really wanted or needed was there. All we had to do was dig and hope.

"You are going to look wonderful," Angela said, as we settled at the table in the main room for a quick breakfast.

She had enormous muffins dusted with rainbow-shimmering sugar crystals and breakfast burritos. She poured the tea, opaque purple, smelling of ginger and peaches, rich and sweet. Felicity and I took turns relating the events of the last two days at Eden. She nodded and frowned and didn't interrupt with questions. We kept talking, offering our theories and trying to rule out what caused the now-you-see-'em-now-you-don't-now-you-see-'em-somewhere-else situations.

"You're worried. That's good. Of course, being who and what

you are, it's part of your nature to worry," Angela said, when we ran out of words.

"You know what worries me the most?" I said, after I took a long sip of that incredible tea. "I'm worried that people *aren't* seeing or connecting what's happening. It's like something is stopping them from seeing how freaky it is. They're glossing it over in their heads and blaming gas leaks and kids playing pranks. It's not like quantum physics, where they can reshape reality by refusing to believe in something. Whatever it is, it's too strong." I shivered when that came out of my mouth, because I hadn't been consciously thinking that up until that moment.

"Don't be too sure of that," Angela said slowly. She sipped her tea and gazed into the mirror-like purple depths. "The guardians, and especially you three with your gifts, exist to see clearly and anchor reality in all the right spots so it doesn't stretch and get too thin. So it doesn't reshape from the power of belief. Or in this case, disbelief."

Angela paused, eyes half-closed. Felicity and I filled our mouths and waited for her to tell us what we needed to know.

"From my viewpoint, my experience," she continued after several minutes of silence, "Neighborlee is a nexus spot. Things that aren't possible or even welcome elsewhere in the mechanized and sense-oriented world, which insists that if something can't be seen or touched or tasted or heard, it isn't real ... are drawn to this town. However, the dangerous part of filling this vital need in the world is that the more the unreal and necessary and potent things are drawn here, the harder it is for reality and truth to fight for solid footing and predominance.

"And reality and truth must, ultimately, prevail. The strange and imaginative and ephemeral are necessary to help us color and reshape reality to be easier to swallow, so to speak. We need truth so the doorways between different levels of reality are not pulled from their anchor spots and warped from their true shape."

"Why?" Felicity whispered.

"What happens when a door is warped?" She waited only a heartbeat while we thought. "You can't open the door, or what is more dangerous, you can't *close* it. People are trapped where they don't belong, help can't get to us, and the things that are ugly or dangerous, or both, can't be pushed out into a place where they are happier—and we are happier without them. Sometimes, the wonderful, amazing things slip through into a place where they never belonged, and even though that might be a blessing … well, let's just say that cycle continues, getting stronger and stronger until no one remembers how the world used to be or has any idea how it should have been."

"Wow," Felicity said, nodding slowly.

When the introspective light left her eyes and she visibly relaxed, as if a burden had been set down, that signaled the end of what Angela was going to give us for that day. Pushing Angela or Divine's for explanations or support they weren't willing to give was equivalent to a death wish. I've seen what happens to people who threaten or anger Angela. Or worse, disappoint her.

"Umm, I'm really sorry about leaving you guys in the lurch tonight," Felicity said, as we were finishing up and the time approached for Will and Phil to return and take us home.

"Don't you feel guilty," Angela said. "We'll be fine. You deserve some time off. In fact, a lower power level, or chord of energy or talents, or however our enemy senses our presence … a lower level will make them overly confident and careless. We have a trap set for them. Besides, if Jake is following through on some of those looks he's been giving you, don't you dare sacrifice tonight." She winked at Felicity and started gathering our dirty dishes onto the tray, to take everything up to her apartment.

"You think?" Her voice cracked a little with relief.

I wanted to laugh, not just from how silly she looked, but the certainty that Angela wouldn't give Felicity permission to just be a girl in love tonight if we really *needed* her participation.

Tonight was for Jake and Felicity, a couple who deserved to be together forever. Not the trio of Felicity and Kurt and Lanie. She laughed when I told her so.

"No, I'm serious," I said. "This is a night to be Felicity the girlfriend, not Felicity the superhero. You deserve time off from saving the world. Or at least our corner of it. Superman gets to take off his costume and be ordinary. Just because we don't have costumes doesn't mean we can't take time off, right?"

Of course, Felicity wanted to go take a second look at something that might be better for tonight than what she had picked out last week. Angela came back with the watering pail, to add water to the wooden tub that held the Christmas tree.

"Can you see the future?" I asked, when she just smiled at me and parted the tree limbs to insert the watering pail.

"You mean my remark about Jake asking Felicity to marry him tonight?"

"You didn't say that. You just hinted. But yeah, can you see the future?"

"You must really be worried about tonight, to ask a question like that," Angela mused. She put down the pail and clasped her hands, studying me for a few seconds. "No, I don't see the future." Her serene expression sharpened to mischief. "Jake came to me for some help with a very special item."

I mirrored her grin. If Jake found an engagement ring at Divine's Emporium, it would be perfect.

Tonight had to be perfect, both for the party and whatever we did to defend our home once again. We had Felicity and Jake's future to defend, too.

~~~~~

I got to Eden just after 1. Gina didn't report any weird rumors or occurrences, so I took it as a good sign that nothing had happened. Of course, the silence could mean the weirdness had ended, or it was taking a break and gathering up steam for later.

My relief lasted about ten minutes. Gina and I were still setting up to go over all her lists and decide what task to tackle first when a warning chill went up my back. I swear the lights dimmed in the office. Gina raised her head and looked over my shoulder at the door.

"Can I help you?"

I turned my chair to look toward the door. Sylvia posed there, lounging against the doorframe with a smug little grin on her face. She wore a glossy black fur parka with a poufy, silvery fringe on the hood and hem and cuffs. I had never considered myself an animal rights activist, but the thought that some furry critter died to decorate *her* riled me.

"Well, hey there," Sylvia purred. She had an inexplicable Southern accent. Maybe she had indulged in a liquid lunch and her carpetbagger ancestors were coming to the fore?

Okay, that was catty, but I didn't like her all through school, and now with the grief she was giving Daniel, I had even more
~~~~~

reason to dislike her. Especially if she was about to waste our time, when we had a lot of work to do for tonight.

"Do you need help with something?" Gina asked, using that cool, polite voice and expression she wore when politicians and self-appointed movers and shakers went on the attack. I hadn't said a thing, but she must have picked up a clue from me that I didn't like Sylvia.

"Are you lost?" I couldn't just roll into the shadows and leave Gina to handle the invasion.

"I know exactly where I am. Thanks for asking." Sylvia gave her fake little giggle and tiptoed across the floor in her stiletto boots. "You can tell me where my Danny is."

"Danny?" Gina said, raising one eyebrow so high it disappeared into her hairline. "Is this a lost dog or a cat? You look like a cat person."

"Mr. Sheridan hasn't come back from his business trip, as far as I know. Have you checked with the main office?" I said a silent apology to all the nice people at the office in Independence for foisting Sylvia on them yet again.

"They don't know anything." Sylvia pouted.

That wasn't her best expression. I've seen some girls use a pout as their secret weapon. Some men just can't resist a cute pout. It melts their brains.

"I can't get hold of Danny anywhere. I tracked down his hotel, and they said he was on his way home. Someone there heard him talking about a New Year's Eve party at a community center." She flashed that triumphant smile that had enough wattage to light up the entire town for a week. "So I came here, and look, you're having a party tonight."

"That doesn't mean he's coming to this one." Gina managed to sound and look bored and bland. No hint of how she felt about Sylvia. She had a future on stage, if she wanted it. "Come on. I'll show you." She beckoned for Sylvia to follow, and led her out of the office, down the hall to the wall of bulletin boards.

Chapter Six

One bulletin board was set up for what Gina referred to as cross-pollination. It held announcements of activities in our sister towns. These were small towns across the state where budgets for activities were small and populations were hungry for learning and doing, so they banded together to share information. Kids from Neighborlee might go on a canoeing trip in Canada sponsored by the community center in a town near Toledo, or a seniors group from Cincinnati might come up to Neighborlee to join an overnight trip to Amish country. Things like that. Right now, the cross-pollination board had at least twenty flyers for New Year's Eve parties, in every county surrounding ours.

Sylvia studied the board, her lower lip quivering with disappointment. I had the excuse of lots of work and a tight schedule to let me escape. I rolled to the main gym with two huge bags of crepe paper rolls hanging off my chair, and diagrams for how Gina wanted it set up. My crew was waiting. I gave her a thumbs-up sign as I rolled behind Sylvia's back. She turned her head so Sylvia couldn't see, and winked.

Her head was turned, so she didn't see the glare Sylvia directed at her. I could see. For a second, I swore Gina got blurry around the edges. That's the only way I could describe it. My chair seemed to tip to the right and lift off the ground.

I never had a fear of falling until that night I broke my back, and even then, my chair tipping usually didn't bother me, because—hey—only a couple feet off the ground. However, gut instinct kicked in, screaming something awful was about to happen. Instinct acted to fight it. I grabbed with my mind for the floor, reached for Gina with one hand, and mentally yanked. Hard. A zapping sensation, like the one time I got caught in Felicity's crossfire, scorched all my nerve endings. Felicity had killed some sound equipment, that time a grunge band lied its way into performing for Home Days and started in on a raunchy number that had a bunch of seniors dropping their dentures. She was a true guardian of Neighborlee, that day.

Gina stumbled into me and my chair hit the tile floor with a loud enough thud I thought my tires would go flat. Something *clanked* inside my head, like maybe my brain would go flat, too. She stared at me and for a few seconds her eyes were blank. Then she laughed and shook her head and looked around.

"Okay, too many late nights preparing for the party. What were you saying?" She turned back to Sylvia.

I really wished I had telepathic contact with the other guardians right that moment, because something weird had definitely happened.

On a positive note, Sylvia had staggered back against the wall while we were otherwise occupied. She went a dirty white under her makeup and looked around with a drowned kitten kind of expression. I actually felt sorry for her for a second. Gina switched into concerned-defender-of-the-facilities mode, linked arms with Sylvia, and suggested she sit down. Would she like some water? Was she suffering low blood sugar? Weren't the holidays just simply insane-hectic? Sylvia let Gina lead her back toward the office, still looking a little pitiful. I glimpsed those bruises again under all that makeup, and really did feel sorry for her. No matter what a conniving, entitlement-attitude witch she always had been, nobody deserved to be in a situation where she had to cover up evidence of physical abuse.

I had to wonder if Sylvia was suffering for being such a disappointment in her family's schemes. Since I'm being honest here, I didn't feel sorry enough to follow them to the office and try to help. I turned my chair around and headed for the gym again. Work to do. Party for several hundred residents of Neighborlee to prepare for, and the clock was ticking down.

A gust of cold air barreled down the side hallway nobody ever used, just before I reached the gym doors. The wind outside sounded like a freight train and I locked my brakes and looked for the nearest handhold, which happened to be the old cast-iron water fountain. It felt like a wind tunnel for about ten seconds, and that icy air cut through my jeans and sweatshirt like I was wearing gauze. When I looked to the far end of the hallway, my first thought was to yell at whoever had left the door open. Then I stopped, because I honestly couldn't remember if there was a door at that end.

"How did that door get open?" Gina blurted, skidding to a stop right next to me. "That thing has been rusted shut since before the factory closed."

I remembered that now. The existence of plenty of other exits close at hand allowed the fire marshal to give a pass on that one inaccessible doorway. Plus it was in a section of the building the general public never went into. The last three doors on either side of the hallway were for storage and held mostly old equipment for a possible future museum about the former factory. In the thirty-some years since they started transforming the factory into a community center, a lot of people had probably forgotten the equipment was even there. When Eden got big enough, busy enough to need those rooms now being taken up with storage, then people would remember.

For now, the Rooney boys were about the only ones who cared that the equipment was there. Until they got hold of things like the helium tank and enough firecrackers to build a bomb, Gina wouldn't worry. Not too much anyway.

"You think they got the door open?" she said, turning to me. I got that momentary shiver, whenever Gina did something like that, as if she could read my mind.

"The Rooneys?" I gestured through the open gym door. The boys in question were busy dragging dozens of folding tables out of the loft area at the back of the room.

"Close, but not close enough to do that. And they like to brag about what they do," she murmured, shaking her head. "Okay, somebody has to get that door closed before we all freeze to death. Where did that wind come from, anyway?"

I shivered again. She was right. Outside, when I arrived, it had been calm and quiet. That deathly calm in winter, when snow muffles every sound and there's sort of a ringing in the air, like the air is chiming against all that snow. That hurricane force wind that had just rushed down the hallway couldn't have come up out of nowhere, and vanished just as quickly.

If Kurt were there, I would have asked him to go close the door. And weld it shut. He wasn't due to arrive at Eden for a few more hours, to help with the sound system.

"Mike, Matt?" Gina stuck her head into the gym and beckoned for the Rooney boys. "Can you give us a hand here?"

The twins were fourteen, scrawny for their age, with ears that stuck out like jug handles and hair that went in every direction. Their mother gave them buzz cuts whenever she could tie them down long enough. That, fortunately, was where their similarities ended. They would have generated ten times as much mischief, switching off and driving people nuts, if they had been identical. Matt had chocolate curls and brown eyes and a hawk-like nose I hoped he would grow into someday. Mike had strawberry blonde hair and gray-blue eyes and a pug nose and stood about four inches taller than his brother. It was hard to believe they were twins, until they spoke. Then it was like hearing them in stereo.

"Whoa! What happened?" Matt said, while Mike whistled, when the four of us reached the end of the hall. There was too much awe and respect in the boys' faces for them to be guilty.

The big double doors that had never been opened in local memory ... were completely missing. Not even the frame. No sign of damage. Just smooth, flat-shaved bricks framing the new hole in the wall.

Gina stepped gingerly up to the doorway and looked out. I rolled up next to her and set my brakes, and then gripped the sides of my chair as I looked down. And down, to a ramp that went to an underground level of the old factory. There used to be a loading dock of some kind, or maybe a deck here, evidenced by the scraps of wood and big rusty iron bolts still sticking into the brick. No wonder the door was left rusted shut. No one could escape to safety even if they could get the doors open.

There was no room for anyone except Spider-man to stand by the door and unscrew the hinges or do anything else to remove it. No footprints across the steep slope on one side leading up to the door. It looked kind of icy there, too. I looked up and saw a regular monster's mouth of icicles hanging down from the roof. No one had taken the doors off from the outside. I had been about fifty yards down the hallway when the doors came open or vanished or whatever happened, and I hadn't seen anyone.

"You think somebody came by with a helicopter and lifted the doors off?" Mike said to Matt.

"Yeah, that'd be so cool." He grinned at his twin. They scurried back to the gym, discussing how they would have removed the doors and what they would have done with them.

"Okay," Gina said slowly, stepping back from that gaping hole. Warm air from the hallway hit the icy air outside and created a haze of condensation. "First thing we have to do is get someone out here to cover that hole before we lose all the heat in the building. We can't hold a party tonight if we're all freezing." She turned and strode back down the hall to her office.

That left me staring at her. How could Gina so calmly ignore the fact there was no way anyone or anything human could have taken those doors? The same thing had happened yesterday with the vanishing circuit panel. Those who knew it happened had been a little too ho-hum-what-else-is-new? Other than Kurt. Granted, what we called the Neighborlee effect was convenient when we were involved in bizarre incidents as guardians, but this was pushing the envelope.

I scooted my chair back out of the doorway, just in case those doors decided to reappear. I didn't feel like getting hit by probably a ton of rusty iron. What if it didn't swing down from some invisible point in an alternate universe, but materialized like a transporter beam had taken it? I didn't want to have even a few of my molecules merged with all that metal, thanks very much. I was overdue for my tetanus shot.

My joke about the people around Neighborlee employing quantum physics to let them ignore what was happening wasn't funny anymore. Whatever was making things—and people— vanish and reappear was also affecting minds. Were Kurt and Felicity and I the only ones who could see it? Were we the only ones who could even remember what had happened and wonder about it? I looked back at the doors and rolled away, to follow Gina. Then I thought better of it and called Kurt.

"I'll be right over with some plywood and Stanzer," Kurt said when I called him. A ringing sound in the background told me I had caught him at his shop. "That's probably Gina or Hiram calling now. I bet with all that cold air gushing in, the HVAC is giving them fits, too."

"Hurry before the whole building vanishes," I said.

Kurt laughed, but it wasn't an amused sound. Then again, I hadn't been joking.

Gina's wail rang down the hallway. I said good-bye, shoved my cell phone in my pocket, and zipped down the hall as fast as my arms could push me. About ten seconds later, I skidded around the corner into the office and found her standing in front of the table where we had been working when Sylvia walked in. The big accordion file marked "NYE RES: PAID" lay on its side across all the papers and diagrams we had been looking over.

"That witch," Gina growled. "I thought you were exaggerating. But I shouldn't be surprised, after my run-ins with her cousins." She handed me several pieces of paper.

A sinking feeling anchored me to my chair more securely than my broken back and numb legs. I knew what would be on those pieces of paper before I read them. The first was Daniel's registration form. It had his cell phone number, a notation he paid by credit card, and had volunteered to help with the talent show. There was a hand-written note that the company was donating several dozen pizzas for the buffet. Sylvia had found proof where he would be on New Year's Eve. Worse: she now had his cell phone number. Common sense said she hadn't had it before, otherwise she wouldn't be hounding us to track him down.

"What's worse is how cheap Grandstones are." Gina tapped another notation, in different handwriting, next to the space for how many reservations Daniel was paying for. The "1" had been scratched out, and next to it was a "2." The second paper was Sylvia's registration, with a note that her fiancée had paid for her reservation.

"So ... get some volunteer cops to stand at the door and tell her when she arrives that Daniel has refused to pay. In fact, get Chief Tanner to do it. Every off-duty cop and city services worker will be here tonight. Most of them would pay for a chance to frustrate a Grandstone," I offered.

That cheered up Gina a little. Still, Daniel needed to have the option not to show up at all. I pulled out my phone to do my humanitarian duty and warn him, but all I got was static. I ended up using the landline in the office, and only got his voicemail. Either he had his phone turned off, or he was talking to someone. Despite the genetic inclination of all Grandstones to gloat, Sylvia wasn't stupid enough to call him and give him warning.

I prayed he was driving through a town that had made it illegal to talk-and-drive, and some cop eager to fill his quota of tickets before the end of the year would pull him over. I prayed

Daniel would be in a bad mood and fight with him, so he'd end up in a cell somewhere until the doors at Eden had locked for the evening.

It wasn't that I considered Daniel a friend just yet, but I wouldn't wish Sylvia Grandstone on anyone. Besides, if he didn't show up at the party, Sylvia wouldn't stay. It was a win-win for everyone.

~~~~~

"Gina?" Hiram leaned into the gym, bracing himself on the frame of the doorway with both hands. He wrinkled up his nose at the streamers my decorating team had hung from every possible contact point in the ceiling.

The intersecting swoops of crepe paper effectively covered up the girders far overhead. The shadowy heights had been known to swallow basketballs and volleyballs and balloons that went too high, never to be retrieved again from the iron webwork. It might not have been the most aesthetically pleasing pattern of pink and blue and purple streamers, but those were the colors the party store in Hadley had donated. They got rid of stock that wouldn't sell because it had started to fade, got a tax deduction for charitable donations, and we got free decorations.

"What, Hiram?" Gina finished taping the skirt onto the beverage table.

"What door did you say was missing?"

Gina opened her mouth to answer, then frowned. She looked at me, met my gaze, and we both shrugged. I glanced over at the doorway, where Kurt leaned in. Over Hiram's head, he twirled his index finger opposite his ear and crossed his eyes. We had been using the "something's screwy" signal since grade school. Then he pointed down the long hallway in the direction of the missing doors.

Logic said (even though it *wasn't* logical) the door wasn't missing any longer. *Duh!* We should have stationed someone at a safe distance from the doorway to watch and make note of what happened when the doors returned.

Yeah, but what was a safe distance? I thought of that chiming in the air when Gina had skipped from one side of the hallway to the other on Monday night.

I stayed at my post, supervising the kids who were having a
~~~~~

grand time, perched on ladders in a kind of stationery relay, attaching streamers to the grimy girders and tossing them from one side of the gym to the other.

"Whoever took those doors is good," Gina said, when she came back twenty minutes later. "I didn't hear them come past us. Why they would play a prank like that in the middle of the day … well, practical jokers aren't that practical, when you think about it." She shrugged and went back to covering the tables.

I had the feeling that whoever had taken the doors and put them back didn't exactly count as "who" or even people.

Just like when the doors vanished, Gina just shrugged and took the reappearance in stride. I decided to trust my crew, who were almost done, to finish their work unsupervised. I wheeled out into the hall to catch Kurt for a local superhero conference.

I found him standing about ten feet back from the doors, hands jammed into his hips, staring at the big, ugly, rusty slabs.

"Mind control, maybe?" I said. He flinched. He had probably been concentrating so hard he hadn't heard me, even though my wheels squeaked a little on the damp tile.

"Mind control?" He turned and stepped back so he could lean against the wall.

"We're just *imagining* things vanishing, but they're there all the time? We only imagined we felt cold air? We only imagined the circuit board missing from the furnace?"

"It would explain the gas man and the Rooney boys passing out. Someone tried to take over their brains, got them so far, and couldn't control them any longer." He shook his head and looked at the doors again. "Do you hear anything weird?"

"Like what?" I sat still and listened, but the voices laughing and talking in the gym covered up whatever Kurt heard.

"Well … it's more like I can feel it than hear it, but it's still vibrations. Like I feel and hear when I get a battery to give up an extra dose of juice."

"Energy at work?" I guessed. He shrugged with one shoulder. "Gina was way too calm about the whole thing, when the doors went missing, and now. How was Hiram when you guys were working on the circuit board?"

"Considering he loves all the antique equipment here like it was his own flesh and blood? Way too calm." Kurt gave me a crooked smile. "Mind control, definitely."

"Wish we could shut the place down, cancel the party. Maybe evacuate the whole town?"

"Evacuate for what?" Gordon said, startling me. He had paused, aimed for the doorway into the gym. Judging from his jeans and sweatshirt, he was off-duty and had come over to help with decorations. He glanced in the gym and continued down the hall to join us. Obviously, we had been talking too loudly.

Kurt and I exchanged a glance, testing how each other felt about what was going on. When people worked together as long as we had, they didn't need to be able to read thoughts. They knew just from expressions and how they reacted to other situations what their answers would be.

He told Gordon about the missing door, adding it to the list of other weirdness going on. Something was affecting people's minds, their perceptions, and the physical reality of our town. Would more things start vanishing throughout town? Would we be so mesmerized by whatever was in the air, we wouldn't notice or care, even when a crater opened up where the town used to be, and we fell down into the pit?

Worse: would we be unable to care when the town rematerialized, back where it belonged, and we were all crushed?

Could this be part of the rivals' plan, or something that Big Ugly had been trying to do all along? Nope, I was in no mood for a party tonight, but I didn't dare go home and hide under my bed. I was a guardian.

"Could be someone playing games with nerve gas," Gordon said. "Think about the way those boys were all acting, going after Lanie. Maybe some new foreign bug they picked up in the military, overseas, that affects the mind."

"Then how come I'm not hallucinating?" I said. "And if I am, how are other people having the same hallucination?" I shuddered a little, thinking about that dart in my neck. Then the blank in Hayward's memories, from Friday night to Sunday morning. All related? Or just different attacks from different enemies, coming from different angles?

"Good point." He grinned and nodded. "You're right, something weird is going on. I'd better contact the Chief and find out if anybody is reporting strange stuff anywhere else in town.

I'd hate to think about canceling the party tonight, but if there's something going on, or somebody is up to something nasty ..."

"Not on your life," Gina said, when we approached her with our discussion. "We need this party for town morale."

"If the party isn't here, I'm sure everybody would be fine having smaller parties at their own houses," Gordon said.

"Maybe before, but this year it's different." She glanced at me. I got a warning prickle up my back. "After what happened to Lanie, well, a lot of people signed up for the party."

"Say what?" was all I could get out.

"They want to make sure you're really okay. And then there are the rumors about your folks." Gina shrugged apologetically. "People are scared something really bad has happened to your folks. The Zephyrs are part of the heart of this town. They make us feel safe, they have great, crazy stories, they make us feel we're unique. This town can be a little boring sometimes, but Charlie and Rainbow always have something going on."

It was a good thing I was sitting down. Gina said Neighborlee was *boring*? In what universe? She had no idea of all the pranks and problems Kurt and Felicity and I headed off at the pass.

I thought back over the escalating weirdness of the last few days. Weirdness was stock-in-trade, normal even, for Neighborlee. People were used to finding logical explanations for illogical things and shrugging off the impossibilities. Maybe it had become such a strong habit, they did it even when they should have asked questions.

"So you see," Gina continued, while that revelation stormed through my brain, "we need this party, just to assure people that Lanie is okay and she and her brothers aren't worried about their folks, and we're going to get into the new year just fine."

"Didn't know you were so important, did you?" Gordon said, his voice soft, but mischief in his eyes. I had seen that look before. It promised me trouble and a giant-sized dose of teasing later on, at the worst possible moment.

"Nope," I had to say honestly. "Never crossed my mind. Are you sure we're not on Candid Camera?"

That got the laughter I wanted. We were able to shake off the somber atmosphere and get back to work. Kurt and I lagged behind them, so we had a few minutes alone in the hall to confer.

If this was a series of nasty jokes, we had to catch the pranksters. If this was a plan or a freakish unnatural phenomenon, there had to be a pattern to pick up. Once we caught the pattern, maybe we could predict when it would next happen, where, and be there to witness it. If not stop it.

"Just make sure nobody else sees me, if I end up passed out in the girls' locker room," Kurt said.

I promised, and he wheeled me into the gym to continue decorating. It was going on 2 in the afternoon, and the doors opened at 6. We had a major miracle to pull off in four hours.

~~~~~

Matt Rooney let out a shriek. In an adolescent boy, a shriek sounds like a junk truck with his voice breaking and peaking a dozen times in about three seconds. I turned around so fast, my load of balloons and plastic clips almost slid right off my lap. Matt just stood staring at the empty air next to him.

It took me about five seconds to realize what he should have been looking at: Mike.

"Where's your brother?" I asked, pretty sure they were playing the oldest trick in the book. While one distracted me, the other would sneak up behind me and try to steal the balloons.

"Don't know." Matt swallowed hard. "He was right there, and now he's gone."

One thing the Rooneys couldn't do was act. I had caught them trying to look and sound innocent enough times, I knew when they were faking. Matt wasn't faking. He was scared. More color drained from his face with every heartbeat.

I looked up and down the hall, and even looked up at the acoustic tile ceiling. Nope, too high for Mike to take a running leap, grab onto the support bars, push a tile aside, climb up and move the tile back into place. Not without knocking down years' worth of collected grit and grime. Besides, the twins had been jabbering away about all the things they could do if Gina would just be a pal and let them play with the helium tank. There was no way Mike could have performed a near-impossible acrobatic trick and kept talking, even if I hadn't heard the scraping of the tiles.

So where had he gone?

More important, why hadn't Matt gone with him? The twins were practically Siamese. They never went anywhere without the
~~~~~

other, never did anything without the other. Which was going to lead to pretty interesting times, once they got a little older and realized girls were fun.

Mike wouldn't have voluntarily gone anywhere without his twin, so why was Matt still here and why hadn't he seen whoever — or whatever — took his brother?

"He's probably playing a trick on us," Matt said after a few seconds. He looked all around, even up at the tile ceiling. Maybe he expected Mike to drop down on us? He offered me a weak version of his usual mischievous grin. "You know how he is."

"Yeah, I do," I muttered.

Okay, strike another point for the weirdness wiping everybody's minds. I gave up on trying to figure things out. We had the midnight clock to set up, and we were running out of time. I didn't want to worry Matt any more than he was. Or rather, any more than he had been.

If Mike stayed missing, would everybody eventually forget he even existed?

We continued down the hall to the room where most of the crew was putting together the gizmo Kurt updated every year for counting down to midnight. We had our own version of the Times Square apple drop. When it hit bottom, it would trigger the release of a huge net to drop hundreds of balloons and confetti.

We had about half the non-helium balloons inflated, most of the confetti ripped up, and the net untangled, laid out across the floor, and connected with the cables by the time Daniel showed up. He had grease stains on his sweatshirt. It was a classic image of the first four Dr. Whos, which probably would have fetched $500 on eBay in pristine condition. I didn't notice him until the wonderful aroma of pizza drifted across the room and most of my crew sat up, sniffing. It was going on 3, time for their afternoon feeding. Thank goodness my parents had taught my brothers how to fend for themselves before they got into second grade. How did parents of adolescent boys manage anymore?

"Is that your cologne?" I asked, when everybody in the room was staring at him and he looked like he might turn and run. Daniel's eyes bugged, then he looked down at the grease stains on his clothes, and visibly realized the hunger-rousing aromas came from him.

"I brought about fifty pizzas from Mancuso's. Hold it." He braced himself across the doorway of the room to block it. That was a pretty heroic gesture, considering that some of the boys helping me in that room were more likely to eat him and still have room for the pizza. "Nobody touches it until the party. It's been locked up in the kitchen. The kitchen crew have permission to use deadly force to protect it." He glared at my boys, who all stared, mouths open, for about ten seconds.

When I couldn't hold back the laughter, the boys relaxed and grinned at Daniel. A few of them were members of our Trek club and knew him from there. The rest had no idea who he was, but he had already proven himself crazy enough to have their respect. Daniel settled down next to me and helped with the assembly-line of filling balloons and sealing them with plastic clips.

"Thanks for your warnings," he said, once he got the knack of twisting the end of the balloon and slipping the clip on.

"Are you going to make a permanent run for the border?"

"Heck no. I figure there'll be enough people here to provide cover. She can't try to cozy up to me if I'm on the move." He gave me a sideways grin. "Besides, I wouldn't give you the satisfaction and an easy out from doing *Terry*."

"You are still the Evil Overlord."

That got a grin from him, and I couldn't help grinning back.

~~~~~

Mike Rooney showed up at 5, emptying his guts in the boys' locker room. It could have been worse. He could have been making a mess in the girls' bathroom at the front of the building, where everybody would be that evening. Hiram heard him moaning and flopping around, and went in, expecting to find some hormonal teens messing around because it was too cold to use someone's back seat and park at the quarries. He waited until Mike stopped heaving, made him wash his face and rinse his mouth, then half-dragged the kid down the hall to the kitchen. Gina and her team of heroic volunteers were going over the list of what food would be served when and how, and who was supposed to be in charge of what.

Matt was there, of course. He wasn't allowed within ten feet of any of the food, but that didn't mean he and his buddies weren't loitering near the door, hoping for pity handouts. He took
~~~~~

one look at his twin and charged. Like most boys, he couldn't hug his brother, so he grabbed him and shook him and then punched him in the arm and shoved him against the wall, all the while chewing him out for scaring everybody. Except him, of course, because he knew his twin was just being stupid and he wasn't in any danger. Was he? Nobody hurt him, did they?

"I don't know!" Mike finally moaned, when Matt stopped shoving him around. He sank down to the floor with his back against the wall. He wrapped his arms around his stomach and shivered.

"What happened?" Gina brought wet paper towels, knelt next to Mike, and wiped his face.

"I don't know. We were going down the hall with Lanie and the next thing I know, I'm on the floor and my guts are turning inside out."

"That was nearly three hours ago." Matt looked about as pale as his twin and sank down to the floor next to him. "Don't you remember nothin'?"

Mike shook his head, which wasn't a smart move, because he moaned and slapped both hands over his mouth again. We ended up bundling him in the back of Daniel's car and he drove both boys home. Mike kept insisting it couldn't be past 5, because he hadn't passed out, he just got really dizzy and everything was black for a few seconds and he ended up in the locker room.

Just like before, nobody thought anything more of it, once the initial excitement had passed. Nobody but Kurt and I wondered how Mike got from one far corner of the building to the other without anyone seeing him. And more important, where had he been for nearly three hours?

To say that the whole situation was getting me hacked off would be an understatement. I seriously considered calling Pete and Harry and telling them to spend New Year's Eve at home. Whatever was going on, I didn't want my brothers involved in it. They were ordinary mortals. Even if I didn't have the power of invulnerability, I had a better chance of surviving the building collapsing around us or turning inside out than they did.

The problem was, knowing my brothers, they'd kidnap me and throw me in the back of a car and take me somewhere far away to keep me out of danger. Then they would come back to

Eden to face whatever weirdness was gathering its strength. That was just the way Charlie and Rainbow Zephyr raised us, I guess. Heroic, but dumb.

We tried to contact London and Sherwood, to find out if their monitoring of the energy around town, and especially Eden, had revealed anything. They didn't answer. They had warned us they might be so busy they wouldn't hear, but the silence still bothered us. We tried to call Athena, and I got that static in my phone like when I tried to call Daniel. Kurt tried too, and ended up going outside to get beyond any interference field. He came back less than two minutes later, accompanied by the Longfellow clan, who had just arrived. We went into conference with Ford and Athena and Wallace.

Ford had been driving around town all day, looking for anything odd, any blips of energy, anything that clicked with his increasingly hazy dreams. He had checked with Angela, and took a test walk down the dimensional tunnel between Divine's and Eden. It made him sick to his stomach. Angela thought there had been a few attempts on the shop's defenses, little more than pressing against the energy to test its strength. Maybe equivalent to someone leaning against a closed window and trying to see through gaps in the curtains.

Athena and Wallace had been working with London and Sherwood most of the day, trying to fine-tune their link with the energy defending Neighborlee. They had brought a bag of equipment and bits and pieces from Kurt's shop, and instructions from the two AI's for refining the sensor Kurt had been working on all Christmas Day. While the intent was to detect and analyze and hopefully figure out how to fight those energy fluctuations if they occurred again, all of us hoped nothing would show up tonight. There was always a chance, after all, that having so many people in the building would provide energy for *defending* Eden, rather than aiding the enemy in breaching the gates.

~~~~~

A chiming feeling of energy shivered around me, and for a second something rippled in the open air of the lobby, about three feet in front of me. I slammed on the brakes and pivoted back onto my main wheels and turned. And nearly knocked Daniel off his feet. Well, that was what he got for walking so close to my chair.
~~~~~

I kept my eye on that ripple. It reminded me of the time cloud effect in the first *Tomb Raider* movie. It faded in another three heartbeats. I swallowed hard, sending my stomach back where it belonged. No way did I want to know what would have happened if I had wheeled into whatever it was. Energy or some kind of semi-invisible monster? I grinned and muffled a snort when I thought of the Id Monster from *Forbidden Planet*.

"Yeah, you think it's funny, but you're not the one who almost got run over," Daniel groused. "What's wrong?"

I swear, he was looking right at the spot where the ripple had been. If he had seen something, wouldn't he have said so?

Then again, I didn't say anything about it to him, did I?

"That's what you get for stalking me," I muttered. My mind raced, trying to figure out what would happen if I told him about the weirdness going on at Eden. "Where's Kurt?"

"Right here," Kurt said, sounding a little out of breath. He dashed through the third set of doors to the gym a second later. He carried his sensor gizmo, about the size of a portable cassette recorder from the 80s. Lights flashed on the screen, multiple colors that did not look good on his skin. He hesitated for just a second, giving Daniel a weighing glance. "Oh, yeah, I feel it. Not as strong as it was about ten seconds ago. Almost dead now. Did you see or hear anything?"

"I nearly rolled into it."

"What?" Daniel demanded. He glanced at the same spot where I had seen the ripple, then gestured at the gizmo. "That looks like something from Star Trek."

"Better," Kurt said. "It actually works."

Chapter Seven

I hurried to introduce them. Then I described what I had seen and felt, very careful not to look at Daniel as I did. I wondered if he was rethinking his insistence that I be *Terry*. Ironic, that my chance had finally come to stop being an advice columnist, and I wasn't all that eager to be free.

Kurt stuck his hand into the middle of the empty air where the ripple had been. Multicolored sparks shot up through the air. Daniel took one step back, then stopped himself. He moved over to stand next to my chair and gripped the handlebars. Maybe he thought he could pull me out of danger if anything happened? Maybe he did it for his own comfort. Either way, I kind of liked having him that close. He still smelled like pizza.

"Whatever it was is gone," Kurt muttered. He went down on one knee and waved his hand through the area. No more sparks, which was a relief to me, but he looked disappointed. "Energy. Kind of reminds me of Felicity when she's really ticked," he added with a grin, turning to face us. "A phenomenon, not something alive."

"Lots of different definitions for alive," Daniel said. "Just ask the writers for *Stargate*."

Kurt gave me a look we almost never used. The one for, *Does he know?* Meaning: Had I told Daniel about us? I shook my head.

"If we knew what kind of energy it was … heck, we still wouldn't have any answers. We need Dr. Who, Samantha Carter, Data and Spock, all rolled together to figure this out."

"We could try praying," I said. As usual, I kicked myself for not thinking of it sooner. God shouldn't be the last resort, right?

"I'm ready to try anything." Kurt got up and stomped back to what he had left unfinished in the gym.

Daniel stayed with me when I retrieved my coat to go outside to make my phone call. I called the church. Pastor Rocky answered the phone. I figured he was gathering up what he needed for the prayer and communion service Neighborlee Gospel Church would hold at Eden, before we moved into the new year. Not many people wanted to spend even half an hour of reflection leading up to midnight, though, so only Pastor Rocky made the effort to lead services.

I gave him a general idea of what was going on. Ford had the duty of keeping Pastor Rocky updated on this new assault on our town, so I didn't have to give many details. He promised to get the concern going through the prayer chain and then told me to save a spot in the first game of Murder for him.

Yeah, Pastor Rocky has always been a cool guy.

"So … you don't think science fiction and church cancel each other out?" Daniel asked, his words a little slower than usual. He walked beside me this time, instead of semi to my left and behind me, as we went back inside and headed down the far hallway to the locker rooms. The opposite direction from the hall with the storage rooms and the temporarily missing door. We had twenty minutes until the doors officially opened for the party. It was time to get washed up and change into our party duds.

"Nothing cancels out God, and I think He's open-minded enough to let us have fun. Besides, Paul said to be all things to all people."

"Paul who?"

"The Apostle Paul." Funny, but I felt kind of disappointed that Daniel didn't know. Ironic. Five weeks ago I couldn't stand him, and now I hoped we had more in common.

"Oh, yeah, him. You talked like he was someone you knew. The preacher at my church always insists on formal titles. You can hear him talking all in capital letters."

Okay, good, Daniel went to church, but obviously not a comfortable one like I had. That was a relief. It was a starting point. A starting point for what, exactly, I wasn't in any mood to consider right then. We reached the locker rooms where all the workers were getting cleaned up. I yelled ahead. Samantha opened the swinging door and held it so I could wheel through. No more time to talk to Daniel. I was relieved I didn't have to explain all the background weirdness that went along with what he had just seen. With the way things had been going that day, he would probably forget all about it in another five, ten minutes.

~~~~~

Doni and Cosmo volunteered to work the registration table,
~~~~~

and I asked them to be on the alert for Sylvia to show up, so we could warn Daniel. She never appeared. We recruited several friends from the Trek club to watch at the other doors, to make sure Sylvia didn't try to sneak in. They didn't open from the outside, but we knew better than to expect rules to apply to Grandstones when they were on the warpath. Our precautions were almost a waste of effort. No action. No known Grandstone henchmen showed up for the party, either.

Looking back, that should have warned us something was up. At the time, all we cared about was being safe from the expected nasty tricks. We shouldn't have been relieved when Sylvia didn't slither through the door.

At 7 on the dot, and no sign of invasion, we exhaled a collective sigh of relief. It was almost an anti-climax when we joined in the ceremony of locking the doors from the inside, so no one could leave until morning. The Fire Marshal would skin us alive if we actually padlocked the doors, even with Fire Chief Porter and a half the off-duty fire-and-rescue team present. We did the next best thing: toy plastic chains and plastic padlocks on all the doors. If there was an emergency, it wouldn't take much to break the chains and let us open the doors. Kurt also had a nifty gizmo on all the doors that set off an ear-piercing shriek if somebody tried to leave without permission. When Gina clicked closed the plastic padlock at the main doors, everyone let out a cheer and raced to the gym to officially start the party.

Gina, Daniel and I lingered at the front doors, watching the parking lot. I had the awful certainty Sylvia would show up at any moment and raise a ruckus when she couldn't get in. A typical Grandstone tactic was to threaten legal action to obtain whatever they considered their rights. But no lights appeared in the parking lot. The walkie talkie clipped to Gina's waist didn't crackle and pass on a report of a crazy blonde trying to get in at another doorway.

"The witching hour ... has not arrived," Gina muttered. She grinned and pretended to wipe nervous sweat off her forehead.

"And there was much rejoicing," I said, and blew one of those tickler thingies that unrolled with an obscene raspberries sound.

"Before or after they ate Robin's minstrels?" Daniel held onto his innocent expression for about five seconds after he referenced that Monty Python line. Then the three of us burst out laughing and our sense of impending doom fled.

Still, I couldn't quite believe Sylvia had the intelligence to realize she wasn't welcome, or the tact to stay away.

~~~~~

Pete and Harry had been in charge of setting up the obstacle course for Murder this year, and they outdid themselves. There were rows of chairs, school desks, ramps, enormous seesaw contraptions that would tip when someone walked too far along a section of supposedly stable flooring, creaky sections of flooring on raised platforms, stairs that went nowhere, ropes and poles that people could climb down and up to get to other levels. They created four levels this year, because it was a matter of honor to surpass last year's three levels. The newcomers, like Daniel, just stared at the layout as we walked into the auxiliary gym set aside as the Murder room.

"So … are we running races?" Daniel asked me quietly, after Pete and Harry and their team walked through the course, demonstrating how everything moved.

"I wouldn't, if I were you." I grinned up at him. "Murder is played in the dark."

"Why?" was all he asked, after several seconds of his mouth moving but no words coming out.

"Murder started as a college drama fraternity game," Cleo, a drama major at Willis-Brooks said. It was tradition for a theater student to introduce the game. "We usually play at the Playhouse on campus, wandering around in the auditorium, going up on the stage, and through the green room and balcony. Essentially, Murder is Hide'n'Seek. Here, the seeker is the murderer, and you're trying to stay alive and keep moving as long as possible, and try to figure out who the murderer is."

She held up an oversized, grinning plastic skull that had been a punchbowl in a theater production about thirty years ago, according to the lore surrounding the game.

"In here are enough slips of paper for each player. Two are marked. The paper marked with an 'M' is the murderer. The paper marked with the 'DA' is the district attorney. Don't tell anyone what you draw. We will turn off the lights and everyone will wander around the course." She laughed when a couple of
~~~~~

the newcomers let out groans or giggles or exclamations. "When the murderer catches up with you and whispers 'you're dead,' you must wait at least ten seconds before dying, and you must die within one minute, as loudly and dramatically as possible. And this is important: you must stay where you die. The murderer will kill as many people as possible in the time it takes for someone to find the first dead body. When you find a dead body, shout 'body' and someone will turn the lights on. All corpses will then report to the morgue." She gestured at a corner of the room with body outlines sketched on the floor with blue painter's tape.

"Anyone who has been murdered must stay in the morgue until the murderer is found and a new game starts. In each round, the DA will take accusations and can ask one person if he or she is the murderer. You must answer truthfully when the DA questions you. If the murderer is not caught, the lights go out and we start all over again until the murderer is caught or there are no more victims to kill. Got it?"

There were general nods and mutters of acceptance. A few people asked some questions to clarify a few points of procedure. That was when Daniel turned to me.

"How are you going to play?"

"Pete and Harry built the course. They know it's worth their necks to make the aisles wide enough for me to get through." I pointed at the ramps. "I can also go up at least two levels, and the surfaces are reinforced so no one can hear me coming, if I'm careful and if I oiled my chair." I bared my teeth at him. "I was even the murderer once and got through four rounds before someone ran into me right after I killed. Kind of hard to disguise a chair, then."

"You can be nasty, can't you?" He had a thoughtful look behind that grin.

He had no idea.

I drew the DA paper. I tossed it back into the skull when it made the second round of the circle of players, to make it available for the next game. We would only play for an hour, then go into the main gym for the talent show, then people could play board games and eat, watch movies in several rooms, or go to the service Pastor Rocky was conducting. Then back into the gym for music and food, games and a raffle for door prizes donated by business in town, until the countdown to midnight. I would do my comedy routine, then another game of Murder or board games or whatever people wanted to do. After that, it basically got unstructured. Whatever people wanted or needed to do, to stay awake until breakfast was served at 6 am.

Fifty people playing Murder meant a lot of noise, a lot of traffic, making it easy for the murderer to find and kill people without being detected. The murderer in the first round moved fast. I barely got up the first ramp and ducked into a niche that let me sit and listen and stay out of traffic before I heard the first scream. Female, elongating into a yodel. It was followed by a loud thud and rattle, meaning someone had deliberately rolled down the corrugated iron ramp. I made a bet with myself that was Mandy. I felt sorry for her, being the first kill of the evening. She had to spend the rest of the game sitting in the morgue. But Mandy would have fun despite that. Especially if Gordon managed to run into the murderer and get himself killed. It was a good excuse for them both to sit still, in the dark, and have some private time amid the silliness of the evening.

I could never understand why the other people at the party didn't want to start things off with a rousing game of *Murder*. Gina said we had over 200 people signed up. Everyone else was in the main gym dancing, or playing board games, or watching movies. It just didn't make sense to me to do something we could do any other time of the year. We rarely had enough people and enough space to play Murder.

The next scream sounded tentative. Male. A voice I hadn't heard before. Probably a newcomer. Or maybe one of the boys whose voices had changed over the summer, so I didn't recognize the shriek. There were no sounds of falling and banging into things, meaning someone who hadn't looked for staging. Also a sign of a newcomer. The grand master murder victim was a theater student at Willis-Brooks. He held his scream out for a record thirty seconds (showing great breath control, he was also in the Show Choir), then threw himself from the top of the Playhouse balcony stairs and rolled through four switchbacks to the bottom, to land spread-eagle, clutching a lily, and a white feather. That legendary game had been played at the drama fraternity's costume ball, and the murderer was dressed as some kind of vulture-like bird from a student-written play. Even with the feather for a clue, it only narrowed the field down to six players, since a lot of people borrowed feathered costumes at that party.

I know, because I was there and wearing one of those vulture costumes. And no, I wasn't the murderer.

Six more people died before someone called out "body!" The murderer managed to kill two people in search of the light switch, so the game was delayed another five minutes or so before the lights came on.

What was I doing all this time, sitting in my niche, out of traffic and harm's way? Every time someone paused in front of my niche, or hands trailed over the indentation, I would yank on a sleeve or try to grab a hand or leg. That always spooked them and got them running, banging into a railing or wall. If people ran and banged into things, they lost track of where they were in the maze, and that made things a lot more fun. Who said that a gimp couldn't play Murder?

I was right. Mandy was the first to die. The rule was that the first body found had to be carried to the morgue, but all the other victims could walk in under their own power. Otherwise it might take another ten or fifteen minutes until all the dead bodies were gathered together.

The murderer got ten people, including Daniel. That was pretty good for a first round, but not a record. Two years before, the murderer got fourteen people in the first round.

I announced I was the DA. Daniel opened his mouth to offer testimony. Mandy jabbed him in the ribs.

"We are not having a séance here," I said, gesturing for them to be quiet. "The dead are not allowed to speak while the living are in the room."

That got Daniel laughing, and even more whispering from Mandy. She wrapped one arm around his shoulder, sitting next to him on the floor where the dead bodies were supposed to be stretched out in their tape outlines, not sitting up. They whispered back and forth like two mischievous rug rats in my Sunday school class. I nearly burst out laughing. Gordon's eyes got really wide, then narrowed. Gordon—jealous? I never thought I'd see the day.

I listened to accusations for the required five minutes. Some people were as silly with their evidence and accusations as others were with their dying techniques. I asked the person who got the most accusations during this round, Gordon, "Are you the murderer?"

He said no, which was a relief. I would have been personally disappointed, because being a cop, Gordon ought to know better than anyone how to cover his tracks.

We played two more rounds. About halfway through the second round of the three, we heard strange sounds coming from the morgue. I thought at first someone was cheating, giving out clues to the murderer's whereabouts. Then I realized someone was singing! It was hard not to laugh, but that would have given away my presence at the top of a ramp.

Several people giggled, scattered through the maze. The song was *Dem Bones*. A few screams followed in quick succession, meaning the gigglers were close to each other and the murderer caught them all in a group. I nearly lost it when the song ended and the morgue chorus got louder, with more voices, and they changed to, *When the Saints Come Marching In*.

A shimmering sort of feeling washed over my skin, like that crossover of sensations between waking and dreaming. That place where sounds have taste and colors have temperature. From the corner of my eye, I thought I saw light move across my bare skin. The sense of energy died out almost immediately, but it felt familiar enough I guessed Angela had come through the tunnel from Divine's to Eden. Good. The more guardians we had on hand, the better our chances if anything happened. Preferably, the more guardians present, the lower the chances the enemy would try anything tonight. Or if they did try, succeed.

Someone found the knot of dead bodies just before the end of the first chorus. I sighed, a little too loudly, when someone shouted "body!" and the next thing I knew, chilly fingers touched my neck and a voice growled, "You're dead." With peanut butter-scented breath.

Harry had been snarfing down peanut butter cups, from a two-pound bag one of his clients gave him as a late Christmas present. I reached back to give my loving brother a swat, but he had already moved on. I made a note to tell him he had really cold hands, then gave myself a push down the ramp. The wall facing the ramp was padded as a safety precaution. I hit it, shrieked out the loudest yodel I could manage while trying not to laugh, shoved myself out of the chair and did a double-twist to land on the carpeted floor while my wheelchair crashed and tumbled over to land on its side.

The crash of my wheelchair hitting the wall shut up the morgue fast, with a collective gasp that created a wind-tunnel effect in the room for about two seconds. I lay where I landed, holding my ribs and trying not to burst out laughing. I loved freaking people out. It always shocked someone that I could play as rough as everybody else. Just because my back had been broken didn't mean I couldn't tumble with the best of them. It just meant my legs weren't any too reliable.

Pete found me just before the lights came on. He knelt next to me, muffling laughter that made him breathless, put my chair upright, and held it for me until I could climb back into it. The morgue was deathly silent as I was wheeled in to join them. Daniel just stared—especially when Pete grabbed my chair by the handles and tipped it, so I could slide out to lie on the requisite body outline on the floor.

Since he had already been cleared of being the murderer, Gordon was nominated as my successor. He ignored all the accusations and directed his one allowed question at Pete, reasoning that family was the most likely suspect. When Pete burst out laughing and said no, Gordon immediately turned to Harry with narrowed eyes. If Harry didn't get Gordon in the next round, he was caught and the game was over.

"Are you okay?" Daniel asked me, after I got back into my chair, the morgue's occupants got comfortable to wait out the next round, and the lights went off.

"I knew what I was doing." I rubbed my elbow, glad that it was dark, and glad I had left my sparkly blue performance shirt in the locker room. Did not want to risk getting dirty, sweaty, or tearing it.

A loud bang from the doorway made us jump. The door rattled, but didn't come open. It wouldn't until someone stepped over and lifted up the simple locking bar Kurt had created, that slid down over the two panic bars and kept it from being pulled open. The Fire Marshal might disapprove, but it wasn't like anyone needed a key or combination to open the door if there was a fire and we needed to get out.

Another bang. Someone pounded from outside. A woman's voice called through the door, muffled, and impossibly familiar.

"No way," Daniel whispered.

Another bang. A cold prickle washed over my skin. A smell like ozone, but sour. Then wood snapped loudly, and the left door swung open. Light spilled into the gym. Several people cried out, mostly from the morgue. Hey, people who played Murder were hard core and knew better than to make noise while they were trying to avoid the murderer.

"Danny!" an unpleasantly familiar voice caroled. "Is my Danny in here?"

Sylvia Grandstone posed in the light streaming through the door.

"How'd she get the door open?" someone said from behind me.

Daniel went pale and his throat worked like he fought nausea. Yes, I could see him because we sat just on the edge of the long spill of light from the door. His eyes went wide, pleading.

"Get behind me, dummy," I whispered, and gestured into the shadow cast by my chair.

"My hero." He scooted around on the floor.

"Hey," Queenie Peterson said, stepping down from the ramp closest to the door. "We've got a game in session. Can't you read?"

For a second, Sylvia stared at her, visibly stunned. Yes, Grandstones could be stunned speechless by the simple action of refusing to be intimidated by the fact they were Grandstones.

"Read? Listen, I don't know who you are—"

"Good for her," someone muttered from the darkness. That prompted chuckles from several others in the morgue, and out in the playing area.

Sylvia reached to shove Queenie out of her way. "I'm looking for someone, so just get off your high horse and be a good little girl before you get in trouble."

"She's going to get in trouble?" Rita O'Malley said, stepping out of the darkness. "The sign on the door says no one is allowed in while the doors are closed."

"They aren't closed now, are they?" She batted her eyelashes at them.

"Give it up, guys," Bettie Kline said, joining the other two. That was three of the Four Musketeers, as Queenie and her friends were referred to. They had been together since Kindergarten, standing up for the little kids, and then taking martial arts classes when other little girls were taking gymnastics.

"This is the Not Nearly Lost Long Enough Grandstone," Bettie continued, with a toss of her head and a sassy cocking of her hip. "They hire other people to do things like read for them. The only people in Neighborlee who think they're important are them. If you can call it thinking."

Sylvia's eyes got big, and I could have sworn there were sparks dancing around her fingertips and the thick cowl neck of her sweater. Then again, it was full of sparkly stuff, and she probably had on about ten pounds of jewelry.

"How dare you?" she whispered. That kind of whisper that comes across as a shout, sharp-edged and icy-hot and penetrating. "I have never seen anyone so rude—"

"You're the rude one," Queenie snapped, and proved she was stupidly brave by stepping forward.

Wonder of wonders—Sylvia took a step back.

"The doors are closed and nobody is allowed in until the first game is over. Those are the rules. What makes you think whoever you're looking for is in here?"

Sylvia took another step back. She tried to look around the three and seemed to realize the room was pretty much darkness. Her mouth opened like she was about to say something. She glared at the darkness, like she expected it to do something. Maybe she expected some of her family's henchmen to pop out of the shadows and support her. Obviously, she didn't know none had come to the party.

When several seconds passed and no doom fell on the girls blocking her way, her mouth flattened and she turned her glare on them. If she had had superpowers, I wouldn't have been surprised if Queenie, Rita, and Bettie didn't burst into flames, just from the intensity of her gaze.

"Danny, if you're in here … well, I can't imagine why you would want to be associated with this low-life riff-raff." With a sniff, Sylvia flicked her fingers at the three girls and turned and stomped away.

Queenie stuck her tongue out at her retreating back and stepped out into the hall to grab the door and pull it closed. I saw her and her two friends exchanging eye-rolls and grimaces before darkness took over again. Whispers and chuckles breezed through the room. A few seconds later, someone let out a death shriek, followed by more laughter, then another death cry. Some people just didn't catch on very fast. They were probably newbies. Hint: laughing when someone died gave away locations to the murderer.

Gordon managed to avoid getting killed in the next round. He accused Harry almost before the last dead body was dragged into the morgue. Game over after only three rounds. That was okay, we were just getting warmed up for the night. We had about ten minutes until the next phase of the party started, so we decided not to start a new game, and headed for the doors.

"Better give this to Kurt, let him know there's something wrong with it," Gordon called. He was the first one to reach the door, and he pulled up the bar of wood with several long teeth, like a huge skeleton key at either end, that held the door closed.

His mouth dropped open and I was sure the same thought hit him when it hit me: How had Sylvia gotten the door open if the lock bar was still in place?

My second thought: I could have sworn I heard wood snapping and breaking, so how was the bar still in one piece?

Maybe we hallucinated Sylvia coming in?

"Hey," Nadine Willis called, "where'd the others go?"

Three people were missing. They couldn't have left the room, because it would have been obvious when they pushed the door open and light spilled in. Besides, the bar was still in place until Gordon pulled it up. So where did they go?

The three were Queenie, Rita and Bettie. Nadine was the fourth Musketeer, so it made sense she would realize the other three were missing before anyone else did.

Okay, I did not have to be hit over the head by this time to figure out something weird had happened. If not the mystery of how the door opened, then the three girls vanishing without going through the door. Fact: Nadine was the ringleader of the

Musketeers. They wouldn't have gone anywhere without her, even if it was just running to the bathroom. They did everything together, as if they had invisible umbilical cords linking them.

"Well, Queenie was saying she felt a little dizzy, before the game started," Nadine said. "They probably took her to the bathroom." She nodded, smiling and relaxed again, and stepped up to the door. Gordon moved aside and let her shove the door open. She turned right and headed down the hall, in the direction of the main girls' bathroom. Mystery solved.

Gordon frowned for a few seconds. He looked at me. He looked at the other people pushing both doors open and heading out. Then he shrugged and held out a hand to Mandy. They got those goofy we're-the-only-ones-in-the-room expressions and joined the others leaving the room.

"That is just not right," Daniel muttered. He followed me out into the hall. We stayed by the door, watching people stream past us in both directions.

How did girls move that fast in such high heels, anyway? I was an athlete and pretty graceful once, but I never could have moved like that with six inches of plastic spike stuck to my heels.

"The other three running off without her?" I asked, without really thinking.

"No, how easily everybody shook it off." He went down on one knee next to my chair so he could look up at me. Which was a nice, considerate gesture. Sometimes I did get tired of having a crick in my neck from looking up at people.

I got a shiver, mostly relief, when I realized that maybe someone else was immune to whatever weird mind-bending effect had infiltrated Eden.

Yeah, we should have done something to cancel the party. There was no way we could do it now, because how could we convince anyone that things were getting weird-for-Neighborlee-weird?

Well, that was an easy answer: Get Angela. She could convince the entire town government to lock down and lock out the rest of the world, if she had to.

"Lanie?" Kurt slid through the crowd of laughing, chattering, dressed-up people. He pulled out the sensor gizmo. "Something big just happened." He held it out for me to see the screen.

I didn't bother looking at the screen because the little graphs and bars and numbers didn't mean padiddly to me.

"Three people vanished while the lights were out, and they didn't go out the only door."

"Okay ..." He turned the gizmo around to look at the screen. "That would explain it."

"Please tell me we're in the middle of filming some new sci-fi movie?" Daniel said.

Before Kurt had to think of answers that wouldn't have Daniel running for the wagon to haul us to the loony bin, Sylvia sang out his name. Yes, literally sang it out, like a really hokey Nelson Eddie and Jeannette MacDonald number, about two sweethearts separated by continents and warring kingdoms. Except that Daniel didn't sing back. And if I remembered correctly, Eddie and MacDonald loathed each other. I was positive if Daniel opened his mouth in the next few minutes, the only thing to come out would be his last few meals.

The traffic had started to thin by this time, so Sylvia didn't need to shove anyone aside with either her glittering talons or the laser beams from her eyes. She wriggled like an excited four-year-old—or a porn queen, take your pick—as she caught up with us and reached to latch onto Daniel's arm.

Poor Daniel backpedaled as fast as he could to get away from her. One problem: my chair was between him and life-saving escape. His only other option was to back up against the wall, but he stopped short before that happened. It would have left him nowhere to go and her on the point of doing a full-body press.

"Darling, where have you been? This place just isn't you. The people are so ...." Her gaze met mine for a second and her lip curled up. I so wanted it to stay frozen in that position. "Common," she finished with a cooing sigh. "Let's get out of here and bring in the New Year properly, hmm? Like we planned?"

"We didn't plan anything." For all the terror I had seen in his eyes a few seconds ago, Daniel stiffened his backbone and actually sounded cold. "I don't know where you got the idea I wanted to be with you—"

"But sweetie—"

"Because I told you I had plans, they were related to business—"

"Yes, yes, I know, taking over the old rag they publish in this town. Don't you know that printed news is so passé? So last century?" She let out a tinkling little giggle and wriggled like she wanted to snuggle up next to him.

I moved forward about a foot. Daniel slid around behind me, and I mentally gave my chair a shove backwards. Essentially the two of them were forming an arch over my head. Not the most comfortable position, but Sylvia let out a scratchy little sigh of disappointment and she let go of his arm and stepped back. Maybe she was afraid of getting gimp germs from me?

Kurt stood to the side and didn't even try to hide his big grin. Until he glanced down at the gizmo in his hands. His smile flattened. A few creases appeared between his eyes as he concentrated on the screen. He looked back and forth between Daniel and Sylvia.

Meanwhile, she slid into that tone of voice she had been using ever since middle school. The one that implied she knew for a fact everyone loved her and she couldn't understand why people kept forgetting that fact and wouldn't lay down so she could walk all over them, because it was only right they acknowledge she was adorable, and she was just brokenhearted over all the mistreatment she so utterly didn't deserve.

"But Danny, honey, this is the most romantic night of the year. After Christmas. Okay, yes, Valentine's Day is pretty romantic. But it's such a cliché. And I know you're just aching because something got in the way and we weren't able to have our lovely little private romantic Christmas together like you planned—"

"No, *you* planned, but I kept telling you no and you don't have the courtesy to listen," he said, his tone somewhere between cold and bored. I swear, I heard his voice in my head adding, *Nor the intelligence to listen.*

I had to learn that tone of voice. The one that implied the person I was talking to was an utter moron and didn't even deserve my expending enough energy to get angry with him.

"But baby-doll, you don't understand…" Sylvia let out a whimper and pressed her fists to her temples. "I'm just not feeling good at all. I think there's something wrong."

"You're telling me," Kurt whispered.

She shuddered dramatically. "Don't you ever turn the heat on in this place?"

"It seems nice and warm now," Daniel muttered.

"My head hurts. And I've just been walking around this horrid, dirty old place for hours, looking for you. I'm just traumatized from worrying that maybe something happened to you. Danny darling, you'll drive me home, won't you?" She fluttered her eyelashes at him and used that disgusting little girl voice she had used on all the high school teachers who were old enough to be her grandfather. "Tuck me into bed? Make sure I'm all right?"

I swear I heard Daniel's stomach make this sloshy noise like it was about to come up his throat.

Daniel grabbed the hand grips on my chair. I hit the hand brakes, because as bad as it was to sit there between him and Sylvia, I didn't relish the image of watching her chase after me as I was pulled backwards as a living shield. I had a mental image of Daniel retreating into the men's bathroom in hopes of warding her off, and using me as a barricade in the doorway. Considering my few bad experiences helping the janitor at our church, I knew how men's bathrooms smelled. Ain't going there, ever again. Nuh uh.

"Please? Pretty please? Be the knight in shining armor I know you can be?" She batted her eyelashes at him again and simpered. "Help out a damsel in distress?" She probably thought she looked innocent and put-upon.

No wonder she never got any Emmy nominations when she worked on that soap for two years.

"There you two are," Gina called, stepping out of the gym main doors. She took two steps down the hall toward us, then stopped, the horror clear on her face when she saw Sylvia with us. "How did you get in here?"

Chapter Eight

"It's not hard. This place's security is worse than a wet paper bag," Sylvia snapped, her face and voice hard. Then she flinched and gave Daniel a guilty look. "I'm just nerve-wracked, Danny. You'll take care of me, won't you?"

"Maybe you need to lie down in the nurse's office. Alone," Daniel hurried to add, when a gleeful look brightened her eyes. "Gina, can you take care of Sylvia?"

"No. No. I'm fine." Sylvia sidestepped, as if she thought Gina would actually try to take her by the hand. Gina had done a lot of disgusting things for the sake of Eden, but even she wasn't that self-sacrificing. "I'm starved, though. My head hurts something fierce. My blood sugar must be down."

"Food is this way." Gina pointed into the gym.

"Danny?" Sylvia held out her hand, like she expected Daniel to escort her.

The big coward took a tighter grip on my wheelchair and turned me toward the doors, as if I couldn't get there under my own power. I was tempted to grab the wheels and prove to him just how little help I needed.

"Lanie, I've got some technical problems to work out. The sound system," Kurt said. "You're helping with the tech crew, so maybe you should be in on this," he added, gesturing at Daniel. Then before Sylvia could start in on her wheedling-whining routine again, he gestured with a jerk of his head and hurried down the hall.

I pushed hard on my wheels, but Daniel turned me around even faster and we got ahead of Kurt in less than ten seconds. He stopped as soon as we got around the corner, looked back, and bared his teeth in something that couldn't quite be called a grin.

"Run while you can," he said to Daniel. "If you don't want to set off the alarms on the doors, I recommend the basement. The men's rooms are kind of cliché. She probably knows her way around men's bathrooms."

Daniel chuckled and the tension vibrating from him, through

the handlebars of my chair, finally stopped when he let go. He stepped back and I turned my chair to look up at him. His smile faded as he looked back and forth between us.

"What's up?" He gestured with a jerk of his chin at Kurt's gizmo.

"Security for the building. And other business that, quite frankly, you would be better off not knowing about." Kurt let his sensor gizmo hang at his side, with the screen facing his leg. And he just waited.

"Okay. I'm the new guy, but ..." Daniel sighed. "Thanks for the head start, anyway, but ..." A shrug. "It's my fault she's here, and I have to protect my family corporation's reputation. Besides, this is my new home, so I better protect the people who are going to be my neighbors." He stepped back around the corner the way we had come.

"That has got to be the bravest man on the planet," Kurt whispered, and then we waited until the sounds of footsteps faded out entirely in the hallway. It was a pretty good guess everyone was in the main gym now.

We moved farther down the hall, around another corner, and conferred in whispers. I told him everything that had happened. It took a few moments of calculating, but he agreed, the big ripple in the energy he had detected pinpointed the moment when Queenie, Rita and Bettie had vanished. It made sense to blame the same phenomenon or weak places in the wall between realities that caused the equipment to vanish, the Rooney boys and the gas company repairman to lose time, and Gina's time skip and change of direction.

"Let's track down Angela and tell her what happened."

"Angela's not here," Kurt said slowly.

Okay, I hadn't told him everything that had happened. When I explained that I thought that first ripple of energy was the tunnel opening between Divine's and Eden, he shook his head.

"Yeah, I felt something, and I thought that was Angela arriving, but she's supposed to come through the closet in Gina's office. When I went to look, she wasn't there." He sighed. "My phone isn't working, so I used Gina's landline. Angela is still at Divine's."

"Then what did we feel? What happened? Or maybe the

question is, who else or what else vanished?"

"It wasn't the same energy type when the girls vanished. I don't know how to ..." Kurt frowned and turned slowly, eyes narrowing, as if he could see through the walls between him and whatever he was sensing.

"Considering I didn't feel when the girls vanished, yeah, that makes sense. I don't feel anything now. Is something happening?"

For answer, he held out his gizmo to me. The little colored bars popped up and down on the screen and the numbers fluctuated, but he didn't hold it still enough for me to read. Not that I would have understood what any of it meant. We locked gazes for a moment, then Kurt turned and headed down the hall, and I was right behind him.

We reached the lobby in time to see Cleo stop in the doorway into the gym and look back and stick her tongue out at Sylvia, give a toss of her head, and saunter into the gym. Sylvia, meanwhile, was yanking on Daniel's arm, trying to pull him to the main doors to head into the night. His mouth a flat line, he leaned back a little to resist her tugging. It was almost a funny scene. Only a few times in my life had I seen Sylvia Grandstone so furious she lost the power of speech.

"What is that?" Kurt whispered, and skidded to a stop. He caught the back of my chair in one hand and brought his gizmo close to his eyes. He stared at whatever was on the screen, then lowered it to stare at Daniel and Sylvia like he couldn't believe what he saw.

I did, because I had seen it before.

Daniel was sort of fading around the edges.

Like Gina had faded.

When Sylvia was angry with her.

Okay, maybe I *did* have to be hit over the head to make the connection. And I admit, I hesitated, because when I made the connection between what happened to Gina — or nearly happened to her — and what was happening to Daniel right that moment, I also remembered what I had experienced. The sense of being crooked and falling.

Besides, this was Sylvia Grandstone who was suddenly demonstrating a talent for ... for what, exactly? Grandstones weren't semi-pseudo-superheroes, or whatever the polar opposites were in Neighborlee.

"Oh, heck," I whispered, as pieces fell together in my head with a crash that Kurt probably heard. "Think she's working for the rivals?"

I grabbed my wheels for a good hard shove, and took a deep breath to brace to mentally push myself and dive in to rescue Daniel.

"Something's happening." Kurt grabbed my shoulder.

What happened next wasn't exactly a flash, because it wasn't really light. The opposite of light? Something snapped into place and suddenly Daniel wasn't faded anymore. He jerked free of Sylvia's grip and his arm went up in the air and for two seconds, I thought he was going to clobber her one. Yeah, I wanted him to give her a good hard smack, kind of like the Destroyer from the first *Thor* movie backhanded Thor and sent him flying, just before his sacrifice gave him back his powers. And yeah, equating Sylvia with the Fabio-of-the-Fjords, even for a fraction of a second, made my head hurt.

I swear, Daniel's eyes seemed to change color, go almost silver, but so briefly I couldn't be sure it wasn't anything more than an illusion from a rainbow shimmer that seemed to flicker across the lobby. Winkies swirled in, coming between us and Daniel and Sylvia, and then Angela stepped out of the office.

"Oh, Danny ..." Sylvia whined. She went to her knees, pressing her fists against her temples.

This time, I was pretty sure she wasn't faking feeling sick.

Daniel sighed and bent down, caught her by her elbows, and hauled her back up to her feet. She wobbled so I thought she might fall off her high heels, and he had to put his arm around her to lead her into the gym. She winced and let out a couple tiny yelps as swirling winkies ran into her. They visibly sparked and blackened and fell to the tile floor. And yes, I proved what a self-righteous twit I can be sometimes, because I felt more sorry for the winkies than I did for Sylvia.

Kurt, Angela and I backed up to the doors leading outside, putting some distance between us and the center of the lobby and whatever might still be lingering, invisible, there.

"What happened?" Angela focused on the now-empty space. I wouldn't have been surprised to find out she had the ability to call up an instant replay to watch it as we ran through the sequence of events.

I related what we had done to ensure Sylvia hadn't gotten into the party before the doors were ceremonially locked. Then I described the ripple I had narrowly missed rolling into, earlier. Kurt added his part of the story, the sparks, what he had sensed when he had stuck his arm into the space where the energy had still lingered. I felt a little stupid: I should have realized there was something up when Daniel obviously had seen the ripple too. Kurt slapped his own forehead when Angela smiled, just a little bit, and reminded us that Daniel's grandfather was a Lost Kid. Even if he didn't have semi-pseudo-superhero powers, he obviously had some sensitivity.

I described the ripples of energy during the game of Murder, which I had thought signaled her arrival, the altercation with Sylvia, and then the disappearance of three of the Musketeers. Kurt didn't even try to explain the readings on the screen of his gizmo, beyond stating that the energy I felt before Sylvia broke into the Murder room was very different from the energy his gizmo registered just before Angela showed up.

"But that could be because whatever was happening to Daniel was giving off a lot of energy. Or sucking it in. I know you said Gina faded around the edges, but I didn't really understand until I saw it happening to him." Kurt swallowed audibly. "I think you scared it away. There was a lot of energy coming from way down below. Like the readings I was picking up last week, but multiplied. Like squaring or cubing it."

"You think Sylvia is doing it?" I said, when Angela finally turned her gaze away from that spot in the air above the floor where Daniel had momentarily faded.

"The thought of a Grandstone having that kind of power, to reach between the dimensions of reality ..." Angela wrapped her jewel-toned shawl tighter around herself and tried to smile. "I much prefer the more logical explanation, that she is simply a dupe of the malevolence we have been fighting for decades."

"Not dupe," Kurt said. "Tube. She's like the hose on a vacuum cleaner, and it's using her to ..." He snorted. "Yeah, Grandstones suck. Big-time."

Angela rolled her eyes. I managed a grin. It made sense, but that kind of implied Sylvia had been present when other people and the equipment had vanished around Eden. Why suck up people? What did she get from the pieces of the HVAC unit, and moving around supplies?

"Triangulation, perhaps," Angela said. "Practice. Getting the range for targeting." She frowned and turned to look back at the office door. "Bother ... someone rang my doorbell. I will be back as soon as I've proven that I really am sitting sick at home." She mustered up a smile for us. "You're both doing very well. Keep an eye on Sylvia. And your boss. Hmm," she added as she crossed the lobby to the office door. "Since both he and Gina had fading moments, it might be wise to keep an eye on both of them for any delayed reactions." A soft chuckle escaped her when Kurt snapped off a salute. Then she stepped through the door.

That shimmer of rainbow light a moment later was very reassuring, since it came from Angela and not whatever monster below the foundations was using Sylvia as an energy vacuum hose. Kurt and I headed into the gym to do our duty as guardians, keep an eye on victims and dupes, and ensure Eden didn't get sucked into another dimension at the stroke of midnight.

As if our entrance into the gym was a signal, Sylvia's voice pierced the generally happy chatter of people filling plates and cups and settling at different tables. I tried not to show my dismay or nausea, and turned to follow my ears. Sylvia was leaning on the end of the beverages table, chewing out Pamelia Quisp, who stood there with an empty two-liter bottle poised on the edge of a punch bowl big enough to bathe a Corgi. My guess was that she had been refreshing the punch and Sylvia either asked her for something she couldn't provide or a few drops had splashed on Sylvia's sweater as she walked by. I looked for Daniel, and he was just turning around from a table, both his hands still holding plates of food.

"You want me to give you a big hard shove, so you can ram her?" Kurt asked, stepping around behind me and putting his hands on the back of my chair.

"Yeah, and with my luck she's got a force field that burns. No thanks." I grabbed my wheels and gave a good hard shove. Kurt didn't follow me immediately, the coward, and I slalomed in between people to get to the punch table. As I approached,

Sylvia's voice dropped in volume enough that the ringing off the crepe paper-festooned ceiling didn't quite obscure her words. Now I could tell my first guess was right. Sylvia was infuriated and felt quite abused that Pamelia couldn't—or more accurately, wouldn't—give her the scotch-and-water she needed to steady her nerves. By the time I crossed the ten yards or so of floor, Sylvia demanded three more alcoholic drinks, and each time Pamelia just shook her head. She finally had the sense to back up and put down the empty two-liter.

"Sylvia, there are kids here," I said, using my coldly angry teacher voice. Amazing how easily it came back after four years. I had some satisfaction in seeing her flinch and turn sharply enough to nearly fall off her icepick heels, startled. For a second, I wished I had thought to give her a good, hard mental shove. She would have to go home if she broke a heel, wouldn't she? Or even broke her ankle?

"What does that have to do with it?" she whined.

Behind her, Pamelia fled. I noticed the circle of open floor all around the beverage table had grown wider. From the corner of my eye I saw Daniel approaching. Okay, I officially could no longer call him the Evil Overlord. He was turning into my hero, just for having the guts to try to control Sylvia in the face of his very evident terror of her. After all, chances were good that if he spent enough time voluntarily in her company, some time during the night she would pull out a diamond ring and flash it around and proclaim they were engaged, and he would be stuck with all those witnesses. Enough people had been duped or intimidated into marrying Grandstones through the generations, they would believe Daniel was either stupid enough or desperate enough or evil enough to ask Sylvia to be his wife. After all, hardly anyone really knew him. Too bad Conrad and Clarice weren't at this party tonight. They were character witnesses.

Back to facing down the Wicked Witch …

"This is a family-friendly party. It was on the flyers. It was on the party sign-up page. That means no alcohol. Nothing dangerous for kids. So you can demand booze until you're blue in the face, but you're not getting any. If you're so desperate for alcohol to get you through the night, you shouldn't have come here at all."

"That's not fa-a-air!" Sylvia wailed, and instantly turned on the waterworks. "Danny, baby-doll, you'll get me out of this awful place, won't you? What's New Year's Eve without champagne?"

"A lot more fun than you can imagine," Daniel said, from over my shoulder. "Go home, Sylvia."

"But I want to be with you, sugar-pie."

Beyond Sylvia, Kurt had stepped up to the far side of the beverage table and was retrieving some cups. I assumed they were for us. He crossed his eyes at me and pretended to be gagging. Daniel must have seen, because he muffled a chuckle before stepping past me, managing to hold both plates in one hand. He reached out the other hand to lead Sylvia away, still whimpering about what an awful place he had brought her for New Year's. Daniel sounded more tired than angry when he replied that he hadn't brought her, he hadn't invited her, she had brought herself.

Kurt's bit of clowning was anchored in common sense and good taste. When we were in high school, he wasn't like some guys who would have taken advantage of every tramp and twit who offered herself to him. Sylvia had chased Kurt, a few times. We hadn't understood why at the time, because we knew the low opinion the Grandstones had of anyone who lived at Neighborlee Children's Home. After what we had learned in the last few weeks, it made sense that Sylvia was trying to woo Kurt to become a henchman, just because he was a Lost Kid and had potential the Grandstones wanted to siphon away for their own use. Several times when Sylvia had chased him, it was to try to convince Kurt to become a designer and inventor for the Grandstone empire. Kurt earned good money in high school, making him a desirable conquest. It was almost funny, each time Sylvia tried to use her wiles on him. Did she honestly think Kurt wouldn't remember the last time she was on the hunt and he was the prize? I kept telling him if he would just take her out on a date and talk about mechanical theories, and disassemble and reassemble an engine for her, she'd leave him alone forever. He never listened to my advice.

When we joined Sylvia and Daniel at their table, she was still playing at being delicate and exhausted, sighing and fluttering her eyelashes at him. And nibbling on a plateful of enough appetizers to keep a Sumo wrestler going. She was so busy impressing on him how happy she was to be with him, and how happy he would be with her, she never noticed Kurt and I were at the same table. So there the four of us sat, like a really weird double date, nobody else talking much. And nobody joining us. Kurt had his gizmo on the chair next to him, situated where he could just look down and check the screen from time to time. Nothing was happening, energy-wise. Everybody else was having a good time.

That pleasant ripple of energy came like a chime announcing the end of a really miserable day at school. Angela was back. That was my signal.

"Where are you going?" Daniel said, when I backed up my wheelchair.

"Bathroom." I waggled my eyebrows at him and gave him a cheesy grin, daring him to try to follow me.

Actually, maybe I did want him to follow me, just to give him a reprieve from Sylvia. She had started eating off his plate. Maybe she would start eating him if he wasn't careful.

"Anybody else having trouble with phone reception in here?" Kurt said, and held out his cell phone. "I'm supposed to get a confirmation call, but … Maybe out in the lobby it'll be clearer." He got up and followed me to the door.

"That's such a bad lie," I said when he caught up with me.

"You don't want people thinking I'm going to the bathroom with you, do you?" He grinned crookedly. "Besides, the signal is still bad. Athena said if London tried to contact her, she's worried she won't get through."

Cleo was a few steps ahead of us, heading for the door. She glanced back and met my gaze and smiled. Turning, she took a couple steps backwards.

"Hey, Lanie, when we go back —"

Something hazy wrapped around her and something shimmered — very like the Id Monster from *Forbidden Planet* — and Cleo vanished.

Kurt grabbed my chair handles and yanked me to a stop. Yeah, like I was going to go anywhere near that doorway until I was sure whatever made her vanish was gone?

Repeat after me: Superhero does not equal stupid and suicidal!

"We are in some big trouble," Kurt muttered.

A shriek out in the hall a heartbeat later had both of us lunging through the doorway. Something tingled against my skin and I thought it sparkled on the metal beads of my bracelet, but that was all the reaction I got. That scream sounded a lot like Diane Rittenhouse, a college girl who had just started working for Angela. Diane just was not the screaming sort. Not without good reason.

Kurt and I whipped around the corner, heading for Gina's office. Sure enough, Diane crouched against the wall, staring at a heap of bodies.

Correction: a heap of groaning girls. More to the point, Queenie, Rita and Bettie. They were all pale and trembling and fighting to get their eyes open, weakly flailing their arms, trying to get disentangled from each other. Angela appeared, looking as serene as always, her hair just a little windblown, like she had broken the speed of light to get there.

~~~~~

"You know, if this was a TV show, we could apply the Jessica Fletcher theorem and figure out who's to blame," Mandy said, as we watched Mrs. Tancredi, the part-time nurse on duty that night, finish taking the girls' vital signs.

All three were nauseated, pale, with dark smears under their eyes and dark shadows in their cheeks that didn't come from makeup. If I hadn't seen them less than an hour ago, I would have sworn they had been starving themselves for two weeks on a new fad diet. Their clothes hung loose on them and they looked drained.

Not a good word, but the most descriptive.

"Jessica Fletcher?" I said, not really listening.

"Yeah, you know, on *Murder She Wrote*. You can watch the opening credits, and usually the most famous guest star is the murderer. Only we don't have any dead bodies. Thank goodness," she added, with a little guilty smile.

"Thank goodness," Gordon murmured. He had tried asking the girls a few questions after we got them to the nurses' office, but they weren't quite up to coherent answers yet. Chief Tanner was at the party, but he was in one of the movie rooms and Gordon didn't want to interrupt him on his night off. Not until he
~~~~~

had something to report. "This can't be a gas leak like they were talking about earlier. What the hey-hah is going on here?"

"If we blame the most famous person here, that would be Sylvia," I offered. "But she's more the vampire type ... which, if you think about it, fits." I studied the girls, groggy and shivery and pale. Like someone who had half their blood drained to provide someone a midnight snack?

I felt sick, remembering how we had joked about *Buffy* a few days before. The show had made light of elemental dangers that were very evil and deadly at their core. All the things I had run into as a guardian, growing up in Neighborlee, had taught me that every legend, no matter how unbelievable and illogical, had a kernel of truth.

At the turning point of one year to another, anything was possible. Especially in Neighborlee. Especially with Big Ugly trying to break through into our world, and the rivals trying to make contact and something or someone gradually draining the energy protecting our town.

Mandy and Gordon were still talking. I had probably missed something vital in their conversation. I shook my head, trying to shake some concentration back into it. From the corner of my eye, I saw a flash of scarlet and gold. Angela had come back in, carrying mugs of hot tea. From the aroma, that wasn't the generic black tea in bags kept in Eden's kitchen. That tunnel between Eden and Divine's was already proving very handy. She had likely gone home and brewed something special to treat the girls. I smelled spearmint and clove and something that made the tension in the base of my neck unravel.

"You're going to be just fine," Angela soothed, and pressed a mug into Rita's hands. Soon all three girls were sipping, and that glazed look faded from their eyes. Color seeped back into their cheeks in a matter of seconds.

Angela came over to the corner where I was huddled with Mandy and Gordon. She watched the girls, her eyes bright with concern and growing anger. Big Ugly and whoever was working with him were going to be very surprised when she finally slapped them back where they belonged.

"Cleo vanished," I whispered, leaning closer. "Just before Diane screamed."

"Ah, so that was what I felt. What did you see? Besides not seeing Cleo?"

I beckoned out into the hallway and she followed me. Gordon followed us, leaving Mandy behind to help Mrs. Tancredi and Gina with the girls. He caught up with us as we joined Kurt in the doorway of the gym.

Kurt described what he saw, both when Cleo vanished and a flicker of light just before Diane screamed. Gordon just listened, not saying anything. He shook his head and pressed his lips hard together, so they formed a white line. I felt sorry for Gordon. Despite having lived in Neighborlee so long, this had to be hard for him to accept and deal with. Maybe his inherited Lost Kid blood would work against him this time, so he couldn't ignore what everybody else seemed able to shrug off.

"I was starting to think what I saw before was just my imagination, that you were practicing a trick for your comedy routine," Gordon said. "Then with the girls ... what's wrong with everybody, that nobody else is bothered?"

"When we have that figured out, we'll know what to do about it," Angela said. "I suggest we keep this quiet. It's no good panicking anyone."

"I think we should shut the party down and send everybody home," Gordon said. Then he stopped and swallowed hard. "Unless it's some sickness. If somebody put drugs in the food, I can't send everybody home. What if they get in accidents when the drugs take over?"

"It's not drugs. It's an unwelcome guest whom most people don't even know is here." She took hold of Gordon's hands, and the agitation immediately left his face. "You are here to protect. The only way you can protect these people, this town, your responsibility, is to be calm and have the patience of the hunter. It would be wise to confer with the Chief when his movie is over, but I am sure he will tell you the same thing. Wait for the danger to show itself. Then you can act because you will know what it is."

"Right." Gordon took a few deep breaths, visibly looking more like his normal self in just a few seconds. He blinked and shook his head, looked at the three of us, seemed about to say something, then shrugged and went back to the nurse's office, most likely in search of Mandy.

"What did you—"

"I did very little." Angela shivered and wrapped her gold fringed shawl around her shoulders. "Most of his agitation came from the conflict between his strong sense of honor and responsibility, and the outside influence trying to lull him back to complacency again." She sighed and closed her eyes and rubbed them with her index fingers. "I am ashamed to admit I feel somewhat out of my depth. If this is our age-old enemy rousing again, or something new, I have no idea yet. Until we have some certainty, how can we act?"

"So maybe we *should* send everybody home?" I looked at Kurt.

"Nope." He shook his head, once. "Keep it contained. Keep people calm, like you said. I've got this feeling ... whatever it's trying to do, it's going to do soon. There's this sense of pressure, like it's working against time or something. We have to stay here to figure out what's going on." Then he grinned at me. "Besides, you have to do your routine. You're not getting out of that."

"Yeah, some friend you are," I grumbled.

~~~~~

"Man, are you all glad to be here, or what?"

I looked out over the audience. For a second, dread shivered over me that didn't have anything to do with stage fright.

How many of them would still be there at the end of the evening? Would the disappearances and time-warping stop with the stroke of midnight, or would the world end, just like some people thought it would when the clock struck midnight on 2000? Or all those stupid Aztec calendar stories, claiming the world would end in 2012?

"I heard there's a New Year's party over in Darbyville that is supposed to be so boring, instead of serving champagne at midnight, they're using embalming fluid."

Snickers rippled through the room.

I let myself slide into the entertaining groove as most of the people in the gym snickered and nodded and grinned. Well, at least most of the people in Eden that night had no idea there was anything going on. If I could contribute to the safety of the town by keeping everyone in one place so they didn't walk into wandering fogs that yanked them into another time zone, I would
~~~~~

consider my evening well spent.

Okay, I had started off my routine pretty well. That was a relief. If I could stop thinking and engage autopilot for my routine, I would be fine. Unfortunately, I looked over at our table to the far right. Angela and my brothers had joined us. Her smile was encouragement. Sylvia smirked and kept trying to inch her chair closer to Daniel. He had this stiff, frozen, polite smile on his face that I imagined the Vor lords wore when they attended parties given by Mad Emperor Yuri: afraid they'd die if they didn't enjoy themselves, and afraid they'd die if they enjoyed themselves too much, and afraid they'd die if they didn't attend at all. My brothers were scrunched together on the far side of the table, as if afraid they'd catch something from Sylvia. They knew what was going on. Maybe living with me so long had made them immune to whatever rewrote everybody else's memories?

"I can't hear you!" I growled, lowering my voice and cupping my hands around the microphone, as if that would make my voice louder. People jumped and laughed a little louder. I moved my chair around a little. "Whew! I was afraid for a second I had fallen into a painting. You know, with these wheels, I keep getting this weird feeling that in a parallel universe, I'm supposed to be rolling luggage."

Some shrieks and groans answered that. Sylvia sat up, actually moving away from Daniel for a few seconds, as she frowned in evident confusion. I swear, I saw smoke come out of her ears. Too much effort trying to figure that one out? Good, I had caused the gears to jam and distract her from planning how to trick him into proposing. For now, at least.

"Hey, have you thought about improving your mind this coming year? Wouldn't it be better to spend your time reading instead of cruising around town, trying to pick up chicks who are too smart to be outside in this weather, anyway?" I pointed at a bunch of high school guys who belonged to the car club. They all jerked and looked wide-eyed, like I had turned a TV camera on them and embarrassed them at a football game.

More snickers. Okay, people were mellow, but they were awake and mentally present. Who knew how alert people would be in an hour or three?

Please, Lord, let everybody **be** *here in the new year?*

I waited for some comments. The peanut gallery along the back of the gym didn't disappoint me. I couldn't hear their words, just their voices and their cheerful, mocking tones. I rambled for a few minutes about books and audiobooks and comics.

"Let's talk … Modern Music. If you really think about it, what each generation thinks of as Modern Music never really changes. It's whatever the older generation thinks is lewd or disrespectful. Basically, people getting drunk, having sex, and killing each other. You know what they called music over 500 years ago, about people getting drunk, fooling around, cheating and stealing and murdering? Opera. Opera is just 500-year-old Rock 'n Roll. Imagine fifty years in the future, two snobby Frenchmen, kind of like Siskel and Eibert, showing how cultured and intelligent they are by going to a revival of *Tommy*."

That got Daniel laughing. Sylvia looked back and forth between him and my brothers, wearing that put-upon, everybody-is-mean-to-me expression Grandstones patented. Well, at least Daniel forgot his dilemma for about ten seconds. Another good deed chalked up to my account. I took my life into my hands and asked for feedback from the audience, with a half-dozen options of what to say next, depending on what they said. I lucked out, because people mentioned jobs and education.

"Yeah, nowadays, you need specialized training for almost any job. I wanna know: can a shoemaker go to boot camp? Hey, you even have to get training to go on those game shows. You think they just take any hyperactive screaming freak off the street? You have to get training on how to jump up and down, and how to scream without blowing all the circuits in the control booth.

"But you know what I'd like to see, after someone wins really big? Just once, I want to see someone, after winning a ton of money, when the host asks what they're going to do with it, just once I want to hear someone be totally honest and say, 'That's easy. I'm gonna quit my job, right after I punch my boss in the mouth.'"

I pointed at Daniel. A good number of people must have found out he was the new majority owner of *Tattler*, because I got even more laughs. From there I went to fad diets and the vegetarian-versus-carnivore argument. I watched the interaction between a few of the couples at the tables directly in front of me.

From the way various people were grinning at each other, and other people shook their heads and rolled their eyes, I had stumbled into an ongoing argument. Well, nice to know my material was still current.

I checked the clock. I had about five more minutes before I needed to end, let people calm down a little, run to the bathroom, get up and stretch, before the next scheduled events started up. I wanted time to compose myself — and more important, let Pastor Rocky compose himself — before we went into the room set aside as the chapel for the New Year's communion and prayer service.

Laughter roared through the room when I griped about people who insisted on asking the person next to them, in a movie theater, what was going to happen next. As if their companion had seen the movie already. So a lot of people had the same pet peeve. I had struck a nerve of commonality among us. Always a good thing for a comedian.

Finally, I was done. I snapped out my final smart-alec line, tipped back into a wheelie, pivoted, and scooted down the ramp on the side of the stage as laughter and groans and clapping roared through the gym.

Whew! I survived. And no one vanished while I was speaking.

God was merciful yet again. Maybe if we could keep everyone in one place for the entire evening, we would be safe?

Chapter Nine

"Life and death are always intertwined," Pastor Rocky said, wrapping up his New Year's prayer service. "No, I'm not talking about that eastern philosophy mumbo jumbo about them being opposites and balance. Life is bought by death. The obvious ways, by plants and animals dying to provide us food. By a seed decaying in the ground so it can germinate into a plant. By Christ giving His life on Calvary to pay the price for our sins, to cover them over, to cleanse us so we can approach God and slowly return to the oneness with our Creator that we were meant to have from the beginning. There is no balance and unity between life and death. They are part of a larger pattern, a broken pattern, in the larger tapestry of God's will. The old year dies to let the new year begin. Night dies to bring dawn.

"What part of you will you allow to die, so you can step into the new life that awaits you with every breath, if you will just open your eyes to see the incredible gift God is waiting to give you? As you count down the minutes until the old year ends and the new year begins, think about letting go, of sacrificing, of dying, and finding new life. It's the scariest and the hardest thing you'll ever do, but I guarantee it's well worth it."

He stepped back and gestured for the church staff who had volunteered to help with the communion service. Pop would have been part of this, since he was a trustee and a deacon. I closed my eyes, fighting tears as the wooden trays with the pieces of unleavened bread were passed down the rows. Mum and Pop made those trays more than thirty years ago. They had discovered early that tithing wasn't limited to money, but to every part of their lives: woodworking, baking, teaching, landscaping, and leadership. I wanted to hold onto one of those trays when it was passed to me. Yeah, as if holding onto it would yank Mum and Pop through time and space, from whatever dimension they had traveled to, and bring them safely home?

I nearly dropped the tray as a glimmer of an idea came slamming through my brain. It vanished just as quickly, leaving a whisper of itself behind. Fortunately, Daniel sat next to me. He took the tray from my hand, holding it long enough for me to slip a piece of bread off it with shaking fingers.

Maybe a communion service to ring in the New Year wasn't the best place to daydream and get inspiration to handle our problem, but where else were we quiet enough that God could talk to us and give us some clues?

Usually, we used the little plastic thimble-sized communion cups for the grape juice, but a couple times each year, for special occasions, we used these beautiful, hand-made glass goblets. They looked like Venetian glass, with streaks of indigo and crimson and swirls of gold and silver beads through them. Pastor Rocky made them when he was going through his artistic phase, back when he was a hippie art teacher at Willis-Brooks. We had a set of two dozen, each one unique in color and pattern, but all perfectly uniform in size and shape, with the purest piercing chime when they were flicked with a fingernail. Filled with white or red wine, they seemed to absorb all the light that came from the garlands of Christmas tree lights that filled the ceiling of the room, spun it around, and threw it back to us. Members of the staff took the goblets, filled them, and stood at strategic places around the room. Then everybody attending the service (I estimated around eighty of us) left our seats and went to someone, took a sip from the cup held for us, and went back to our seats to sit in silence and just think.

Without meaning to, I ended up in the line going up to Pastor Rocky. He rested his hand on the top of my head as I took my sip of the wine, and that wasn't the usual procedure. Instead of saying the words I had been hearing since Mum and Pop first brought me home from the orphanage, speaking Christ's words as He gave the cup to His disciples, Pastor Rocky leaned close and whispered to me.

"Be strong, faithful servant. Those with a great gift have a higher height from which to fall, and a more severe judgment if they shirk their duty." He smiled at me, a glimmer in his eyes that might have been tears, as I tipped my head back to just stare at him. "The Lord is with you, Lanie. You and your friends. You put yourselves between this town and the darkness, and the Lord will bless you for it. Remember that wherever you go, our prayers go with you. Where two or more are gathered in His name — "

"He is there among us," I whispered. I choked, wanting to cry, wanting to ask a thousand questions. I could see it in his eyes, the truth, the information I needed waited there. All I had to do was ask the right question. Was that God, the Holy Spirit looking through Pastor Rocky's eyes, or just some spiritual knowledge, ready to be tapped?

If I hadn't been sitting down already, I might have fallen from the wave of dizziness that seemed to turn the entire community center on its side. My skin tingled and burned. A shimmer of energy washed over me.

Heck, that wasn't the Holy Spirit. That was Big Ugly trying to open a dimensional door, or Sylvia was being the conduit for something nasty yet again. My chair seemed to try to tip sideways and I was afraid to look around and see Daniel start to go blurry again, like maybe she was trying to teleport him out of the communion service. Maybe this Grandstone really did burst into flames when she stepped onto holy ground.

And the moment was over, that pivotal second when I could have had answers if I knew the right question. I let myself get distracted. I yielded to the temptation to snark, and to worry.

"God bless you," Pastor Rocky whispered. He blinked, and that holy gleam vanished.

Feeling somewhat deflated, I rolled back to my place in the back row. Daniel and Harry and Pete were already back there, having gone to other lines. I hunched over myself in the chair, feeling chilled, thinking hard, but not quite sure what images were spilling through my head. It was all a fog, with tantalizing glimpses of images and fragments of ideas.

When the last person had taken wine from the goblets, Pastor Rocky led the way back to the communion table at the front of the room, and his helpers put down their empty goblets. He tapped the edge of his goblet with his fingernail and the pure, true tone rang out. The others tapped theirs. The sound filled the room. I glanced sideways at Daniel, and his mouth dropped open. Neat trick, huh? All twenty-four handmade goblets rang with the exact same note, perfect pitch.

Taking their note from the goblets, Myrtle Sitser led the church staff into the *Doxology*. On the second line, the rest of us joined in, and those who could stand, did. As the last notes rang through the room, we all started filing out. Nobody said a word until we were outside.

"Wow," Daniel murmured, when the four of us emerged, the last of everyone. "Maybe it's a good thing you only do that once a year." He shook his head. "You only do that once a year, right?"

"Christmas and Easter are pretty amazing, too," Harry said.

"Danny!" Sylvia appeared among us so fast, I honestly expected a puff of black smoke and a whiff of brimstone.

Okay, that was the wrong thought after such a solemn moment, when we should have been thinking about starting the new year right. Hadn't Pastor Rocky been encouraging us to try to establish new thoughts, new thought patterns, new habits of actions and reactions? That included being more charitable to those who hacked us off something fierce.

Sorry, Lord, but some habits are really hard to break. Especially when we were floating along on a spiritual high point, and got rudely yanked back down below sea level by the last person any of us wanted to see or hear.

Why couldn't whatever was making people vanish have swallowed Sylvia for a few hours?

"What in the world were you doing in there?" She tried to weave her arm around his, but he managed to sidestep her and hold his arm tight against his side.

"Getting right with God," Daniel said quietly. "You might try it some time, before it's too late."

"Oh, honey, no need to be so serious and gloomy. It's New Year's Eve. We're gonna celebrate." She leaned closer, tipping her head up. I swear, she expected him to kiss her, because she looked both disappointed and stunned when he turned away.

"So, what's next on the schedule?" Daniel asked me, and grabbed hold of the handlebars of my chair again.

I bit back a comment about him using my chair as a crutch. Any minute now, Sylvia would realize she wasn't going to catch gimp germs from being within my breathing space. Then he wouldn't be able to hide behind the invisible wall of contamination that warded off the able-bodied world.

"Board games and the countdown," Harry said. "At 11:30, Kurt's going to unveil the clock. He tries to do something new to it every year."

"What's so big about a clock?" Sylvia grumbled and scooted up next to Daniel as he pushed me back to the gym. Well, she was closer this time, but she still wasn't touching him while he was touching my chair. I could have pushed myself without any trouble, but I was willing to do my part to help protect Daniel.

"What's so big about the clock is that it's enormous," Pete said, mimicking Sylvia's grumbling voice and her hip-swaying walk. He caught me watching him, turned red, crossed his eyes at me, and skidded through the gym doors before I could burst out laughing.

"We're not exactly Time's Square," Harry said, as we followed into the gym, "but who'd want to be?" He gestured at the end of the gym, where the lights glowed through the huge tarpaulin covering the midnight clock. The body of the clock was about four feet wide and rose up into the rafters. They weren't strung with streamers at that end of the gym. It was a pretty impressive sight, even covered up with the tarp. I could imagine how it would gleam and sparkle and shoot off sparks in psychedelic patterns when the tarp was pulled away at 11:30.

Until then, we had board games to play at every table, lots of food, and those door prizes being given away every five minutes.

Sylvia went back to grumbling. First, the big crystal plastic buckets of ice lined up along one wall weren't sitting on the tables. Next, she didn't want to wait for the midnight toast to open the bottles inside. Then when she confiscated a bottle, it held sparkling cider.

"What's the good of going to a New Year's party if there isn't any champagne?" She plunked the bottle down in the middle of the table, right on top of the discard pile for the card game we were playing, which she, grumbling, refused to play.

"There's more to a party than booze." Mandy sighed and shook her head, lifted the bottle off the stack, and got up to take it back to its ice bucket.

"Yeah? Name one thing more important than getting smashed at a party." Sylvia plopped down in a chair and scooted up close to Daniel. She tried to lay her head on his shoulder, just as he reached for a card. "Please, Danny? Take me away from here so we can get some champagne?"

Daniel shifted aside so she had to sit up to keep from falling over. He didn't answer, just picked up a card and immediately slapped it down on the deck. The other six people at our table leaped into action, slapping matching cards down on the table until the last one in line (poor Harry) ended up drawing twelve cards. Well, not a record, but pretty good for so early in the evening.

"You're boring!" Sylvia stood up so fast, her chair folded up and slammed to the floor with a crash. She turned bright red and tears filled her eyes when not a single person reacted to her shriek.

I didn't get to see what happened next, because Athena hurried up to the table. Kurt wanted to see me, and couldn't call me. The phones still weren't working well inside Eden.

Athena led me down the long hallway that had become far too familiar in the last few days. The one that nobody used because it dead-ended at the door that was rusted shut. The same one that had temporarily vanished. The door of the left-hand storage room was open. She gestured for me to go in, and stepped back to lean against the wall opposite the door, very visibly standing guard.

The sound of retching greeted me before I turned to go through the door, which made me pause. Working with little kids should have immunized me to odd and disgusting smells, but only an idiot blithely rolled into a room where someone was heaving up their insides. At least, not without checking how to stay out of the line of fire and any natural drainage in the room.

Kurt stood over a skinny, sweaty guy dressed in a navy and gray pinstripe suit and lavender shirt. His hair was pale, washed out, but with a hint of red in it. Like a fire that had been doused with dirty snow. The guy gagged and choked a few more times, holding a wad of paper towels to his mouth. No spatters on the floor. Okay, simple nausea I could handle. Kurt was holding out his gizmo, nearly touching the guy's back, like a doctor in a science fiction movie would touch a patient with a medical scanner. For all I knew, his sensor gizmo could do that.

"Someone is using a variation of my trick," Angela said. She sat in the shadows on a pile of something swathed in brown paper and plastic sheeting, and watched the guy.

At the sound of her voice, he raised his head and wiped his

sweaty face on his sleeve, and his eyes kind of bugged out when his gaze landed on me.

"They didn't get you?" he blurted.

"You know Lanie?" Kurt raised his gizmo like maybe he would swat the prisoner if he said the wrong thing.

"I saw pictures, the few times they let me see anything." He sat back on his heels and looked around the room, full of shadows and dust and old pieces of equipment and tools that hadn't been cleaned out when they turned the old factory into a community center. "This place is actually a step up from where I've been the last twenty years."

"It's completely gone," Kurt said, and gestured again with his gizmo.

"What is?" I asked. "And who are 'they' who didn't get me? The ones pulling the strings with Parker and the other boys?"

"Do you recognize him?" Angela asked me, before the guy could swallow and wipe his face again and respond.

"Rodney," Kurt said, when I shook my head. The name meant nothing to me. "The guy who vanished after the really suspicious fires, while you were in England and Venice."

"The old men took him? Or the rivals?" At the back of my mind, I made a note that we needed to find better names for the mysterious parties who had been snatching away Lost Kids with any semi-pseudo-superhero powers.

"Since he smelled like the Colonel did when he got dumped on the porch," Kurt said, "I'm guessing the rivals." He took a step back and offered a crooked grin. "He had some of that stuff in liquid, in what amounts to a squirt gun, but he fell and landed on it. Broke it. Knocked himself out for about an hour, from what we can tell. Angela and I found him when we were tracking down residual energy from that big surge. That's what's gone. The energy still clinging to him."

"Okay, so … he was sent in to knock someone out and take them away? Who?"

Angela held out a packet of papers. That chalky smell that had clung to Hayward clung to the papers. The top few were maps of Eden. The rooms currently available for use, as well as the master plan made up by the board of directors years ago, with the vision of what the entire old factory would be turned into when the slow, one-step-at-a-time renovations were completed. I knew what it looked like because I had done a few stories on the progress of Eden for the *Tattler*. For Rodney to have that map meant that whoever sent him here tonight had connections. Access to information and materials only a limited few possessed.

I choked as I finally made the connection between this skinny, pale, sweaty guy who quite frankly looked like those old pictures from the liberation of concentration camps, and the guy a few years older than Kurt, who had vanished from Neighborlee Children's Home when we were kids. The last one who had been taken away before that quiet, pale girl named Jane. We had her pictures among the files Mrs. Silvestri had entrusted to us, in our attempt to figure out what happened to all the Lost Kids who were suddenly claimed by long-lost relatives and vanished just as mysteriously as their relatives appeared. Always after strange incidents occurred around the orphanage and in town.

The thin stack of papers included the schedule of events and locations of different activities for the evening. Also a little scary that he had it, because Gina hadn't distributed that schedule until people signed in at the registration table in the lobby, and only people who had paid could get in the doors.

The last few papers were pictures of Angela. And Athena. And Wallace. And Bethany.

Honestly, my first reaction was as close to pity as I could ever get for someone who was stupid enough to threaten Angela.

Followed by fury. I had known Athena and Bethany since they were babies. I had babysat them. I had taken them to the zoo, to movies and summer fairs, let them eat themselves sick on cotton candy and fry pies, cheered their triumphs, and cried over their losses. The rivals had sent Rodney to gas and kidnap my girls? Yeah, and Wallace. I was mad for his sake, too, but mostly because hurting him would hurt Athena.

"What made them think Bethany was here?" slipped out before I really thought about it.

"They don't know everything," Kurt said. "But we're going to know everything they know, right?" He crossed his arms and looked down on Rodney.

"I don't know anything," Rodney said. "I swear. They keep me in this place like a prison camp. It's always cold, and there's nothing for miles in any direction, and I only get to leave when they want me to set things on fire. That's what I can do."

"We remember," I said, and I kind of felt sorry for him.

"He's told us a few things," Angela said, "but we're not living lie detectors. We need to know what the plan is for tonight and who sent him, what they want, and who else is in here that we have to watch out for. Rodney, give Lanie your hand and speak as simply and truthfully as possible. For your own good."

I had to muffle a chuckle when Rodney went a few shades paler, which I would have thought was impossible. Very clearly, he thought that lying to me would cause him pain or some kind of damage. Angela hadn't said that, but she was very good at implying without lying.

My pity for him increased a couple more degrees when he gave his hand into my grasp. It was nothing but skin and bones, and a little shaky. The poor guy spilled immediately, and the longer he talked the steadier his hand got, and his sweating dried up. Like he was relieved to tell everything he knew.

Which wasn't much, as he had said. Kurt and Angela asked questions, to clarify the story Rodney stumbled through, and I got flashes of images in my head that verified everything he said.

The people who took him away from Neighborlee Children's Home claimed to be distant cousins. They turned him over to a group of people who seemed to be homemade military, at a place that looked like a combination of Stalag 13 from *Hogan's Heroes* re-runs and an abandoned mining town in the middle of Siberia. The people in power all wore jumpsuits of dark blue and dark green and gray, but there didn't seem to be any rank designations or even divisions of duties indicated by the colors. They essentially showed who was in charge. The inmates wore jeans and T-shirts. Nothing personalized, everything pretty drab. The ones who cooperated and accepted what their keepers taught them lived on one side of the camp, in nice quarters. The ones like Rodney who were afraid and angry and just didn't trust anyone, lived in the barracks, kept in a haze by drugs in their food and in the air of their quarters. The only time they were brought out of the haze was when their keepers had jobs for them to do.

Drugging them kept them from using their powers to try to escape. When Kurt asked, Rodney admitted yes, he had seen Jay

Parker, Steve Muldoon and Toby Malone at the camp. He had met them a few times and was called in to verify details about the layout of Neighborlee.

Rodney said there were six others living in the barracks with him, all younger, who had been brought from towns other than Neighborlee. When they first arrived, they all cried for their families. He never asked, but things their keepers said made him think either their families had been frightened into turning their children over for "training," or they had been paid well.

"I would wager if we were able to do some research, all of them are descendants of Lost Kids," Angela said. "They left Neighborlee and the Grandstones or whoever they ..." She tipped her head slightly and studied Rodney with narrowed eyes.

He had flinched when she said Grandstone.

"What do you know about them?" Kurt said.

"I'm supposed to meet her and help her catch ..." Rodney gestured at the papers lying on the swathed equipment next to Angela. "She brought me through and when I got sick, she pushed me so I fell and spilled the drug on myself, so she left me in hiding to sleep it off. After she kicked me a few times." He winced in memory, and I winced too, feeling the echoes of bruises in his ribs and butt.

"What do you mean, she brought you through?" Kurt said.

"That's probably what all the power surges are, or whatever is going on," I guessed. "Sylvia is the anchor. Maybe she's wearing something that, I don't know, lets her draw energy from people? That's probably what all those disappearances were before, you think? Practice runs?"

"Triangulating," Angela said, nodding slowly. "Reaching blindly into Eden, figuring out locations by feel, drawing items to her, and putting them back."

"I find it really hard to believe a Grandstone would have the mental focus and energy and just the intelligence to pull off something like that," Kurt said.

"But she could have some innate talent, some powers she inherited from the first Grandstone, and the rivals found out how to wake it up, you think?"

"So you're helping Sylvia grab people." He turned back to Rodney. "What else?"

"Set fires, for distraction. I'm supposed to be her energy source." Rodney shrugged and looked down at himself. "Some of them call me the Battery. They feed me really good most of the time, and I have a trainer back at the camp to keep me in good shape, and then I get sent out on missions and … I end up like this."

Kurt and I exchanged pained glances. Again, I had to feel sorry for Rodney. We asked him more questions, but there wasn't much more we could learn from him. He and Sylvia were the inside people. She was pretty much helpless without him, and he couldn't get out of Eden without her to open the door and shove him through again, back into the hands of his keepers.

"We won't do that, of course. You are one of ours, and we must make up for being unable to protect you when you were a child here," Angela said. "Athena?" She turned to the door, and a moment later Athena looked in. "Did you hear all that?"

"Recorded it, too." Athena held out her phone. "What do we do now?"

"The most important thing is keeping you and Wallace and Angela away from Sylvia," Kurt said.

"And keeping Sylvia from hooking up with Rodney again," I added.

"I will be returning to the shop in a few moments, and taking Rodney with me. I believe the smart thing to do is turn him over to Franklin, and send him somewhere safe," Angela said. "Athena, you will tell Ford everything we just found out. He has likely felt some reverberations from all the activity throughout the evening, so he is already on the alert. He will be responsible for watching out for you and Wallace. As soon as you can get through to her, tell London everything, and have her focus on protecting Bethany." A smirk twitched the corners of her mouth, and a little bit of malicious delight touched her eyes. "We shall spend the evening playing keep-away with Sylvia, and have a delightful New Year's Eve celebration despite her and the enemies hovering on the outskirts of our town. When morning comes … well, we shall deal with the fallout in the new day and new year."

~~~~~

Kurt and I had a good view of the gym from the main doors, and we could see our table, where Daniel and Mandy, Gordon
~~~~~

and my brothers were playing a variant of Jenga, created by the shop class at Neighborlee High about seven years ago. The playing pieces were about fifty percent larger than standard Jenga pieces, three times as many of them in each set, and painted six different colors. Creating the game and assembling the pieces and selling them had been a fundraising project for the art department. Players rolled the dice that had colored circles on each face of the cube instead of dots or numbers, and whatever color showed on top dictated which colored block of wood they had to remove from the tower. As Kurt and I paused in the doorway and studied the scene, Gordon pulled a piece out from about halfway up the tower. It wobbled. I had to resist the temptation to mentally steady it. I had to save my energy for any emergencies that might crop up throughout the night, after all. Besides, it would have been cheating.

We studied the room, looking for Sylvia. I found Chief Tanner, sharing a table with Fire Chief Porter and several EMTs. Good to know where they were, if we ran into any trouble.

The gizmo tucked inside Kurt's jacket, held against his side by his arm, started ticking softly, about the time I found Athena. She was standing next to Ford, bent down and talking to her grandfather. The rest of the family, including Wallace and Cosmo, were all focused on her. I wondered why no one at any of the tables around them didn't notice they weren't laughing and talking, and the game sat neglected in front of them.

Then that ticking got loud enough to be noticed.

"Is it supposed to do that?" I asked, as Kurt turned to step out of the doorway, back into the lobby. He reached into his jacket to pull it out.

"I didn't *know* it did that." He frowned at the screen.

He held it high enough I couldn't see it from my chair level, but the swirling colors were bright enough to reflect off his face. Probably not a good sign. Then Kurt's eyes got wide and he looked up from the screen.

I turned to look where he was looking.

That ripple returned to the lobby, brighter, a swirling shimmer now. It expanded in the space of a couple breaths, from something the size of my fist to a garbage can lid to the size of an eight-seater round table. It spun and the colors darkened, so it was like a dirty rainbow-streaked oil slick.

I don't know how, but I had the sudden impression it was angry and hungry and somehow didn't see us, sitting and standing only ten feet away. The spinning grew agitated in another few seconds, and I had the impression of whitecaps, like on an especially stormy Lake Erie, while the flat swirling went from two-dimensional to three-dimensional. It rolled through the air, hovering about three feet above the floor.

Heading toward the office.

Gina's office. Where the end of Angela's tunnel back to Divine's was anchored in the closet. I opened my mouth to shout something to Kurt. We had to do something, I just didn't know what.

All the lights in the building died, just for a few breaths.

There was a loud *crack-snap-buzz.*

The lights came back on before anybody in the gym behind us could react.

The expanding oil slick hanging in the air was gone.

All the hairs on my arms and the back of my neck stood up stiff, aching in the roots. Delayed reaction. I wanted to laugh, needed to laugh, but for a few seconds I felt as if all the air had been sucked out of the lobby.

"Angela," Kurt said.

He beat me across the lobby and into the office. Gina's door was locked. Angela would have pulled it closed behind her when she went back through with Rodney. Knowing that was no comfort. Kurt grimaced and grabbed the doorknob. It clicked loudly and opened. That lock knew better than to argue with him when he scowled like that.

The door of the big storage closet in Gina's office hung open, and a few items had fallen off the shelves. A ream of paper had broken open, a box of pens, some markers, paper clips, and a huge bag of leftover candy from the Christmas pinata. Kurt waved his gizmo at the otherwise empty closet.

"Don't ask if everything is normal, because I don't know. There's no such thing as normal in Neighborlee."

"Normal for other people, or normal for Neighborlee?" I muttered.

That got a snort and a crooked, aching kind of grin from him.

"What just happened?" Ford Longfellow demanded, as he stomped into the office. Athena, Wallace and Jinx were right behind him.

"You call Angela," Kurt said, showing me his cell phone, which was entirely dead, drained of power. "I'll tell them."

I banged my knee on the desk in my hurry to snatch up Gina's landline and call Divine's. Angela answered on the fourth ring. I tried not to worry, because she did have to get from the back door of the shop, where the tunnel was anchored, to the phone behind the counter in the main room. Still, it felt like forever. I heard Athena say, with some rising concern in her voice, that her phone and tablet were both dead, so she couldn't contact London. Then Angela picked up the phone.

"Are you all right there?" she demanded.

"The light show came back, in the center of the lobby, about the time you and Rodney were leaving," I said. "How about you?"

"Rodney took the worst of it. I'm afraid he has an automatic reaction to any call for energy. He complies and shuts down all his natural resistance. I'm going to get him on his feet and wait for Franklin to come take him, then I'll rejoin you."

A faint chiming sound came through the phone as I finished relaying what we had experienced on our end. Angela told me to hold on, because her computer was calling her. That felt a little odd, because Angela didn't use her computer except for inventory purposes. And yes, when Athena or Wallace came to the shop and they had a conference with London or Sherwood. While I waited, I listened to others conferring with Kurt on what they had experienced during the brief blackout. They had just agreed that Kurt would help Athena and Wallace get past the alarms on a side door. They needed to get outside and find a place to plug in so they could contact London. The two AI's were monitoring the energy surrounding Eden and Neighborlee this evening, after all. Then Angela came back on.

"Sherwood is as close to frantic as I've ever seen him. He's lost all contact with Athena and Wallace. He says it's like a big black hole there."

"Tell him they're going to get outside, past the interference, and try to make contact. Does he know what's going on?" I asked.

"He and London agree with my theory. Sylvia followed us to Gina's office and had a temper tantrum when I closed the door." Angela snorted softly. I could envision her shaking her head at the typical Grandstone reaction. "She tried to latch onto me. Your theory is right. She's wearing talismans that draw energy, it's not something she herself is doing. Then something awakened, something huge and angry. It joined forces with her and we had a few seconds playing tug-o-war before whatever was sucking at me snapped and broke. Again, Rodney had the worst of it. He'll be all right, though, as soon as he can put a few hundred miles between him and his keepers."

Ford was standing close enough when I hung up the phone and turned around, I was sure he had heard some of Angela's side of the conversation. Kurt, Athena and Wallace were gone, probably making their escape. I waited for Kurt to come back before I related everything Angela had told me.

We agreed, there were only two things we could do. First, we needed to track down Sylvia and keep her from getting at her targets. Until Kurt's gizmo went off, detecting the energy signature of her type of interdimensional tunnel opening up, we had to assume she was still at Eden. Second, we had to go on as if nothing had happened.

That turned out to be easier than we expected. Everyone else in the building seemed to have forgotten that momentary blackout. Then when we checked, not a single person's phone or tablet had any energy, but nobody had noticed. They didn't check their phones or get on social media for the next few hours, and that was just plain weird. Had the oil slick monster (perhaps the true face of Big Ugly?) done a mind drain on everyone? Mind control? Or was everyone just choosing to ignore the inconvenience? Mass amnesia? Just how were we supposed to enjoy the evening with the amped-up weirdness staying on our minds?

Ford and Jinx went back to their table to report to Charlotte, Doni and Cosmo. Doni and Cosmo got up after a little while and left. I didn't see them come back, and when Kurt finally returned to our table, he said he had helped them get outside, so Cosmo could help Athena and Wallace get back in contact with London and Sherwood.

Sylvia didn't return. When I asked when she had left and if anyone knew where she had gone, my brothers shrugged and Daniel just grimaced. Mandy and Gordon frowned, as if maybe they had completely forgotten Sylvia had been whining and trying to run thing, generally doing what Grandstones did best: make others miserable if things didn't go their way.

At about 11 or so, Ford left the gym. When he came back, Angela was with him. She joined our table with her usual serene smile and a little nod in answer to the questioning looks Kurt and I gave her. We certainly couldn't ask her to report on how Rodney was doing and if she had learned anything from the computer gang. Not in front of the others at the table. They had a right to enjoy their evening, after all.

Gradually, we were able to relax, I managed to push some of my concerns to the side of my mind, if not the back. We ate and played games and Pastor Rocky's retro band—minus Pop—played Big Band-style songs, and some people got up to dance.

I won the last prize drawing of the night, at ten minutes until midnight. A basket of aromatherapy candles from Common Scents. As I wheeled up to the stage to take the basket, the slowly streaming lights on the midnight drop clock shifted to strobe effects. All the games stopped and everybody put away whatever we were playing and cleared the tables. The delivery teams hurried to the table with the ice buckets, and ran to deliver them, the bottles of sparkling cider, and stacks of plastic goblets to every table, so we could have our toast at exactly midnight.

Kurt poured and Angela passed the plastic goblets around the table. She looked tired, and I wondered just what she had been doing to protect us and didn't mention. How many times during the night had she gone back and forth between Divine's and Eden, to convince the watching enemy she was home, and alone? Had anyone attempted to penetrate the shop's defenses, to get to her?

I honestly felt useless, doing exactly what Angela had told us we needed to do: wait and watch and be ready for whatever happened.

At one minute until midnight, LCD numerals appeared in the base of the clock, measuring off the seconds. The band resumed playing, and Chief Porter, who played saxophone and worked as their emcee, began the countdown at thirty seconds.

Happy New Year! We all shouted in unison. The band belted out *Auld Lang Syne*, and the balloons and confetti fell from the ceiling as the four sections of the net disengaged. We drank our cider and hugged, and spat out bits of confetti that got in our cups no matter how quickly we drank.

At fifteen minutes into the new year, Sylvia still hadn't come back to our table.

~~~~~

To be honest, we didn't expend much time or effort looking for Sylvia. We didn't want to find her. And as the minutes turned into an hour, I played with the idea that the oil slick had swallowed up Sylvia. But if it took Sylvia, did that make it cannibalistic? Or just stupid? At the very least, it had turned on its allies. *If* Sylvia and the rivals were allies. Maybe this was a new player in the effort to break open the door Neighborlee held shut.

Oh, great, just what we didn't need. I wasn't going to ruin our New Year's celebration by offering that theory. It could at least wait until the second or third of January, right?

We moved back to the Murder room. More people joined us. Something about running around an obstacle course in the pitch dark after midnight made a lot of people adventurous. People who usually ran on solar batteries--like me—got kind of loopy that late in the evening. Even bolstered with lots of high-calorie food from the decadent buffet Gina and her crew had arranged.

I wasn't the DA or the murderer in this new game, and I got killed in the very first round. That was fine. I sat in the morgue with Gordon and Mandy and we talked about anything and everything. The only disappointing part of getting killed early (by someone with a shaky, very young voice, who probably felt guilty killing the poor crippled lady in the wheelchair) was that I didn't get a chance to torment people with some little telekinetic tricks. Making a swinging wall move. Tipping the teeter-totter board before they stepped on it. Things like that. Yeah, kind of nasty, but I had to get my jollies one way or another, right?

We decided Sylvia had gone into a bathroom to sulk, with the misguided idea that Daniel would tear Eden apart to look for her, worried sick and feeling guilty. Well, he was having too much fun with new friends to think about someone who wouldn't listen when he said he didn't want to be with her in the first place.
~~~~~

When she didn't return to the table, he shrugged and relaxed and had fun.

"So what's this new church Pete was snickering about with some of his buddies?" Gordon said, after the third round of the game started, and we had five more people sitting in the morgue with us. The others went off into the far corner of the Morgue with a flashlight and a deck of Phase 10 to play.

"New church?" I had to wrack my tired brains for a few seconds. Then I laughed. "Church of the Blue Spruce. They're starting a cult."

"What?" Mandy laughed. "Some kind of school project? World religions class or something?"

"Nope, Sunday school, at my church. See, it's more like a revival of a cult started when I was in the youth group."

"Why Lanie Zephyr, here I thought you were a nice, respectable, church-going girl, but you've got a wild side." Gordon grinned. "That is, even taking into account your psychotic addiction to Star Trek."

"Takes one to know one." I stuck my tongue out.

A shriek echoed down the hall from the main gym. Gordon went into automatic police mode, reaching for the gun that wasn't hanging on his hip as he leaped up from the floor and nearly knocked down the door before he lifted the lock bar. Mandy and I were close behind.

We got into the gym as Gordon was just getting down on his knees next to Pamelia. She lay on her side in a fetal position, crying, bleached white, holding her arm. Multicolored strips of crepe paper lay underneath her. The same colors we had hung from the ceiling. My stomach twisted when I spied an extra joint between her elbow and her wrist. I looked up at the ceiling. A big section of streamers hung straight down, torn ... by something falling through them, it looked like.

"She fell from the rafters," I told Gordon, while he was still trying to get Pamelia to unfold so he could look at her arm.

"How did she get up in the rafters?" he growled. Then his face softened, a sympathetic grizzly bear trying to hide his fangs. "Hey, Pammy, it's okay. We're gonna take care of you." He slid his big hands under her shoulders and braced her as she tried to sit up, still shaking like she was trying to breathe and cry at the same time. "Hey, can somebody get the nurse?"

I honestly expected to find out Mrs. Tancredi had vanished too, but she came running almost before Gordon's voice finished echoing around the room. Which, when I thought about it a while later, didn't make sense. The room was full of people now, all gathering around, muttering, staring at Pamelia. There wasn't any open, empty space for sound to echo. It should have all run up against those bodies and been muffled.

Then I looked up at the ceiling, at the blackness beyond the rafters and the torn crepe streamers. Were the shadows hiding the roof, or was there suddenly a lot more empty space beyond?

"Hey, Gordon, I really think it's time to break up the party. This is getting … weird," I said.

"Ya think?" He glared at me, then a second later his look softened. "Something is seriously wrong here, and it's not just Pammy falling from the ceiling when there's no way she could have gotten up there. How come I'm remembering freaky stuff happening, and I couldn't remember half an hour ago? I'm a cop, for heaven's sake!"

"Gas leak?" Mandy offered. She pulled open the medical kit Mrs. Tancredi had brought and helped dig out the splints.

"The food tasted funny," Pamelia whispered. "Maybe somebody drugged us?"

"That's it." Gordon stood up and looked around. "Where's the Chief?" He pulled out his cell phone out, and a second later cursed when he realized it was dead. How come he had forgotten?

A clatter erupted from the stage, where the band had left their equipment. I heard the cymbals bang-clang and thuds from a drum falling and rolling. What had hit the stage to knock things over?

A woman shrieked. Two high school kids stumbled through the crowd to us. The kids were smart enough not to say anything, but they grabbed Gordon by his sleeves as if they could drag him back to the stage. I heard voices raised and more people moved away, creating an aisle to the stage.

"What's up there?" I asked, catching Pastor Rocky as he moved past me.

"Looks like somebody passed out up there. This has turned

out to be one interesting New Year's." He gave me one of those reassuring, warm smiles they probably taught in seminary.

Gordon got to the stage and stumbled to a stop. He looked back at me, then slowly stepped up on the stage. Something got heavy and hard in my chest and sank all the way to my toes at the expression on his face. He beckoned for me. I had to obey.

I recognized the black slacks and glittery sweater and stilt-heel shoes when I got through the last wall of people around the stage. It took me a minute or two, because people weren't willing to move aside, even at risk of getting run over by my wheels.

"Ricky?" Gordon called, looking past me. "Where's the Chief? We need to move fast. Get everybody on the force who's here and have them contain the building. Nobody gets out. Then somebody has to find a working phone and contact the station. Report a homicide."

The people behind me let out gasps and mutters. I had a really bad feeling. Mostly because my strongest feeling was relief.

I am not a nice person. I have a strong sense of honor, a strong sense of responsibility, a strong inhibition when it comes to doing stupid or vulgar or risky, immoral things. At the same time, I get really nasty when people are selfish and totally oblivious to other people's feelings and wishes. So the thought that Sylvia was dead didn't promote feelings of sorrow and pity right away. All I could think of was something along the lines of, *Thank goodness, Daniel doesn't have to put up with her anymore.* My second thought was along the lines of, *This is so not fair to Gina, after all the hard work she did.* Finally, as Pastor Rocky stepped up next to me and his face wrinkled in sorrow and concern, **then** I thought, *Okay, and where is Sylvia's eternal soul right this minute?*

Well, dumb question. The only time Grandstones went into a church was to try to throw the congregation out so they could build a parking lot.

Chapter Ten

Sylvia Grandstone was dead. There was no doubt about it. Nobody alive had that bluish tint around the lips and the glassy eyeball stare. She certainly wouldn't be caught alive lying like that, getting creases in her designer clothes. If that wasn't proof enough she was dead, one heel had snapped off her boot. She never would have put up with that, even if she was in a coma.

She was dead.

Maybe she and the rivals weren't working with the oil slick that had been floating around Eden? It had been increasing the seriousness of its attacks over the last week. First knocking people dizzy and switching them a few steps down the hall (Gina), then stealing a few hours and knocking people out (the gas repairman and the Rooney boys), making the Musketeers vanish for an hour, returning sick and dizzy in a heap, then dropping someone from the ceiling and breaking her arm (Pamelia), and finally killing Sylvia. Suffocating her and draining her of energy and life. If it had increased its impact on people, what was the next step up from suffocating and draining people? Eating them and not even leaving bones behind?

Then I remembered something.

"What?" Gordon demanded, stepping down from the stage. "That look on your face—you know something."

"Cleo," I said. "She vanished from right in front of me, and she hasn't reappeared yet."

"Why didn't you say—" Gordon stopped himself with a visible struggle. He took a few deep breaths and raked his big hands through his hair. I thought he stopped just short of yanking out handfuls of it. "You did say. I remember that now. Okay, there's been something weird going on with everybody's head, because I'm remembering things now and I know I didn't remember them even half an hour ago. Maybe Pammy is right, and we were all drugged. Hold it right there!" he bellowed.

Gordon, when he wants to be heard, can shake the rafters. In this case, some last balloons and confetti came down in reaction to his roar. He stepped around me and shifted into high gear, racing to head off a handful of people who looked like panic had finally registered in their tired brains and were heading for the door.

I saw Chief Tanner and several people from the fire department surrounding Pamelia and taking care of her. Knowing the Chief was there made me feel better. No criticism of Gordon.

He spent the next twenty minutes delegating people to guard all the doors and make sure no one left, and round up everyone who hadn't been gathered into the gym by Pamelia's scream. Chief Tanner organized people, searching Eden to get everyone in one place, and make sure no one else had gone missing. Pastor Rocky and I were left to guard Sylvia's body, while Gina and Brenda and Mrs. Tancredi shifted Pamelia to the nurse's office. Angela came over to sit with us. We didn't sit on the stage, and we arranged our chairs so we guarded the stage without looking at Sylvia or putting our backs to her.

Pastor Rocky let out a "huh," that was partly a chuckle. When I looked at him, he held out his cell phone. The screen was lighted. How had he gotten power? I checked my phone. It took a few seconds to light up after I turned it on. I made a mental note of the time and tapped a note to myself to check with London on when any big changes occurred in the energy field. Maybe with Sylvia's death, some connection broke? Or battle between invaders and defenders just overloaded everything and stopped blocking everyone out?

When I finished that note, I heard Pastor Rocky talking on his phone, giving directions to someone to call the deacons and trustees who weren't at the party, to get their assigned prayer chains going. He couldn't give details, but some strange events were happening at Eden, and he needed the congregation to surround the town with prayers.

"Fat lot of good that's going to do," I muttered. "We had people praying before all this started."

"Prayer is never a waste of time." Angela scooted her chair closer, and rested her warm hands over mine, clenched in my lap. I realized then my hands were cold. "I know how hard it must be, to feel useless and helpless, but you have to consider that even if you were on your feet right now, you still couldn't have changed or prevented anything. You and Kurt chose to come here and keep watch in the hopes of averting disaster. There was a chance we could do nothing because none of us knew anything for sure."

"We still don't know anything," I snapped. But amazingly, I did feel a little better. Not much, but somewhat.

"Well, that ruins the Jessica Fletcher *Murder She Wrote* theory," Mandy said, coming back into the gym to join us. "If Sylvia is dead, then she isn't the guilty party."

She sighed and pulled up a chair, strategically angled so she didn't have to look at the crumpled form amid the band equipment. Angela and Pastor Rocky both looked confused. Mandy explained the old technique for deciding who was the murderer on the old TV show, usually the most famous guest. That got wry smiles from them both.

"We have double duty. We have to keep people away from the food, too. The lab will need to take samples of everything, in case drugs are involved. Gordon is herding everybody into the Murder room. It's the second-biggest room, even with the obstacle course set up in there. When they can finally take care of the body, we have to go in there and join everybody else."

"Is everybody accounted for?" I asked.

"Everybody but Cleo and the people helping with Pam." She wrapped her arms around herself and shivered. "I think this is a sign God wants me to start going back to church." She offered Pastor Rocky a weak smile.

"Isn't that kind of arrogant?" He snorted when her mouth dropped open. "You're assuming God caused something awful to happen, just to get *your* attention."

"Well, no, that wasn't quite ..." Mandy sighed. "How come we didn't notice all the weird things that were happening before? And how come we're remembering everything so clearly? That's the worst part of this."

"Whatever had the power to block your minds has either lost that power, or it doesn't care about distracting you anymore, would be my guess." Angela frowned, staring off into the distance at something that wasn't anywhere but inside her mind. I had seen that look often enough, I felt a surge of hope. Angela was going to come up with an answer pretty soon. Even if she didn't share that answer with anyone right away, just the thought that there would be an answer made me feel better.

Or maybe I could feel those prayers starting to pile up all around Eden like a big, thick, electric blanket with the control turned up to ten.

~~~~~

Basically, I felt we weren't in an old *Murder She Wrote* episode, but a warped version of *Murder on the Orient Express*. Sylvia had hacked off practically everyone at the party, either in the past or just tonight.

Just like in the Agatha Christie story, practically everybody had motivation for offing her. Unlike the movie, I was pretty sure nobody even loosely defined as human had anything to do with her death.

"If only someone else..." I felt sick when I realized what almost came out of my mouth.

"If someone else what?" Pastor Rocky asked.

"I think what Lanie was about to say is that if someone had to die, why couldn't it have been someone else. Then we could have blamed Sylvia," Mandy said. "Wrap it up nice and neat. And no matter what she said in her defense, nobody would believe her. Except that we would expect her to hire someone else to do the dirty work because she wouldn't want to break a nail or mess up her designer clothes." She scooted over to my chair and wrapped an arm around my shoulders. "It's been a long day and there's something going on here that's bigger than all of us."

"There's nothing bigger than God," Pastor Rocky said. "I'm living proof of that. You throw a big enough challenge at Him, He throws it back at you."

"Yeah, but I've heard your sermon on that. God gives us jobs to do to make us grow. But what if the job is so big it smashes us, or we can't figure out what God wants us to do before we get smooshed by it?"

"Sometimes the best thing we can do is be a thorn in someone's foot," Angela said. "Enough irritation to slow them down."

"Yeah, but I can't imagine it's much fun for the thorn," I groused.

About that time, the police finished making sure everyone they could find was accounted for and the doors were secured. The four of us were relieved of duty. That meant we had to go
~~~~~

into the Murder room. Now the name was all too appropriate.

We settled down wherever we could. I had the advantage of bringing my own chair. There were only about a dozen folding chairs and a few comfortable chairs with cushions that had been liberated from a few offices in the center. Everyone else had to sit on the floor or on the ramps. Pete and Harry and their friends had already gotten to work dismantling their maze to provide seating room, and impromptu benches and seats for everybody jammed into the room. It was kind of cozy with so many people there. With the maze taken down, it was nice to see how big the auxiliary gym really was. And warm. And unusually quiet. It wasn't just the acoustics from the dropped ceiling that had been installed here. I felt a little safer, being able to look up and see a real ceiling instead of the darkness and rafters, covered over with those streamers. As long as I didn't think about what could be lurking in that dark gap between the old rafters and the acoustic tiles.

Yeah, sometimes it didn't pay to have a superhero-sized imagination. Especially one that knew there were a lot of weird things beyond what most people in Neighborlee knew.

See, believing what I do about the spiritual side of things, that tells me evil does have a lot of power. Temporarily, of course, but it's hard to keep that in mind when our side seems to be losing the battle between good and evil. I looked over at Pastor Rocky, who sat with Queenie, holding her hands, and talking to her with that expression I could only describe as Good Shepherd. Having Pastor Rocky there should have been reminding me all along that we weren't alone in this struggle. On the team of defenders for our town, I was representing the Boss.

That's enough to make someone shrink up and feel like a size two in a size-twenty wheelchair. Lost and bouncing around with no anchor.

Okay, Lord, there's still time to get through this. The first four innings have been lousy, but there's still time to redeem the game and strike out the enemy. What's worse? Having Big Ugly involved, working with the rivals? Or a new enemy on the scene? Or multiple enemies? Please, God, give me wisdom. Wake me up, because despite all the stress, I'm getting wiped. Please, Lord, don't let anyone else vanish before we can get out of here.

What would happen if police officers started disappearing? Would the mind-warping effect start up again, so no one would remember or even think about the anomalies?

Please, Lord, could this be a bad dream, too?

Why hadn't I spent more time studying Mum and Pop's DVD that they snuck back home to us under the noses of the military? Whatever they were investigating in the Bermuda Triangle must have something to do with what was happening here. According to what Athena and Wallace had found, my folks had vanished into thin air, without any detectable traces that the military scientists could pick up. People were vanishing and reappearing...and kids had been appearing around Neighborlee for decades. Was it all tied together?

"I can hear the gears running fast and I can smell smoke," Kurt muttered, as he leaned against the wall next to me and slid down so he squatted, looking up at me.

Mandy and Angela had pulled up chairs so we sort of faced each other, but could watch the room, too. I think we were all waiting for Cleo to show up again. I wondered right at that moment if anyone else remembered that she had disappeared.

"Everything is tied together. It's all a pattern. The only problem is that we see the back side of the tapestry being put together, so all we see are the knots and lots of loose threads."

"You know what's really ugly?" Gina said, settling down with us. "People saw Sylvia come in this afternoon, asking about the party. They saw her slinking around, looking like she was on a mission earlier this evening. Practically everyone knew who she was, and they know the Grandstones' reputation. They've decided she's to blame for all this. A couple have decided that somebody found out Sylvia spiked the food, and they killed her for it."

"And when people convince themselves of something like that, no matter how unlikely, it slips into their court-sworn testimony," Daniel said. I nearly jumped out of my chair, because I didn't realize he had come up behind me. He offered a tired, blood-shot eyes smile. "How come I'm starting to feel guilty?"

"She made her choices, and all this weirdness going on has nothing to do with you. If you hang around Neighborlee long enough, you'll figure out things like this happen regularly," Mandy said. Then she shrugged and rubbed at her eyes and yawned. "Only not so extreme."

"Well," Gina said, "if it's any consolation, some people think most of what they've been seeing and experiencing is a hallucination, from the drugs."

"What about the things that happened before they started eating, and before Sylvia showed up?" I had to ask.

Before anyone could respond or get angry at me for destroying what should have been a comforting explanation or theory, my cell phone rang. Felicity.

"Jake asked me to marry him!" she shrieked before I could finish saying hello. Then she babbled all the details—where they had gone for the evening, what they ate, the music playing. All the important stuff a woman in love cared about.

The others grinned and wandered away, leaving me to suffer her gush of exuberance by myself. This was a good thing, because as soon as she slowed down and let me congratulate her, I had to ask a really important question.

"Have you told him about us?"

"Do I have to?" Fortunately, Felicity still sounded giddy and happy. I didn't want to burst her great big, brain-stealing bubble of joy, but someone had to have some common sense and anchor the rest of us to reality. We had discussed the possibility of one of us facing this moment, and telling the love of our life about our abilities, about the three of us, our theory about the kids who appeared around Neighborlee. We had to prepare for the eventuality, but we had never really come up with a definitive answer. Some of our actions and plans depended on the person doing the asking or being asked.

Bottom line: Felicity had to tell Jake. Especially if she got upset or really excited when they were alone together, and she killed every bit of sophisticated electronics in their house. Or at his office. That was something we had worried about, because with Jake running a security firm, he had invested in lots and lots of sophisticated electronic surveillance equipment. She could bankrupt him just by having a fit during a bout of PMS.

"Yeah, you have to."

"Eventually."

"No, I think you need to tell him pretty soon. We have this enormous problem the three of us have to untangle, which means you either tell him and let him help us, or you spend a lot of time away from your brand-new fiancé while you're working on it with us. Because we really need you, Felicity. Things work out right when the three of us are together."

"Okay." She blew out a long, loud sigh. "I get the feeling the Neighborlee freak wave hit really hard tonight. What happened? And how come Angela being there didn't put a big bubble of protection around the party? I didn't think anything bad would dare to happen while she was around."

"Well, I figure that bubble was working overtime, and what happened was toned down a lot from what it could have been," I retorted.

"Oh, that's comforting. So, give me the scoop before Jake comes looking for me."

I told her the bare bones: things vanishing, the Musketeers getting split up, the ripple that almost swallowed me, Cleo vanishing in front of me, Pamelia's broken arm, and then Sylvia disappearing and showing up dead. She was silent for a few seconds, just enough time for me to imagine her expression. I felt guilty for breaking up her happy buzz, but she had called me, after all. She agreed to come by the house at noon, giving me enough time to get some decent sleep.

"Guess I picked the right guy to fall in love with, huh?" she said, with a hint of tired laughter in her voice. "Jake has no idea how much his slogan of ensuring the security of our town will take on a totally new meaning."

"We're glad he's going to be on the team."

"You hope," she said, her voice dropping to a whisper.

We had to face the possibility of Jake getting so weirded out by the revelation of our superhero powers that he would dump Felicity, or maybe even leave town.

Please, Lord, let their love be so strong and solid by now, he'll be more upset that she didn't ask him to help sooner, instead of upset that she kept secrets from him at all. Let him bring ideas to this fight that we never could have come up with.

And please, would it be too much to ask for a big time-warp to settle in, and take us back to Christmas, and make it that this never happened at all? Please?

The police slowly worked their way through Eden, clearing

all the rooms, then through the witnesses, clearing people. The clock crept past 3 and headed toward 4 in the morning. Most of those waiting to talk to the police and be released to go home were sitting in silence and shadows, dozing in their chairs, leaning against the walls, some even managing to sleep lying on the floor.

Pastor Rocky had been wandering around this whole time, offering comfort and encouragement to anyone who looked stressed. How he managed not to look like a zombie, I had no idea. He was my idea of a superhero. I had to wonder just how much spiritual counseling he had done tonight. That got my thoughts turned back to Cleo.

Please, Lord, don't let Cleo be dead. And not just because she's a great kid and runs the best game of Murder I have ever played. Because if I misunderstood what she told me last summer and she's not secure in You, I sure don't want her to suffer for eternity just because she didn't sign up for her Eternal Life Insurance policy.

Which brought up the first flickers of guilt I had felt for Sylvia. It was a given her soul hadn't been insured with Jesus Christ Mutual Life. Yeah, and when would she have listened? I wasn't exactly a good Christian girl in high school, and she wouldn't have talked to me anyway. I was almost at her alleged level, being a star athlete, but I wasn't glamorous. My parents wouldn't sell any of their property when Sylvia's uncle wanted to build a country club on the edge of town. That made me the enemy. Nope, she wouldn't have listened to me, just because the Zephyr family stood in the way of the manifest destiny of the Grandstone clan.

"It's too bad we were never able to do anything about Sylvia," Pastor Rocky said, as if he had been reading my mind. "We should feel sorry for Sylvia, the whole Grandstone family. She must have suffered a lot of pain and emptiness in her life, to strike out at the people around her like she did, and to wear those masks all her life. She always had to fight to convince everyone around her that she was important. If she sat still long enough to think about it, she probably would have been deathly jealous of you, Lanie."

"Me?" I choked on laughter. A Grandstone jealous of *me*?

"Because of your broken back, the heroics from you and Kurt and Felicity when you saved Toby's life, you three will always be town heroes. You went at it with the attitude that it was necessary, and that was all there was to it. People like Sylvia don't understand the concept of filling others' needs without recompense and praise." Pastor Rocky gave me that exhausted but serene smile that always confused me. The same smile that made some people over the years ask if there was some fantastic new drug mixed in with the communion grape juice.

Someday, if I lived long enough, I wanted to get to the spiritual depth and height that Pastor Rocky had reached, so I could understand that kind of thinking.

"The three of you are town heroes and very important to everyone. Especially you, Lanie, with how you go on with life as if your wheelchair doesn't change anything."

"Except my height, maybe. And getting me a primo parking spot everywhere I go," I had to quip. That was my defense mechanism. Dang, but Pastor Rocky was making me uncomfortable.

Then I had to look up, right at Daniel, who had been listening to all this with a growing, puzzled frown. I knew what would pop out of his mouth, seconds before he spoke.

"What heroics are you talking about?"

Angela gave him the bare bones version of what happened on Senior Prank Night, when three seniors borrowed some city equipment and nearly got one of them killed. Kurt and Felicity and I had followed some rumors to the quarries and got there in time to save Toby's life. The dismay on Daniel's face when he heard how my back had a close encounter with a runaway truck made me squirm. So help me, if he said something about how much I must have suffered—

"So, did the city sue you for breaking the truck, Lanie?" he asked instead.

For about five seconds, our little knot of people just sat there, our mouths dropping open. Then we burst out laughing.

"You've been hanging out too much with Lanie, I can see." Pastor Rocky winked, patted Gina on the shoulder, told her to call him if she needed help, and got up to continue his rounds of counseling.

"I'd heard some rumors. And with that ruckus last week, no matter how much they tried to keep it out of the media, something leaked … I thought it was all exaggeration," Daniel said. "So, like the three of you are local superheroes?"

It was a good thing I wasn't drinking anything at that moment, or I might have spewed. Pete was drinking a can of ginger ale, and he started choking. Kurt just grinned and shook his head and shared that look with me that basically translated as, *If they only knew.*

From there, the talk devolved to superheroes in general, which was a relief from all the seriousness we had been wrapped up in. It was funny when Daniel brought up the idea that Marvel Comics had basically been running a superhero school, promoting ideals of heroism and sacrifice and patriotism and responsibility to generation after generation. We were speculating on how many Navy SEALS and Marine commandos and firemen had grown up reading comic books and wanted to be heroes in one way or another about the time Cleo reappeared.

Gordon found her, dizzy and puking into the drain in the furnace room. He had the sense to take her to a bathroom to wash her face and rinse her mouth, get her some ginger ale to settle her stomach, and wrap her in a blanket. Even better, he brought her to us, instead of making her sit all alone in the nurse's office and wait for someone to come examine her. He brought the police medic to check on Cleo, who just shivered and insisted she didn't know what had happened. One minute she was heading for the bathroom, the next thing she knew she was lying on the dirty floor of the furnace room with the most vile taste in her mouth.

The police medic blamed drugs in the food. Gordon later told me he was a new guy, fresh from training, and probably wouldn't last long in Neighborlee. He wanted everything concrete and simple. The medic revealed he had heard some older officers speculating that Sylvia had done the tampering. Her family usually had some grudge against the rest of the town.

"I don't know what kind of regularly recurring weirdness they were talking about," the medic said, as he finished checking Cleo and packed up his kit, "but they say it looks like the Grandstones have been behind it all for years."

"What? You mean like using our town, the water supply, whatever, as a testing ground for drugs?" Harry said with a snort. He locked gazes with me, his mouth twitching as if he couldn't decide whether to be disgusted or fall to the ground, rolling with hysterical laughter. Not that Harry would ever do that. He just threatened it from time to time.

"Stranger things have happened. You're going to be fine, I think, but I wouldn't go anywhere alone for a while. Have someone drop you off at home," he told Cleo, "and make sure someone who wasn't here tonight checks up on you every few hours, okay?"

"How soon do you think we can go home?" Daniel asked him. The medic shrugged and left. Yeah, I wouldn't put any bets on his future on the force. He hadn't yet learned the unspoken rule that in Neighborlee, people stuck together and helped each other as much as possible. The only time we kept secrets was when it was a little too much for some people's brains to handle.

We were in the far back corner of the room, where we could talk in some relative privacy, so it was no surprise that everyone else seemed to be getting called out in groups of three and four, questioned and examined, and sent home ahead of us. When the room was about two-thirds cleared out, Gordon came in and settled down with us. He looked as wiped out as I felt. So much for his night off.

He shook his head and reached over to take hold of Mandy's hand. For such a big bruiser of a guy, Gordon could be pretty sensitive, even romantic. That was all she needed to get that melty look in her eyes. I felt like a peeping tom, sitting there and watching this unspoken communication between them, just locking glances and holding hands.

"Tonight didn't turn out like I planned at all. It was supposed to be my night off."

"Hey, heroes never get time off. Didn't they tell you that when they issued you your cape and your magic decoder ring?" Kurt said. That got a tired bark of laughter from Gordon, and brought back that frown on Daniel's face.

"It's not too late to make this night memorable in a positive sense," Angela said, as she stood. She gave us that warm little smile of blessing and nodded to everyone in the circle. "I think I'll be going now. Happy New Year, despite it all."

Gordon watched her go. Then he turned back to Mandy and got that crooked, goofy grin that revealed what a Teddy Bear lay under his Sasquatch exterior.

"She's right, y'know? Mandy, we can't leave for a—" Gordon yawned, managing to cover his mouth before everyone in the group got a good look down his throat. "Sorry about that. I was planning on doing this privately, but Angela's right. Besides, maybe it's better with witnesses." His grin got wider, crookeder, and goofier, if that was possible.

Mandy let out a squeak as Gordon slid off the chair and landed on one knee in front of her while he dug into his shirt pocket. He brought out a ring that looked tiny in his big hand. It was a wide band, with three strips of color; emerald, sapphire and diamond chips. No, it wasn't a traditional engagement rock, but traditional never would have suited Mandy.

She got to her feet and stared. I couldn't decide if she was freaked by the sight of Gordon on his knee in front of her, or the glitter of that ring, or the significance of what was happening. And Gordon just sat there, the ring in his hand, his throat working like he couldn't force the words out, and his eyes bigger and more puppy dog pleading with every second.

"I think he's asking you to marry him, Mandy," I said. Well, I was their commanding officer, and someone had to get the ball rolling, because both seemed pretty incapable of speech about then. "What do you think?"

She nodded like a bobblehead in an earthquake and her eyes got all shimmery with tears. For a few seconds there, I swear she forgot how to breathe.

"Hey, Gordon, you have to put it on her finger," Pete prompted in a stage whisper. He and Harry were fighting laughter, their faces turning bright red. Who would have thought it? Gordon and Mandy, both paralyzed, both speechless.

He managed to find her hand without taking his gaze off her face. Both their hands were shaking so much, it was a miracle the ring didn't fall off before he got it in place.

"Mandy, now you get to kiss him," Gina prompted.

Mandy let out a squeak and threw herself at Gordon. They landed on the floor, laughing and kind of breathless. Have I mentioned before that Gordon and Mandy are perfect for each other? She was the only girl who could knock him off his feet, and he was probably the only guy who could make her look delicate.

Our gang turned and got out of there as fast as we could. We were witnesses that he had asked and she had accepted, and it was time to give them some privacy.

"Man, first Felicity and Jake, now Gordon and Mandy," I muttered. "What's the world coming to?"

"Save us from the bride magazines." Kurt shuddered in mock terror.

"You might be next," I told him.

"Hey, don't make threats like that," he retorted, "or I'll take out your center bolt and put you up on blocks."

"Would you really do that?" Daniel asked.

"Kurt's about the only one who could get away with it," Harry said. "But not for long," he added, when Daniel stopped short and stared at all of us.

We were still laughing as we stepped into line to be cleared at the different checkpoint stations filling the lobby. The medic took saliva samples and drew a little blood from each of us, asked if we had felt dizzy or nauseated or disoriented during the evening, and got our names and addresses and phone numbers.

"It's after 4 in the morning, and you're asking if we're dizzy or nauseated? You know how long we've been up and haven't been able to eat or drink?" I snapped. The guy had the sense to take a step backwards. A couple of the veterans on the force traded grins. Seems the new guy wasn't that well-liked. Probably trying to force his training on experienced men who knew how things really worked in Neighborlee.

The jerk had me so riled, I seriously considered warning him about the green blood cells that proved I was from another planet. I didn't, because while everyone else would know I was ticked and joking, he would take me seriously. I would probably be committed for psychiatric examination.

~~~~~

By the time I got home that morning, I was ready to sleep in my car. However, I knew the moment I woke up I would need the bathroom, and I didn't need the panic that would set in as I struggled out of my car and into my chair and into the house in the freezing January 1 morning air. Plus, Felicity would panic and blow the circuits in the entire town if she came home and found me passed out in my Jeep. I really wanted to get out of my sparkly
~~~~~

blue shirt because it itched like crazy, and fatigue and stress sweat smelled a thousand times worse than good old-fashioned hard work and nerves sweat. I didn't want my first smell of the new year to be disgusting.

I made it out of my Jeep and into the house, with my hands shaking and my eyes starting to cross. I washed up and slid into my pajamas and then into bed. I stayed awake long enough to feel that illusion that the bed was spinning underneath me and I was falling.

The next thing I knew, I opened my eyes to bright sunshine on snow, bouncing at just the right angle to get through the gap in my curtains, off the dresser mirror, and into my eyes. Meaning it was around 10, 10:30 in the morning.

Yawn. Wince. I could really have used another hour or three of sleep, but now that I was awake, there was no use trying to fall back asleep. I would just lie there and think and make myself stiff and headachy. Besides, I didn't want to be caught still in my pajamas when Kurt and Felicity showed up.

Felicity. She would still be giddy and high about her engagement. I wanted to see the ring. Angela wouldn't have sold Jake the ring unless she thought he was good enough for Felicity. I wondered if Angela's approval was a guarantee Jake wouldn't head for the hills once he knew the full truth about us.

My head was still swimming from some odd dreams I couldn't clearly recall. Getting washed up and dressed in my comfy camouflage sweats and puffy slippers with the Mercury wings on the heels did a lot for waking me up and clearing my head. I needed to think straight.

Pete and Harry were still sawing wood in their bedrooms when I wheeled down the hall to the kitchen. I got the coffee pot going with Pop's special brew tea, pulled a breakfast casserole out of the freezer, and slid it into the oven before I turned it on. Then I hit my office and checked my email. Not that I expected some answers to be in my email, but I could at least whittle down the load waiting to be read and answered before putting breakfast on the table.

I skimmed through my email, checked my office email and saw six new Terry letters, and closed down out of the Internet. That casserole was starting to smell pretty good. I still had half an hour until it was ready, although the boys would probably wake up soon with their stomachs growling louder than any alarm clock.

By the time Harry stumbled into my office and asked if I wanted oatmeal bread toast or corn muffins with the casserole, I had made notes on the snarky answers to give all six letters. Not a bad start for the new year.

Kurt showed up just about the time I had dished up the first serving of casserole. He always had good timing when it came to food. I hooked my thumb over my shoulder at the two dishes and mugs sitting on the counter, waiting for him and Felicity to join us. He grinned and filled his plate. I sat at the end of the table, with the places to my right and left empty, waiting for Felicity and Kurt. Pete and Harry had taken the places at the other end of the table. I lifted the cell phone from across the room and hit the speed-dial. Felicity was awake, and asked if I wanted her to bring a jar of fruit salad when she came across the driveway. Why not? Breakfast was going to be full of heavy thinking and talking and planning how to deal with the fallout from last night. Even if Sylvia wasn't working with the rivals and possibly Big Ugly, we had to shield against the impending wrath of the Grandstones, because their daughter was dead. They would find someone to blame and probably work some world domination plans into their search for Grandstone-style justice.

"I didn't really say anything to Jake about all this," she said as she settled down at the table with her full plate, after filling mugs with fruit salad for everybody and passing them around. "I want to get a good idea of what's going on before I get him involved. Seeing as how I'm going to have to explain a lot of things to him, along with explaining us."

"If I could have, I wouldn't have asked you to break the truth to him right now," I said. "The timing is lousy."

"The timing sucks worse than gravity." Kurt thunked his mug of tea down on the table for punctuation. "Somebody is out to get us. Big surprise? Whenever you set yourself up to do the right thing and help people who can't watch out for themselves, that paints a great big glow-in-the-dark target on your forehead."

"And your back," Pete added. He waggled his eyebrows at me, and it took a few seconds to remember that Pastor Rocky had said almost those exact words the Sunday before Christmas. Weird kind of Christmas sermon, but it had been appropriate at the time. Maybe God was preparing us mentally?

"Well, you know, maybe the timing is good. We'll find out if he has sticking power right away, instead of waiting a few months, a year, until something else freaky shows up and he decides to run for it." Felicity couldn't deflect the tiny wrinkle of worry forming between her eyebrows, or how her bottom lip trembled a little. She was crazy about Jake. She had kept their romance slow and low-key, just because we had known this moment would come for one of us eventually.

Pete and Harry proved themselves useful members of the team. They remembered lots of details from last night, and revealed that they hadn't experienced any of the momentary amnesia everyone else did. Why were the boys immune? They weren't Lost Kids. Maybe spending lots of time with us provided immunity, like an inoculation? That reminded me of Daniel's reactions to some of the "Oh, hey, why did I forget that?" moments. We speculated that he hadn't suffered any memory loss either. Maybe because his grandfather was a Lost Kid? So what did that imply for future efforts of guarding our town, if Daniel not only remembered, but didn't shrug off weirdness with the, "Ho, hum, what else is new?" attitude a lot of people of Neighborlee displayed?

Kurt's, Felicity's and my phones all played *Where Is My Hairbrush?* at the same time. They both jumped and looked a little started, because neither of them had been into VeggieTales, and there was no way short of worldwide insanity they would program that song as a ringtone.

"Sherwood is calling," I explained, and tapped my phone screen to accept the call. I put it on the table, propped up on the butter dish so most of us could see his adaptation of Cosmo's face. He wasn't smiling. Ominous, because Sherwood always smiled. The more problems and tasks we gave him, the better he liked it.

This was all business, and he talked fast, like he was in a hurry to finish reporting and get back to work. London was keeping an eye on Bethany and frustrating attempts to investigate Athena, Wallace, and Cosmo. Someone was focusing a lot of effort on trying to infiltrate the FlopDrop site their college team had created last winter for an advanced computer class project. The walls were holding, but London and Sherwood were developing a super-virus to boomerang on anyone who tried to invade. It would backtrack them and paralyze their computer systems. If the enemy persisted, it would destroy their online presence, their credit rating, and any other vital records that would require them to spend the next five years in repair and rehabilitation.

"Man, I want those guys as my friends," Pete murmured. He flinched and turned bright red when Sherwood laughed. Maybe he had thought he was quiet enough not to be heard?

Sherwood asked me to tell Angela and Ben Miller, Bethany's father, that she was fine, but things were getting uncomfortable out in Hollywood. Publicity for her movie was heating up and it was still months away from release. Bethany's agent and other people around her insisted this would rocket her to stardom, but now she wasn't sure she wanted to be a star. She had been happy with commercials and recurring roles in family-friendly sitcoms. She was considering coming home and dividing her time between the family diner and community theater.

It had to be bad, for Bethany to want to give up on her dream. I trusted her instincts and common sense.

"Angela especially needs to be warned, because London and Athena think Bethany staying away is like Athena's mother staying away. To stay safe. To keep people from noticing any inherent magic she might have. No," Sherwood hurried to say, when Felicity and I both flinched. We were positive Bethany didn't know about her heritage. "Athena hasn't told her yet, but maybe Bethany should know, so she can make the right choice?"

"We'll tell Angela. Bethany will listen to her if she doesn't listen to anyone else," I promised.

The next item in his report worried us. Sherwood now had proof that most of our phone problems last night were due to several layers of conflicting energy. Someone else had wrapped energy barriers around Eden. Or they had warped the defensive energy of our town, making it fight itself, like a compromised immune system. Maybe it was a result of the dimensional access portals Sylvia and her allies had used. Sherwood couldn't be sure, because the disharmony shattered and energy levels dropped by half when Sylvia landed in the gym. He couldn't be sure if that was the moment she died, or the effect she had on the disharmony had simply ended when she reappeared in our dimension—meaning she had been prisoner in another all the time she had been missing from the party.

Several attempts had been made during the night to enter Divine's, both during the party and after everyone went home. None had been more than physical attempts to pick locks on doors or pry windows open. The shop's defenses hadn't had to do more than alert Angela to each attempt. Each time she stepped back through the tunnel and turned on a light or the radio, the person outside ran away. In each case, the presence she detected had the distinct unpleasant resonance of a Grandstone. Probably Reggie or his brother Freddie, since their father and uncle weren't physically up to breaking-and-entering any longer.

Hayward and Rodney had made a clean getaway and were on their way to the safe house where the Colonel had planned to hide Toby and Steve just last week. Since I could verify that Rodney had seen very little and been told very little at the "camp" where the rivals had kept him all these years, we didn't have much hope of getting enough information to identify or locate the rivals. We had to be satisfied that he was safe, at least. Maybe over time the fragments of details he remembered would form large enough pictures to help us.

"Here's the really interesting part," Sherwood said.

Now a hint of eager, geeky little boy touched his eyes. Sometimes I really had a hard time remembering he was an Artificial Intelligence.

"We managed to backtrack some sour notes, dominant notes, leading to the discord portions of the energy enclosing Eden. We think now some threads of energy they formed were trying to drain energy from the people inside, having a good time. There were two distinct resonances to the discord. One thread led below Neighborlee. Since the other thread of resonance felt manmade, we have to label the draining thread magical or at least alien, until we know better."

"Big Ugly," Kurt murmured.

"It's nasty. The discord is like acid dripping into your ears, trying to get into your brain." Sherwood shuddered, but then he smiled. A nasty smile. "We learned a lot from it. London and I couldn't figure out how to turn it back on its maker, but we copied it, adapted it so we could control it, and we turned it on the manmade thread."

"I like how you think." Kurt's grin turned as nasty as Sherwood's.

"We did what we could to tangle that thread signal, go back to the source and really mess up things. Once they shut down, they'll have a hard time turning anything on again. We installed a worm version of the acid. If we're lucky, they have no idea it came from us, because they were too busy attacking to notice us coming back up the pipe at them. The enemy should be crippled for a good long time."

"If we're not lucky," Felicity said, "they're figuring out right now what you did, and who did it. Because didn't you say they've been trying to break into FlopDrop? Isn't that like your home, your Internet core or roots or whatever?"

"London migrated off the FlopDrop servers before I was born. Thanks for being worried, though."

"She's got a point," Harry said. "If they're not crippled, then you basically poured boiling water down a rat's nest, and they're smart enough to follow the water trail back to you."

"Any time they try to tag and follow and do anything to our originals and the rest of the team, they'll get zapped. We've been learning as we go. Every time they attack, we ride the signal back through their defenses. We're using their weapons against them. We'll be all right."

We had to take his word for it. Sherwood gave us a recording of the report and conversation we had just had, to send to Athena and Wallace and Cosmo, and play for Angela when we reported to her later in the day. We didn't have much of a chance to discuss everything we had learned once Sherwood signed off. Not ten minutes after he returned to his tinkering, Gordon called.

Chapter Eleven

Sylvia's body had vanished from the county coroner's office. Documentation proved chain of custody was unbroken from Eden to hospital to coroner's office. Preliminary photos had been taken, for identification purposes and to start the inventory of Sylvia's possessions and outward condition. Nobody had notified her family yet. Even though enough witnesses at the scene had identified her as Sylvia Grandstone, they wanted to take fingerprints and dental records, just in case. Someone at the coroner's office likely had experience with things not being what they seemed, when it came to Neighborlee.

She had been put in a drawer in the morgue. The door was locked. Security cameras showed no one had gone in or out of the morgue for the half hour she was there. Then a night shift technician recognized Sylvia's name from the soap she had been on. He and two other techs came down to the morgue to prove it was really her, and discovered the drawer was empty.

Gordon knew there was nothing we could do, but he thought we had a right to know. Grandstones needed to punish someone whenever they didn't get what they wanted. The loss of Sylvia would just make them more vicious and illogical in their reactions. We had to prepare.

We moved from the kitchen to the family room, to be a little more comfortable, and worked on writing down and organizing our memories of the night before. We intended to meet with the Longfellows and add their memories and impressions of last night to ours, to find anything we had forgotten or hadn't considered important at the time. With our semi-pseudo-superhero metabolisms, we went from our late breakfast straight into snacking. Thinking and remembering and discussing was draining and built up an appetite.

After just an hour of that, we needed a break. Felicity rubbed her eyes with her fists like a little girl. For a second there, she reminded me of the first time we had met. Kurt had been escorting me home after earning the wrath of Sylvia once again.

Felicity was on the edge of the playground at the children's home, studying her reflection in a puddle and playing with her newly discovered ability to change her hair color and curliness. Some other kids on the playground noticed and made fun of her. Right before she set off her first EM burst, Felicity had looked tired and lonely and troubled. Just the way she did now, turned sideways in the corner of the couch.

Dang, she hadn't even showed off her engagement ring yet. Shouldn't there have been some balance in our lives, or at least some time to let her be normal and giddy over Jake asking her?

"We're going to solve this and fix things," I told her, reaching over to grab hold of her hand. "I believe God put us together for a reason. It'll work out. We just don't have any idea how yet."

"There are times I really want to believe. You have some peace I really need. Especially with Jake ..." Felicity sighed, loud and deep, and dredged up a smile from somewhere. "Okay, I think it's time to bring him in. Especially since I just figured out what that phone call was when he dropped me off this morning. Someone on the board wants his input, as a security expert. If we don't let him in on what we know really happened, he's going to be heading for migraines and ulcers from the start."

"Especially when we tell him Sylvia killed herself," Harry said. He shrugged and gave us a crooked grin when we just frowned at him in unison. "Think about it. Rodney said she was the one opening the doorway, right? She brought him in, and she messed up enough that he got sick, so she went stomping off to do things her way, just like Grandstones always do. She messed up, fighting with Angela, opened a black hole, and got sucked into it and drained herself."

"Maybe," I said, thinking back to that swirling of dirty oil slick and what Sherwood had said about the discord from below Eden that seemed to be trying to drain energy away.

"So maybe Big Ugly isn't on their side at all," Kurt said, nodding, after I explained what I had been thinking. "It just took advantage of the trouble Sylvia caused."

"It sounds to me like the rivals woke him up and made him cranky. Remember what Angela's doctor friend said, and our theory about trying to make contact. Maybe Sylvia's team was using the energy generated by all the people being in Eden last night, to try to make contact or even open the doorway for Big Ugly," Felicity said. "Either it got mad, or it was sucking on all the energy she was feeding it and messed up."

"What if it's still there, waiting for another feeding?" Pete said. "What if the other guys woke it up enough that it won't go back into hibernation like it usually does after it tries to break out and you guys slap it back?"

"As soon as Eden is cleared for normal activities and they take down the crime scene tape, traffic increases, the energy being generated by all those people goes up … and the draining starts up again. And maybe this time Big Ugly has enough energy to make even worse things happen than people falling through time slips," Kurt said.

"We won't let it," Felicity said. "At least, we need to get into Eden while it's empty and force a showdown with that thing. We're kind of like bait, right? The three of us with whatever makes us different. It'll come out and maybe we can trick it into being stupid, and we fight it and drain its power down enough to make it go back to sleep. Like we always do. Right?"

"Getting into Eden is going to be the tricky part," I said.

"Gordon." Kurt rubbed at his eyes. "We're expanding the circle to let Jake in, why not Gordon? He has some Lost Kid blood in him. He seemed to be more immune than most people last night. What could go wrong?"

I was pretty sure he was partially sarcastic. Still, the idea needed to be examined from all sides before we took that big step. It wasn't like Gordon needed to know all the facts. He wasn't going to marry one of us. Not like Jake. For a second I hesitated, wondering if we had told Felicity about Gordon proposing to Mandy.

"Think it over," I said. "Gordon plays by the rules. Even if he doesn't turn us over to the people with straightjackets and rubber walls, he might still report us to the Chief, who might feel duty-bound this time to report us to the Feds. Yes, he protects Neighborlee like he knows what's going on, but sometimes something is big enough and dangerous enough, you don't keep it secret from the big guns." I held up my hand to stop him when Kurt opened his mouth to retort. "At the same time, Gordon is the only one I'd trust to at least consider friendship ahead of duty."

"He's been through enough weirdness with us by now, he shouldn't be surprised or have a heart attack or something," Felicity offered.

"And if he decides we're aliens in people suits and he has to turn us in?" Kurt said.

"Wait a minute." Felicity's laugh sounded like she had been gargling gravel. "I thought you were the one voting to tell him the truth. Now you're talking like he can't be trusted."

"I trust Gordon as much as I trust Jake," I offered. "The thing is, if he chooses duty over us — if he doesn't get royally ticked with us for making him choose — how do we protect ourselves?"

"If his freak-o-meter doesn't make him blow a gasket, I guess you have to kill him," Pete said. "Better start now thinking about how you'll dispose of the body."

He was joking. At least, I hoped he was joking.

~~~~~

If we were taking our lives into our hands, it was only right that we enjoy our last meal in freedom. Felicity called Jake and I ordered the deluxe ribs-and-wings-and-pizza package from Mancuso's. Jake arrived at the same time Harry got back with the food, and we gathered around the table and feasted. Felicity finally showed off her ring, and we congratulated them and asked about their plans. It was the most perfect thing I ever could have imagined. A swirl of shimmering rainbow through a long, lozenge-shaped, old-fashioned-looking diamond. Not so big it got in Felicity's way in everyday living. Delicate yet sturdy, and kind of dreamy.

Too soon, Jake made the mistake of asking what happened at Eden, because yes, he had been called by several members of the board of directors for his input as a security consultant. So the meal wasn't quite as fun and lighthearted as I could have wanted. Still, that made it easier to ask him if he wanted to come with us when we went to Eden to investigate something. If Gordon would help us do that. As soon as Jake agreed, Kurt called Gordon and gave him the bare bones of our request: Would he help us get into Eden to walk around and test some theories? Gordon didn't hesitate to agree, and in twenty minutes we were out the door.

We had decided Felicity wouldn't tell Jake about us being semi-pseudo-superheroes just yet. If we met up with Big Ugly at
~~~~~

medium energy level and survived, that would prove to Jake we weren't delusional lunatics when we made the grand revelation. And maybe he would be impressed and glad enough just to be alive, he wouldn't walk away from Felicity and cancel the engagement before it was twenty-four hours old.

Did I mention despite my snarky attitude, I'm a cock-eyed optimist?

Gordon was waiting when we pulled into the parking lot of Eden, the four of us in my Jeep. I left my brothers behind. Same old thing about them being ordinary mortals and my sisterly duty to protect them. Gordon was waiting by the front door, dressed in jeans and a sweatshirt, meaning he was off duty. He carried Gina's six-inch diameter key ring and had unwound some of the crime scene tape from across the door. I assumed that meant he had official permission to let us into the building.

"If you touch anything, change anything, take anything away, my career is on the line," he said. "We're allowed in because you were witnesses, but the Chief isn't real happy about it," he said, when we were all inside the lobby and shivering.

The heat had been turned off. Someone probably held to the theory of a gas leak at the root of the weirdness, even though no one had been able to find one for the last three days.

"So, what are you looking for?" Gordon added, when we just stayed in a lump in the lobby and looked at each other.

"We'll know it when we see it. And it's a good sign if we do see it." Felicity stepped away from me and looked around. "The only time you ever saw it was here, right? So we can pretty much stay here. No need to go walking around, you think?"

"Saw what?" Gordon said.

"A stargate on acid, maybe," Kurt said.

"Either I'm still wiped out, or I ate some of the sabotaged food, because that makes sense." He tried to smile. "The problem is that some of the freaky weirdness, people vanishing and losing hours from their lives, that started before Sylvia showed up."

"Actually, it looks like she was in town long before Christmas, just staying off the radar," I offered. "I wouldn't blame drugs, though, because how could she get into people's houses?"

"Why do you have to be so logical? I know a couple dozen people who want so much to blame the Grandstones." He sighed.

"Just to have ammunition to fight back when the family finally makes a fuss over her body vanishing."

"No word yet?" Jake asked.

"On the body or their response?"

"Wait," I said. "They know Sylvia's dead, they know her body vanished, but they haven't declared war yet?"

"Freaky, huh?" Gordon crossed his arms and hunched his shoulders. "I swear, part of the reason the Chief agreed to this was because he's desperate for some answers, even if they're dripping with Neighborlee weirdness."

"You got that right." Felicity rubbed her sweater-clad arms. "Nothing yet. I'm almost hoping I'm wrong."

Jake watched her, a few frown creases forming between his eyebrows. "What do you expect to happen?"

"Lanie and I saw something last night," Kurt said. "If it comes out of hiding, that might explain some of what happened. Not that it will really do any good, because only someone who grew up here will believe it."

"That's not much good if I can't put it in an official report for the Chief," Gordon said. "He can't file an explanation that sounds like the lunatic fringe of fandom, who wouldn't know reality if it gave them a black eye. What did you see? Or think you saw?"

"On a wild guess … some kind of interdimensional wormhole effect. Something is trying to get through, or just reaching through to take something from us." Felicity shrugged. "I wasn't here last night, or I'd have some experience to solidify …"

There was a new stillness to her, a tightness in her jaw, a hard, determined light in her eyes. She was like someone getting ready to go into a dangerous situation, with the possibility of not getting out in one piece, and refusing to feel afraid. I turned to look where she was staring.

I'm proud to say I remembered to pray, and it was more than just the standard panicky *Help, God!* type of prayer that seemed to be all I could manage in tight situations lately.

This face of Big Ugly hadn't changed much from the last time we faced it. Still a hazy oil slick hanging vertical in the air, all dirty rainbow-shifting, a few sparkles with utter blackness at their core. Gut instinct insisted I was dead meat—and maybe not even recognizable as dead meat—if that thing got its metaphorical claws into me.

A whirlpool in the middle of the oil slick pulled my gaze down into it. I felt like I was falling, even though I knew I was securely seated in my wheelchair. Any second now, I would fall out of my chair, just from trying to resist the sensation. I turned my eyes away before my supper came up my throat.

"Somebody please tell me they're filming a movie," Gordon said.

I looked around at the others, and they had turned their gazes away, too. At least long enough to keep from throwing up. The oil slick just hung there in the air at the far end of the lobby, alive and alert and waiting for something.

"Why is it just hanging—"Kurt let loose a stream of curses and moved back.

The whirlpool glided forward.

I wanted to snark at him about speaking too soon, but I was too busy holding onto my chair and my dinner, with my mind racing to figure out what to do. Something had changed in that swirling vertical oil slick.

It angled toward Felicity.

She took a step backward.

She *tried* to take a step. Her feet sort of sank into the pale green speckled tiles. Like maybe reality wasn't quite as solid as it used to be. Kind of the opposite of what happened to the narrator who visited the outskirts of Heaven in Lewis's *The Great Divorce*.

Kurt made one of those lunges that big, strong, heroic guys are good at, and reached for Felicity. The floor stuck to his feet after the second step. He went partially to his knees when the rest of his body kept moving. I could almost hear his ankles snap.

"Lissy!" Jake managed four steps, reaching for Felicity, before his feet got stuck.

Interesting. The guy *without* superpower had less trouble. Maybe Big Ugly didn't sense him as clearly as us?

Gordon picked up a folding metal chair from the rolling chair rack directly behind where I sat, and flung it right into the spinning mouth of the thing.

The chair vanished.

Felicity managed to take a step backwards.

Leave it to a cop to think of a simple, somewhat violent, cave-mannish, brilliant solution.

"Keep it up! It weakened for a second." Felicity sounded like she was choking.

Gordon grabbed another chair and threw it. Something shot out of the spinning center and slapped at him. It was like a tentacle, kind of sparkly in a dirty, dull way. He ducked back out of the way just in time. Maybe there was a limit to the length of the tentacle? It retracted and shot out again, just a little longer.

"No you don't!" I growled, picked up a chair with my brain, and swatted at the thing. It forgot about Gordon. Another tentacle shot out at me, again falling short. Gordon picked up another chair and hit the tentacle. Big Ugly shook. The tentacle snapped off and evaporated. Another tentacle leaped out at him. I flung a second chair.

We took turns lobbing chairs at the vortex. Big Ugly couldn't seem to comprehend there were two of us attacking it with chairs. I mean, if I was a mad scientist who designed the thing, I would have made it have more than one swatty tentacle at a time, right?

By the time we ran out of chairs, Felicity unstuck her feet from the floor long enough to get to Kurt and Jake. They grabbed hold of her and headed for the door. Yeah, good idea — but we ran out of chairs. The vortex scooted around like it was on roller skates and blocked the door.

Meaning it understood what doors were for.

"Okay …" Gordon staggered over to me. "What was that?"

"What was what?" I rubbed the sweat off my face. Anybody who says telekinesis is simple is lying. I swear it uses up five times as many calories lifting something with my brain as it would if I could lift it with my hands.

"Whatever it is that lets you do your lifting, it's visible."

Kurt and Jake stagger-dragged Felicity over to us, so the five of us were all together in one lump.

"Visible. Like … the Id Monster visible?" I had no idea why images from *Forbidden Planet* kept coming into my brain.

"Something was coming out of you and lifting those chairs. Neat trick." Gordon swallowed hard and rubbed sweat off his face, meaning he had been working just as hard. "But kind of freaky."

Big Ugly had recuperated, maybe digesting all those metal

chairs we tossed down its throat. It expanded and the swirling got faster and I swear, it seemed to be staring at Felicity again and licking its metaphorical chops.

"It wants Felicity. Maybe all the energy she has in her EM bursts," Kurt said, staring at the thing. Maybe he got the same impressions I did, meaning I wasn't delusional. Scary thought.

Gordon and Jake gave us a *What the heck are you talking about?* look. Felicity shifted from confused to ticked to mad. The panicky, frozen look she had been wearing until Kurt and Jake yanked her free, while we distracted Big Ugly with folding chairs, was gone. Now she was zapping mad.

Now I knew what Kurt and Gordon had been talking about, when they said they could see what I had been doing with the chairs. Felicity glowed. I saw little slithering lightning bolts traveling across her skin. Not across—below the skin. Soon she was crisscrossed with these glowing threads, a lot of it concentrated around her eyes and hands.

"That's it," she growled, and shook free of Kurt and Jake.

They were trying to hold her down, like they thought she'd go airborne and fly into the mouth of that thing. It seemed to be creeping up on us and expanding, so it extended through the ceiling and floor in those few seconds we talked.

"I've had enough of you. Do you hear me? Nobody messes with my town!"

Then Felicity kind of … exploded.

She flung her glowing hands at the thing and lightning burst out of her skin, through her clothes, in a halo effect. I wouldn't have been surprised if all her clothes burned off, there was that much power. Three thick, solid streaks of light shot out of her eyes and mouth, and two more from her hands, and they all converged into one shimmering, glowing, blinding bright, kind of snaky stream of power that hit the center of the oil slick of Big Ugly dead-on. Kind of like the power streams from the Ghostbusters' guns during the penultimate scene of the movie.

Everything went electric blue tinged with white. That oil slick look evaporated and my impression of something licking its chops changed to overwhelming surprise. Then horror. I swear, I felt something shriek in the back of my head. Like a really bad melodrama villain in a cheesy space opera shouting, "No, this can't be happening, I'm invincible!" Just before exploding into space dust. Followed by a moment of silence, when the tattered remains of his big, floppy black cloak fluttered to the ground.

No explosion. Just this subliminal popping sound, and Big Ugly blinked out. Just vanishing. Like turning off a light switch.

Talk about anti-climactic.

"I did it," Felicity whispered. She sank back into Jake's arms, shaking. But it wasn't scared or weak shaking. It was the *We're alive and we shouldn't be,* and the *Freaks rule!* kind of shaking. Then, being the smart chick she was, she grabbed Jake and planted one on him. Well, yeah, they were getting married, they were allowed to do that kind of stuff now. Only not in public, okay?

Gordon must have been thinking the same thing, because he kind of turned sideways away from them, and gestured for Kurt and me. We huddled together. They were pale. I was glad I was sitting down.

"Want to tell me what's going on?" Gordon demanded, and he sounded a lot like a police officer. I wondered if he was cranky because he wanted to grab Mandy and celebrate surviving with her, like Jake and Felicity were still celebrating behind us. Only thank goodness they weren't making any sucking sounds. That would have been gross.

"What do you mean, what's going on?" Kurt grabbed hold of the handles of my chair and leaned on it for support, kind of putting me between him and Gordon. The coward.

"I saw what Lanie and Felicity ... something came out of them. I've read enough science fiction, seen enough movies, I can guess and come up with some descriptive language to ..." He sighed and scrubbed his face with both big hands. "Power. Telepathic abilities becoming visible. But ... oh... heck." He raked his hands through his hair. "That whacked-out Parker kid wasn't totally psycho, was he?"

"No, he has powers of his own. It's easier for him to believe he got them from me when my back was broken, than to accept he's a mutant freak from outer space like the three of us," I snapped. Then, because I was exhausted from what had just happened, I laughed. Not a good laugh. Kind of sick. It had been a rough couple of days.

Gordon stared at me for a few seconds, then he laughed too.

He pulled up the rolling chair cart and sat down on it. The ancient cast iron groaned under him. He rubbed at his face again and looked up as Jake and Felicity unstuck themselves from each other and moved over to join us.

"I heard part of that," Jake said. "The three of you? So, if Lanie lifts things with her mind and Lissy shoots lightning bolts, what do you do, Kurt?"

"He fixes things. Makes cars without distributor caps run, borrows other people's talents. He can zap things when I don't have control." Felicity shivered and held up her hands, waggling her fingers for a few seconds. "Whatever that thing did to me ... I can think straight now. It was draining me. Feeding off me. It ... I don't know ... unblocked something inside my head. I don't know how I know, but it burned away whatever was interfering with my control."

"You mean you can turn it on and off now, and you won't be frying any more computers or coffee machines?" I said, catching on. That would be great. Having that bright blue electrical tape in my house to mark off the no-zap zones really did interfere with the décor.

"I think so. We won't really know until I'm pissed again, and nothing gets fried." She grinned at Kurt, who grinned back, teeth bared just a little snarky-fierce. Felicity had unintentionally killed some of Kurt's nifty gizmos when she got upset in close proximity to something he was working on. It would be nice if that didn't happen anymore.

"So ... you really can fly?" Gordon said, turning back to me. What was with this guy, that he wouldn't let go of that one thought? Oh, yeah, he was a cop, and technically on duty, since he had the keys to let us into Eden to investigate.

"I used to be able to," I said, nodding. "Before I broke my back. Not really flying, like Superman. Controlled gliding. Big, long hops from one place to another."

"My talent lets me borrow hers," Kurt said, settling on the other corner of the cart Gordon sat on. "I can put controls on it, like I do with Felicity's talent. The three of us go flying at night sometimes, to patrol the town."

"Patrol the town ..." Gordon nodded, and a wicked grin caught one corner of his mouth and lit his eyes. "You wouldn't believe some of the stories I've heard from the guys on night patrol. Some big, bat-thing on clear nights. A guy reports it only once or twice, then he gets razzed by the others enough times he doesn't say anything more. Or look up at the sky."

"Oh, great," Felicity muttered. "I thought you said nobody would see us if we were careful."

"I don't have an invisibility screen." Kurt shrugged, looking like he fought not to laugh. Because it really wasn't a laughing matter. Even though Gordon must have found some humor in it. Or maybe that was just the stress of what we had been through.

"So … what else can you do?" Jake still had his arm around Felicity's waist, like they were glued together in some way after that celebratory kiss. I was glad to see he tightened his arm, pulling her closer, instead of starting to move away.

"Well, I can change the color and length of my hair, when I'm really bored and concentrate really hard. No dye or curlers needed. And I think my gift for animals is part of whatever makes us... us," she said. "And no, I have no idea if I'll pass it on to our kids." She let out a loud breath. "But Lost Kids can marry ordinary Humans and have kids, because Gordon's great-grandmother was a Lost Kid, and so is Mr. Longfellow. So I hope you still want to have kids, like we were talking about last night. So … that about sums it up. Please don't take back the ring?"

"Hey, I staked my claim and you said yes and nobody and nothing is getting between us. Not even what just happened." Jake put her out at arm's length, holding her shoulders so tight I could see his fingers digging in, and he shook her a little. "You said there were a few things you had to tell me, and I'm guessing this was it. You didn't really mean to have it come out like this, though, huh?"

"Not really." She blinked fast, and I knew she was fighting not to cry. Felicity and I have always despised those leaky waterworks kind of girls who cry when things get mushy and cry when things are fantastic and cry at happy endings and sappy stories. Ugh.

"So … you're marrying Wonder Woman, huh?" Gordon laughed when Jake went still and his eyes widened a little.

"So, yourself," Kurt said. "You're not going to turn us in to the Chief and the Men in Black, are you?"

"Neighborlee looks after its own," he said, getting up from the chair cart. I swear the big iron thing groaned in relief. "This is one of those times when you ignore the weirdness and close ranks against the outside world. From what you were saying about patrol, what you two were obviously doing last night ... the three of you are protecting the town, just like I do. That's cool with me."

"So, maybe we should figure out what you're going to tell your boss," Jake said.

"So maybe we should report what just happened to Angela, before we do anything else," I said.

Jake was going to ask why we would involve Angela. I could see it in his eyes.

"Angela has been guarding Neighborlee for a lot longer than any of us really want to think about," Kurt said. "Believe me, the worst thing you can do is leave her in the dark when something like this happens."

"She's like an advisory in the Young Wizards series," Felicity added.

Jake frowned for a moment, then his eyes lit up. Okay, he not only knew the literary reference, but he liked those books. Just more proof he was perfect for Felicity. And he was going to fit into the team just fine.

He was just as oblivious as the rest of us, and he was the professional. Jake should have known better than the rest of us just how stupid it was to sit there and wipe away the sweat and laugh. The rest of us should have known better, because after all the years of dealing with Big Ugly and all the other shadowy threats thrown at Neighborlee, we knew the fight was never really over. We should have remembered that we couldn't predict the length of the reprieve between battles.

You know how in the really nasty horror movies, where the heroine staggers out of the woods or out of the water or out of the haunted house? And she keeps trying to get moving, putting a lot of distance between her and whatever lies in bloody fragments behind her? Because she knows the movie isn't over yet, but she can't move? And all of a sudden the thing just rematerializes, madder and stronger and bigger than before?

Yeah, the vertical whirlpool of Big Ugly erupted into existence again, spinning faster, the oil slick darker and dirtier.

The five of us staggered backwards and grabbed tight onto each other. Later, we theorized that Felicity's EM burst had temporarily short-circuited it. Maybe even all those metal chairs we threw down its throat had helped feed it.

Big Ugly had come back even stronger, more intent on swallowing Felicity whole. And taking the rest of us for dessert.

And we had been stupidly sitting there, thinking we had won, talking about stupid things like, "Oh, yeah, didn't we ever tell you we're freaks?"

Stupid, arrogant freaks who didn't have the sense they teach in horror movies to get out of the haunted house before the monster came back for a final try, swinging two hatchets this time instead of one. If there had been a soundtrack playing in those few seconds, it would have sounded like a mix of *Psycho* and *Jaws* and the *Darth Vader March*, all playing at chop-and-liquefy volume.

The ground was shaking under our feet.

"This is it!" I yelled. Or tried to yell. It was more like wheezing, with all the air getting sucked out of the lobby.

"Kurt—grab hold." Felicity reached out one hand for him and her other hand grabbed onto me. "Circuit, like we're flying."

He nodded, his gaze meeting mine. Sometimes, when we really concentrated hard on sharing our talents, we got this buzzing sensation when we held hands. That buzzing came back. For the first time, I felt Felicity as the source. She was finally able to tap into her power, instead of Kurt jury-rigging things. It flowed through us all, joining us together. We were like a booster in the city power grid, reinforcing what came out of her and sending it back to her. She glowed so brightly, I had to close my eyes. Yet I could still see as she gathered up all that juice and shot it at Big Ugly.

This time it roared. The trophies in the display case on the far side of the lobby rattled. A couple tipped over. The acoustic tiles jumped in the ceiling and dirt showered down on us in a really disgusting, powdery rain. The tiles rippled under our feet.

The whirlpool swelled up instead of fizzling, and the power kept blasting out from Felicity like it didn't have any end. The dark oil slick look got darker, with a radiance behind it. Like the way old film strips got all melty on the screen just before they burned through and there was a flash of light in those few seconds before the teacher realized the projector was stuck and she raced across the room to turn off the machine. Yeah, that feeling. Only a thousand times brighter and hotter.

Then with a jolt, everything kind of fell back into place and the rumbling stopped. In that silence, this time I felt like a door had slammed down, closing solid and sealing up.

"It's not gone," Kurt whispered. He finally let go of the two of us and dropped down to the floor to rest his forehead in his hands. "Just like the other times. It's just going away to rest up and recover and build up its strength. And figure out what to do differently next time."

"Just like the other times?" Jake wrapped his arms around Felicity and held her up. Not that she was in any danger of collapsing, because I swear I could hear energy crackling all across her skin and see sparks dancing on her fingertips. She was juiced for sure. "How often do you guys do this?"

"We get years between," I offered. Kurt glared at me, but there was laughter sparking behind his eyes. "Usually."

"Usually," Gordon said, punctuated with a snort. "I'm going to hold you to that. Don't think I could do this every few weeks."

"We don't," Kurt said. "This is a geometric progression up from what we usually face and what we usually manage to do. The last time we felt Big Ugly this active was …" He gave me an apologetic little nod. "It got involved that night at the quarries. We're pretty sure it interfered with the defensive energy around the town, so Lanie couldn't heal like she should have."

"You're saying that thing hit her with the garbage truck?" His voice cracked.

"It made the truck go out of control, and made Toby's jacket get stuck," I said. "I felt energy at work, that weird buzzing we all felt." I looked between Gordon and Jake. "You both felt that?"

"Oh … yeah," Jake said. "And I don't want to go through that again any time soon. How are you feeling, Lissy? How did you do that? I didn't know …" He leaned back a little, eyes narrowing, and I could almost hear the clattering in his brain as he put things together. "The other night, when everything went off in my car … was that you?"

"That was the old Felicity," Kurt said. "She's always had trouble with her EM pulses. Any equipment she killed, it was accidental."

"Until now," I said, listening to my gut instinct.

"Yeah." Felicity swallowed hard and tried to smile. "It's controlled now." For a few seconds that power hissed and crackled in her voice, too. "I can access it now. I can feel where it's waiting. And it's just waiting, not constantly building up and fighting me. No more accidents anymore."

"You really think it's over?" Gordon rubbed at his face again and put out a hand to lean on the upright post on the chair cart. The cantankerous thing tried to roll out from underneath him. He settled for taking a few steps back and leaning against the wall.

"For now." I fought down a giggle as a mental image came up. Of something stomping away in a huff, foiled for now, but like Kurt said, retreating to come back with a better, more dastardly plan. I swear I sensed an attitude in that fraction of a second before Big Ugly vanished, somewhere along the lines of, *I'll get you, my pretty, and your little dog, too.*

Please, Lord, let us find a really big dog to help us, when that thing comes back?

"I've got my own control now, my own trigger and aiming mechanism," Felicity said. "Fighting that thing kind of burned away whatever was blocking me."

"You burned it out this time," I offered, "instead of just feeding it."

"Speaking of feeding it." Kurt raised his head, and he was laughing quietly, wearily, with a kind of drained look that I suspected we all wore. "How are we going to explain all those chairs missing? I'll bet you anything that nothing comes back out of that hole now."

Chapter Twelve

"Blame the drugs in the food last night," Gordon said with a shrug.

"Is that the official story?" Jake asked.

"It sounds a lot more plausible than claiming we fought off an invasion from another dimension. I think the best thing to do is stand back and keep our mouths shut and let them come up with a story that works for them. The less attention we draw to ourselves, the better."

"So you're on our side." If I could have jumped out of my chair and pinned Gordon to the wall with a big, fat kiss, I would have. But I was too tired and he was Mandy's property, officially now, so I wouldn't. No poaching on another woman's territory.

"Hey, you stick with your friends. I know better than to mess up a good thing. Kind of like ..." Gordon sighed and scrubbed at his face again. "Kind of like going against Divine's."

"Trust your instincts, Grasshopper," Jake said, trying to sound like the old wise teacher in *Kung Fu*. He grinned and pulled Felicity in for another kiss when she giggled.

Yeah, we were all kind of loopy about then, but we were alive and the town was safe.

At least, safe as long as someone didn't poke too deep into explanations and got out their super-duper science fiction-type paranormal phenomenon measuring gizmos. And what were the chances of that happening in small town nowhere Ohio?

Kurt called Angela to make sure it was all right for us to come by Divine's. The discussion of what had happened at Eden didn't take up much of the evening, probably in consideration of Jake and Gordon, whose minds had been stretched and their sanity strained enough already. Instead, we turned it into an engagement celebration for Jake and Felicity.

~~~~~

Things were really quiet for the next week or two. Gordon was deeply involved in the investigation into what happened at Eden. Jake, as the local security firm, was involved in
~~~~~

recommending different testing labs, translating some of the information the various scientists and engineers gave the city into understandable English for the council members who didn't go far out of the county for their higher education. Most of the people who grew up in Neighborlee stayed in Neighborlee. Except the people who just didn't fit in, or got their brains polluted by big city thinking and decided the small-town mentality was limiting and backwards. I always considered it protective and nurturing. But then, Neighborlee was my personal responsibility.

The weird part? The silence from the Grandstones. They considered the news of Sylvia's death and the disappearance of her body a childish joke in bad taste. They insisted Sylvia had never come home for Christmas or New Year's. In fact, Reggie and Freddie were both heard to say that Sylvia never came home for holidays or any kind of visits, and she wasn't missed.

That, combined with what we had discovered about the Grandstones' actions over the years, corrupting Lost Kids, gave us a few theories. Either the Grandstone clan had written off Sylvia as a lost cause because of her failure to capture the heir of the Sheridan empire. Or they denied her presence at New Year's because she had failed so utterly and they feared retribution from the real bosses in the war to rule Neighborlee.

The media was quiet, too. The Neighborlee effect meant that the media, local and national, didn't pay much attention to what happened at Eden. Conrad cooperated with the request of town officials to keep things quiet. The newspapers and TV stations ignored the visits of official investigative teams. Maybe because very few stories left the borders of Neighborlee.

Between the people who didn't want to remember the events of New Year's, and the ones who didn't want to talk about it, and maybe some lingering residue of whatever made people forget the weird events shortly after they happened, there just wasn't much talk in town. Sometimes we had to wonder if we had hallucinated everything. I was willing to wake up and find out I had been sick and dreamed the whole weird week.

No such luck. A few people did remember and talk about events, but furtively. Gina remembered, and I felt sorry for her because she felt responsible. Despite everybody who mattered assuring her she did the best she could. The entire board of directors commended her for keeping people calm and protected. Then they sent her on a cruise. If she didn't email me several times about the balmy weather in the Caribbean and asking if I had heard anything about the investigation, I might have suspected she had been sent somewhere to shut her up. Like the rivals had arranged for her to disappear, so they could pump her for the truth of what had happened.

(We really did need to come up with a better name for them.)

Well, the board did it to reward her for her hard work and keep her from thinking she was going to lose her job. It was a good time to go away. She had nothing to do and would have brooded, sitting at home, because nobody was allowed into Eden during the investigation of the crime scene.

Jake and Gordon brought us an unofficial copy of the report. Those scientific and technical personnel very clearly had no experience with the weirdness we dealt with regularly.

Sonar and other highly technical equipment uncovered fault lines deep beneath the town. They were related to the "natural" tunnels that had been found while digging the quarries. Supposedly. Toxic elements had been leaching into the soil and the groundwater. The engineers threw around geological and engineering terms, claiming chemicals and other poisons had been filtering through the ground for decades, coming from factories several cities and counties away. They pointed to all sorts of factors that made it plausible (for them, maybe) for the poisons and gases to have migrated and collected into these caverns under Eden. The building had been a manufacturing plant decades ago, which contributed to the toxic elements. The engineers said the fault lines and tunnels were no threat to the stability of the building. Short of a major earthquake, of course.

When we got to that part of the report, we all just raised our heads and looked at each other and variously shook our heads or rolled our eyes and made *yeah, right* sounds. Maybe under normal conditions, the building could stand up to an ordinary, everyday, scientifically plausible earthquake. If a totally impossible earthquake was going to happen, it would. At the worst possible time. With nudges from outside sources that nobody would believe in. Except maybe guardians.

The supposed experts theorized all those alleged toxins in the ground and water table had been stirred up by shifting in the soil, caused by the rapid series of freezing and thawing that Neighborlee had been suffering since October. Various poisons had been mixed together and had worked their way up into the foundations of the building, and from there leaked into the air system. By themselves, nobody would have suffered anything more than headaches and fatigue. Hiram was conscientious to the point of being OCD about cleaning air ducts and filters and such every month at Eden. The regular flushing of the ventilation system would have eliminated the buildup of gases before anyone was seriously harmed.

What is the dividing line between *harmed* and *seriously harmed*? Sick is sick in my book. The person suffering headaches and nausea and dizziness is just as miserable as someone with a migraine and anaphylactic shock, as far as I'm concerned.

When warmer weather returned, the natural venting that occurred in the warmed, aerated soil (and a whole ton of other scientific terms I didn't bother writing down) would have removed the threat. However, the gases had built up to an unusual level in Eden because of the new roof with extra thick insulation. Gee, when the city decided to conserve energy by insulating, they didn't realize they were poisoning themselves, did they?

Thanks to exhaustion, bad eating, the excitement of the holidays, the dyes in new clothes, fumes from various products given as gifts and made in China, and a whole host of other phenomena, the people who gathered at Eden on New Year's Eve were triply vulnerable to what they had been able to ignore for the last two months.

Then the report got serious and a little scary.

Until then, we had been kind of snickering and smirking at the theories presented by the experts. Seriously? The time warps and people being drained of energy, and the battle with Big Ugly, trying to suck Felicity into an alternate dimension, were delusions resulting from a *toxic chemical buildup*?

Sylvia had come loaded for bear on New Year's Eve. The analysis of some of the food at the party and residue in several glass vials found in the lining of her expensive coat revealed a new type of drug. It was easy to extrapolate that she had managed to insert some of that drug into food laid out on the buffet tables. She had only contaminated a little of the food. The drug was so new, it would take months of testing to determine what its effects and intentions were and the designer and source.

Supposedly, all the toxins in the air of Eden might have only made people feel ill, but the drugs had tipped the partygoers over the edge into hallucinations. The new, unknown drug was the catalyst that brought everything else together.

Seriously? People vanishing? Pamelia falling from the ceiling and breaking her arm? No one had seen her climb up through the streamers without breaking them and she didn't even remember climbing, and there was no ladder anywhere to be found in the gym that night. Including the kids who vanished *days* before they ate any of the food? The disappearing equipment and party supplies days before Sylvia showed up at Eden? Someone must have asked those questions, because there was an addendum to the report stating Sylvia had been seen in town for at least two weeks before Christmas. (Okay, so that meant I hadn't been hallucinating. Comforting?) The theory was that she had been sneaking around and sabotaging Eden the whole time.

What's the saying? *There is none so blind as he who refuses to see.*

Or maybe more accurately: he who wants so desperately to see something else?

Now the silence from the Grandstones made sense. They were disavowing Sylvia and showing no concern for her death and missing body to protect themselves from being implicated in her actions.

"They will be lying low for quite some time," Angela speculated. "Busy trying to convince everyone that they are innocent and injured, too busy to cause trouble for us for some time. It's rather sad that they are so bound up in their schemes and manipulations, they can't even mourn properly."

"Can we hope things are going to be quiet on our side of the war?" Kurt said. "For a while? Enough time to catch our breaths?"

"Hmm, there are some developments that might prove to be interesting. I'm waiting for a follow-up to that note our hoped-for allies left with Franklin when they brought him back here."

"You're not going to tell us any more than that, are you?" Felicity accused.

Angela just wore her usual little smirk implying she knew far more than she was willing to reveal. After all this time, I was willing to let her keep things secret and have surprises, because I knew Angela would never leave us ignorant to our harm. When we needed to know, she would tell us.

"I would be grateful for some really boring routine for a good long while. You pushed the freak-o-meter to its limits." Gordon's lopsided grin meant he was our friend, not the cop speaking. "You gave it some new limits. But you're *our* freaks. Our town protectors. And like Mandy said a few days ago ... not that she knows what's going on, but something makes me think she suspects, and I think she ought to be let in on the secret because ... well, come on, we're getting married, y'know?" He shrugged, then rubbed his face with his hands, like he needed to yank his thoughts back on track. "You've proven that you're working for the good of the town, and I'd be really stupid to threaten the balance you've kept going for so long."

"Yeah, we were talking about it," Jake said, nodding to Gordon and visibly taking up the thread of what he was saying. "I love Felicity, and you two are good friends, and you're the same people you were in November. I don't want to lose her and I don't want to lose you guys, either. The way I see it, finding out about your mutant stuff is like discovering you have a hobby we never knew about."

"Some hobby. Kind of on the scale of difference between building model planes and building a working spaceship out in the barn, yknow?" Kurt said with a grin.

"Kind of, yeah, and seriously? It's something I would expect of you. But we can live with that. Maybe we can't live without it." Jake lifted Felicity's hand to his lips and kissed the finger with his engagement ring on it.

"Not that any of us have had time to think much lately, but the way I figure it," Gordon said slowly, "I guess I've always suspected something. Known something is weirder around you three than the normal weirdness that's in our town. If I can, I'd like to help with this whole hunt for other Lost Kids, tracking down the ones who got taken."

"Some more brains tuned into it might be helpful," Kurt said, nodding.

"I'd rather be working with you than against you. It's safer being Spider-Man's friend than siding with Jameson."

The rest of us laughed. We needed to laugh. If Gordon could think of Marvel Comics at a time like this, then he was back to normal and we weren't going to lose him to the mental blindness that was a self-defense mechanism when the freak-o-meter went off the scale.

"I can tell Mandy, bring her into this, can't I? I mean, how can I keep this secret from her? And she'd be a really big help with organizing material and finding information maybe you can't."

"Yeah, it'd be good to have Mandy working with us," I said, speaking for all three of us. Kurt and Felicity nodded, but I knew they'd agree even before I looked at them for their reactions.

Our team was having a population explosion. Stanzer before Christmas, and now Jake, Gordon, and Mandy. Maybe this was a sign of things changing. For the better or the worse? I realized a long time ago that God doesn't grant abundance, He doesn't wake up opportunities or new talents or support, *unless a need is approaching.*

Gordon brought Mandy over for a meeting at my house two days later. The wide-eyed, quiet look she gave us when she walked in the door meant Gordon had told her everything. I wondered if she'd be bubbling with questions or just quietly watch us all evening. The purpose of this meeting, besides bringing things out in the open, was to finally take a serious look at the DVD of information my folks had sent from Bermuda before they vanished. We had me and my brothers, Kurt, Felicity and Jake, Stanzer, Gordon and Mandy, Angela, Ford, all the Longfellows, Wallace and Cosmo. We moved the TV around so we could see it in the kitchen, and gathered around the table so Felicity could make a map of the whole world, as Mum and Pop's information displayed on the screen. We included the information Col. Hayward gave us after Christmas.

"The thing is," Kurt said, after we had worked until nearly 1am on a Friday night and the map of the world was filled with notations. Felicity had started drawing rings connecting things together. "Is Big Ugly really underneath the town? Is it solid, physical, or just a doorway, with the enemy on the other side? And the really big, million-dollar question: *is* it tied into all of this?" He gestured at the map and put his hand on Felicity's, just as she finished drawing a big circle. "You guys see what I'm seeing?" He didn't wait for anyone to do more than lean closer and look at the map. "All these color codes, for strength and frequency of appearances and energy waves and all that other junk ... they don't come within a hundred miles of Neighborlee. And there are three other spots around the world where the same thing happens. Is Big Ugly part of *all* the blank spots, or does each place have its own interdimensional suckage monster? Do we have a bunch of these things to fight?"

"Or are the blank spots associated with other places where Lost Kids are showing up?" Mandy asked in the silence as we digested that.

The three of us must have had the freakiest *duh* expressions ever to grace the planet. Pete and Jake burst out laughing. Stanzer just grinned and leaned back in his chair. Gordon gave Mandy an admiring look that clearly said, "She's mine, all mine," and he thought he was the luckiest guy on the planet.

<center>~~~~~</center>

How does life go back to normal after all the things we went through in the space of a few days? Especially considering we hadn't recovered—mentally, at least—from all the stress and ruckus leading up to Christmas.

Well, I guess this was an example of God giving the strength. Or at the very least putting a haze in our minds so we kind of stumbled through and didn't really notice how strange it was that we didn't have more traumatic reactions.

I went back to practices for the Ezekiel's Wheels, and started performing on Friday nights at the club. The money was welcome, but more important, I worked out a lot of my stress and wobblies from New Year's Eve by sniping and exaggerating and griping during my comedy routines. Daniel didn't show up for my first three performances like he had threatened. He was busy with the corporation expansions, and dealing with the fallout from the Grandstones. They blamed him for Sylvia allegedly going silent and running away to Europe with a broken heart. They held with that story for quite a while and didn't renew their campaign to rewrite history and claim most of Neighborlee belonged to them. Looking back, we should have realized what a clear sign that was of the Grandstones being afraid. Of something or someone.

Stanzer met with a few of us the second and third weekend into January, to eat pizza and study the map and try to get more information from the DVD over and over again. We added a few more details to the map.

We spent a lot of time talking about expanding our search for other abandoned children to the entire planet. That was a huge undertaking that kind of scared us. More possibilities meant more work, more false trails, more disappointments. More chances of getting the wrong attention. We hadn't survived this long, protecting Neighborlee's eccentricities from the outside world, to take a chance on winding up in Area 51 now.

Fortunately, we had a professional hound dog on our side now. Stanzer agreed with our need for increased caution. Any ideas, any clues or information Gordon found as part of the investigation, we would turn over to him to handle and follow up on. We settled in for a long wait.

Then Jane came to town.

It was Thursday, one of those unseasonably warm January days that threatens to go straight through spring in three days and turn into summer. I didn't pack a lunch, from laziness and because the leftovers in the house weren't worth mentioning. I decided to leave the leftovers for Pete, since he cooked the night before. That was not generosity, it was punishment. So I wheeled down the street from the *Tattler's* office to enjoy the warm breezes, the wet streets free of slush or icy ruts, and went looking for something really bad for me to eat for lunch. Thanks to my hyper metabolism and all the extra practices for an upcoming game, I never worried about developing writer's butt or wheelchair thighs. I wasn't paying attention until I got across the street. Old habit had me stop and look in the window of the Spindelmutter building, mentally urging the new owner and the spa to be there, at long last.

The brown paper lining the windows was missing. I could see myself in the glass. That usually didn't happen with visions. I stopped, shook my head, and rolled back a couple feet to really look this time.

The brown paper was down and Debbi Kunardi, a realtor friend, stood by the counter, with papers spread all over. I rolled back a few more steps, popped the front wheels up the first step, and heaved myself up. I mentally yanked on the front door to get it open and hold it so I could roll through.

I get careless when I'm excited. So sue me.

"Hey, Deb, what's up? I thought maybe someone had broken in when I saw the paper out of the windows," I said, sliding to a stop with wet wheels on the extremely dusty, old wooden floor.

"Oh, hey, Lanie." Debbi wore her professional mask, which clued me in right then there was a client somewhere in the building.

Sure enough, I heard footsteps in the stairwell that led from the top two floors. Spindelmutter's had a storage room and workshop on the second floor and an apartment on the third floor, with an enclosed staircase to the roof, where they used to set up a wading pool and cabana and lawn chairs in the summer.

"So, is somebody thinking about setting up shop here?"

Please, oh, please, oh, please, let this be the spa I saw in my visions. Please, God? Haven't I earned this? And please let her give massages and facials and those detox treatments?

I had a sudden flash of the perfect wedding or bridal shower presents for Felicity and Mandy: a luxury day at the spa. *Please, let this be the spa? Huh, can I have it? I've been really, really good, haven't I, God?*

"It's perfect," a woman said, appearing in the doorway of the stairwell.

She was one of those quiet, wheat-colored people who seemed rather plain at first glance, blending into the room. Then, after a few seconds, her nice facial bones and deep, blue-green eyes, and the faint hint of reddish streaks in her hair seemed to fade into focus. And a really nice mouth, one corner quirked up like she wanted to smile. She was thin, aerodynamic and athletic thin, not the disgustingly anorexic skinny that had been encouraged in girls since I was in high school.

"Jane, this is Lanie Zephyr. She works at the *Tattler*," Debbi said. "Lanie, Jane is opening up a spa."

"Yes!" I startled both of them with my growled shout and the downward *cha-ching* pump. Jane grinned at me, and I knew we were going to be good friends, and not just because I had been waiting not-so-patiently since that first vision. "You have no idea how much we need a place like yours in town."

"You don't even know what kind of spa she's setting up," Debbi said, laughing.

"Hey, as long as the massage rooms are wheelchair accessible, I don't care. And you have those detox masque things and aromatherapy candles and oils and stuff? And you do bridal party packages?" I pressed my hands flat together like I was praying, earning an even bigger grin from Jane.

"Even if I didn't have them at my old store, I'd bring them here. You're the bride?"

"I'm crazy, but I'm not totally insane. Nope, two of my really good friends got engaged at New Year's, and I want a super splendiferous gift, and a spa day would be perfect. So I take it that means you do offer them?"

"As soon as I get set up," Jane said, nodding. She tipped her head back and looked around the big, open room with the brick walls and vaulted ceilings with fancy gingerbread cornices and all the woodwork around the windows. Stuff that was in fashion eighty or ninety years ago when the building was first built. "This place is perfect. And best of all, I can live right over the shop."

"You know, a tea room where you sell candles and loose tea and other stuff like that, where people can have book clubs and meetings and stuff would be really good for the second floor," I offered.

Jane went perfectly still, like a gazelle that scented the lion. Her eyes lost their focus, and I swear they turned crystalline gray for about two seconds. I hadn't seen that part of the shop in my visions, but I had hoped. Nothing like putting in my vote before the spa was set in stone, was there?

"I've always wanted to do something like that, but my old place was too small. And the people in the town weren't ... of the right mentality for that kind of thing, if you know what I mean." Jane's smile was slow and thoughtful.

Did I say she was the gazelle that scented the lion? I was wrong. She was lion who had just scented new prey.

I realized I was staring at her, trying to match her face with a memory. I was positive, the longer I looked at her, I had met her before. I knew her, but from the politely curious way she looked at me, she didn't know me.

"Lanie, can I hire you to talk to some people I'm having come look at the empty unit in the Dexter building next week?" Debbi said. "If Jane hadn't already signed the lease, I think you could have talked her into it."

"Probably," Jane said, nodding.

My stomach decided to grumble audibly at that point. "Uh, sorry, I was on my way out to pick up lunch. I should get going and get back to work. I'm at the *Tattler.* If you want a guided tour of town, want to meet up with people and find out what's going on, stop on by," I offered.

"That's great. Where are you going for lunch? That'd be a good place to start getting to know the town."

By the time I skidded down off the front step and continued down the street, Jane's sketchy description of what she was going to do with the old Spindelmutter building pretty much matched what my visions had shown me. I was nearly rubbing my hands in anticipation. That would have made it really hard to push my chair. I invited Jane to come to the Ezekiel's Wheels game the next night, but she had to drive back to her place and start packing for the move.

Funny thing, but when I asked where she was from, she said it wasn't worth talking about, and she was glad to put the lazy, spoiled town behind her. When I asked why she chose to move to Neighborlee, Jane got one of those funny looks on her face that I had seen Kurt and Felicity wear when there was a whole lot of information we couldn't share.

"My guardians, my backers, actually, recommended I set up shop here. They say I'm a perfect fit for the town, and I'm needed here. The old farts have never been wrong before," she added with a shrug and a smile. "You'd have to meet Demetrius and Beau to really understand what I mean. Not that they smell bad, but ..." She shrugged again and we all three laughed.

It didn't strike me until later, when I came back, with my lunch warming my lap through my coat and jeans, that she said guardians, like she didn't have any parents. It made me curious about her background. Curious enough to call Stanzer and give him the license plate number of the car I saw sitting in the alley with out-of-state license plates.

Then I grabbed my wheels, jolting to a stop hard enough my

lunch nearly slid off my lap.

Those blue-green eyes … that wheat-colored hair.

Had I been looking over her shoulder in my vision? Was Jane the woman who had gone transparent and flew to where Col. Hayward, Toby and Steve were being kidnapped by the rivals?

Was she their rescuer? The one who had held Hayward for a day before dropping him on the doorstep of Divine's with a gap in his memory? And a note implying future partnership?

Was she friend or foe? What exactly had brought her to Neighborlee?

~~~~~

I mentioned meeting up with Jane to the others on the team, but not my suspicion I had seen her in my vision. I didn't want to prejudice anyone against her until we had some details to work from. We needed time to figure out our strategy if she was an invader.

Yet if she was against Neighborlee, the town should have worked its defensive magic to repel her. Shouldn't it?

I went to Angela with that question. She gave me one of her serene smiles and said she knew about Jane. In fact, she was the one who had suggested Jane move from her previous shop and town to Neighborlee.

She told me nothing more, and I knew better than to pressure Angela for information she wasn't willing to share. As long as she wasn't being caught by surprise, we were good. Right?

Stanzer met with Kurt, Felicity and me for his first report on the events at Eden. The center had just been cleared for activities again as of January twentieth. He also had a full report on Jane.

"Her name is Jane Wilson," Stanzer said, coming into Felicity's living room.

I had been helping with her weekly cook-and-store session. She cooked lots of dishes and divided them up into plastic divided meal dishes, so all she had to do was pop one into the microwave. It saved time in the long run. We used to do the same for me, until my brothers moved in for the duration.

"Who is Jane Wilson?" Kurt said, stopping halfway down into the easy chair that was guaranteed not to have any dog hair on it. One of his newest inventions was a sonic button installed on the underside of the chair that emitted a frequency that kept the
~~~~~

dogs away. He hadn't worked out the bugs yet. It was still the size of a hockey puck, so it hadn't been patented and offered for sale. He would be independently wealthy when the day finally came.

Stanzer looked at me, raising one eyebrow that clearly said, *Didn't you tell them?* Which led to looks from Felicity and Kurt clearly saying, *What were you supposed to tell us?*

Yeah, what need did we have for reading minds?

I gave a quick rundown of meeting Jane a few days before, and my visions of the spa opening in those stressful weeks before Christmas.

"Okay, so you knew she was coming." Felicity nudged Sheba off the couch, flipped the tiger-striped throw off of it, and gestured for Stanzer to take a seat. Then she stopped and a dawning light of understanding made her nod. "Okay ... there's probably some reason you were supposed to watch for her coming."

"I wish that gift of visions was a little more reliable," Stanzer said. "Like with an on and off switch. I could use your help looking for my people. I think Jane Wilson is one of you," he said, once he had settled down and pulled a bunch of photos and reports from a battered accordion folder he had brought with him. He handed the photos to Felicity, who sat next to him. When she finished each one, she passed it to Kurt. His easy chair was on the right-hand side of the couch, closest to Felicity, while my wheelchair was on the left-hand side by Stanzer.

"How do you know? What does her background check say?" Kurt asked.

"Her background is kind of sketchy before the age of twelve. She was raised in a school for the gifted in Pennsylvania. Big estate, hidden in the fringes of the Appalachian National Park. The corporation that runs the school is called Hoax, Inc. They specialize in investigating suspicious activities, such as our New Year's Eve ah ... incident." He raised an eyebrow, reminding me so much of Spock, with that Vulcan smirk of superiority or stifled amusement.

"You think she works for Hoax, and she's in town to investigate Eden?" Felicity said.

"I don't know. She's been in this insulated little backward town. You know the kind, where you drive down the street and you swear you can hear the banjo music from *Deliverance*? She had a little spa there, closed up shop right after the Christmas shopping season. What's really interesting is that this town had a character everyone referred to as the Ghost."

By this time, Kurt had finished looking at the photos and paperwork and got up to hand them to me. The photos were of Jane and a town a lot like Neighborlee, lots of old buildings around a square, with open farmland stretching out beyond it on several sides.

"Seems the Ghost is a local legend, but fairly recent." Stanzer grinned and shook his head. "It was fun investigating, because even though the Ghost has been officially gone for going on three months now, everybody had something to say about him."

"Officially gone?" I prompted, when he paused just long enough I knew he was looking for the right words.

"The Ghost was kind of like a local Superman. Rescued kids from trees, stopped the bullies from sabotaging trucks or creating crop circles, breaking into the waterworks, that sort of thing. They called him the Ghost because he was invisible. You knew the Ghost was there because things would happen. Seems he could fly and walk through walls. What's more interesting is that the people in town got lazy. They complained when the Ghost didn't show up to fix problems. Like some farmer would forget to fill his equipment with gas and get stuck halfway through a job. Instead of taking responsibility, he'd go to town and sit in the bar and complain that the Ghost didn't show up to help him get the crop in before the rain came. Things like that. Well, the Ghost got ticked off and quit. Just a few weeks before Jane announced she was closing up her shop."

"Okay, makes sense," Felicity said, nodding. "If she was working for Hoax, then maybe she was stationed there to watch the Ghost at work?"

"How can you watch—" Kurt jerked sideways, out of Felicity's reach, when she scowled and swung at him. They both grinned, muffling laughter.

"That's what I thought, until I did some more investigating into the Ghost—who delivered his resignation letter to the town trustees meeting." Stanzer pulled a piece of paper out of his folder and glanced over it. "Seems Jane opened up her shop about a month *before* the Ghost first made his … umm, appearance."

"What are the names of the two men who run Hoax?" I said, following a hunch.

Stanzer gave me a narrow-eyed little frown and studied me for a few seconds before shaking his head, his face relaxing into that *I'm not even going to ask* expression.

"Demetrius Huff and Beauregard Taylor."

"The old farts," I said, grinning. "Okay, you suspect Jane is the Ghost. That's why you think she's one of us." Then something that had been niggling at the back of my mind since I met Jane did a cannonball into the front of my brain. I felt about as startled and soggy as I would if someone cannonballed into the Neighborlee pool while I was walking by. "Jane. That Jane! Felicity, get Mrs. Silvestri's pictures?"

She grinned, meaning she understood what I was thinking. She hurried into the long storage closet Kurt had built when we first converted my garage into a cottage for her.

It was the length of the outer wall, with shelves from floor to ceiling down one side and rods for hanging clothes on the other side. She always joked she could roller skate the length of her closet. It kept everything safely out of the way of her dogs, and organized. Which was more than I could say for my house, with two brothers constantly rearranging everything on me. In less than two minutes, Felicity came back out with the photo albums she had been putting together.

Mrs. Silvestri had managed to take pictures of all the children under her care during her long, sometimes bizarre career as director of the Neighborlee Children's Home. Whenever any children were spirited away under unusual circumstances, she moved copies of their records, and especially their photos, to a special file no one knew about. That was a good thing, because the official files had a way of vanishing as if they never existed. We didn't know about her private files until many years later, when we helped her move into her retirement condo.

"I can't remember much, except she was little and pale and her name was Jane and …" I swallowed hard. "Sometimes it seemed like she was invisible. She was near your age, Felicity."

"Okay, that helps." She flipped through the album. We had arranged it by the dates that previously unknown relatives showed up to claim Lost Kids who were suspiciously involved with odd events.

Kurt, Felicity and I participated in the program where graduates of Neighborlee Children's Home came back to work with the children, with craft nights and helping with homework and guiding them where they showed talents. We kept watch for anyone who might be developing special talents. So far, things had been unusually quiet. Maybe there was no stress, no special need for someone to exercise an unusual gift. Or maybe they were quiet, minor talents that could be exercised and practiced without attracting attention. Kurt's handyman skills, or how I learned to hover without anyone noticing.

Felicity found the picture. A school picture of a pale, thin-faced girl with big green-blue eyes looked at us, wide-eyed and kind of uncomfortable. Like she expected the guy behind the camera to jump out and bite her. Stanzer came around behind my wheelchair, so he could see the album sitting on my lap, and he put a picture of Jane down on the facing page. There was maybe fifteen years' difference between the two, but the eyes were the same, only not so wide and wary. Jane grown up had a nice tan and her hair didn't look like she had combed it with her fingers and tied it with a rubber band before she got to the photo room. Jane grown up ran a spa and knew how to take care of her hair.

If she was the Ghost, who could turn invisible and fly, why wouldn't she have a whole lot more confidence than she did as a little girl with budding, bizarre gifts, in a noisy orphanage?

"One way to find out if she's the Ghost." Kurt grinned and leaned back in his easy chair and laced his fingers behind his head. "I'll spend a lot of time with her and see what sort of interesting gifts I pick up. I've never walked through walls before. Should be fun to learn."

"Just make sure you don't get too far away from her. I'd hate for the talent to wear off while you were stuck halfway through those really thick brick walls of the Spindelmutter building." I opted for a snarky tone, since the alternative was to feel sick at the image of Kurt stuck half in and half out of solid brick. That was the only drawback of his ability to borrow talents. Too far away from the person whose talent he borrowed, the talent wore off.

"Ouch," Stanzer said, visibly catching on. "Could I make a

suggestion? Just talk to her?"

"Wait until she's settled in and find out if she's investigating what happened at Eden, make friends with her, then talk to her," Felicity said.

The rest of Stanzer's report, giving us updates on the continuing investigation into New Year's bizarreness, was an anti-climax. I didn't care. We had something new and fascinating to investigate, and maybe, just maybe, we had a big break in our search to find the other kids who were like us.

END

Neighborlee, Ohio

(Title, Original Title, Release Date)

Confessions of a Lost Kid (Growing Up Neighborlee) 05/20
Semi-Pseudo-Superheroes (Dorm Rats) 07/20
Virtually London (London Holiday) 09/20
Living Proof (that no good deed goes unpunished) (Living Proof) 11/20
Night of the Living Proof, 01/21
Quitting the Hero Biz (Hero Blues) 03/21
Bride of the Living Proof, 05/21
Shrunk: The Exile of Maurice (Divine's Emporium) 07/21
Return of the Living Proof, 09/21
Allergic to Mistletoe (Have Yourself a Faerie Little Christmas) 11/21
Dawn of the Living Proof, 01/22
Angela's Knight (Divine Knight) 03/22
The Living Proof Gets the Blues, 05/22

ABOUT THE AUTHOR

On the road to publication, Michelle fell into fandom in college and has 40+ stories in various SF and fantasy universes. She has a bunch of useless degrees in theater, English, film/communication, and writing. Even worse, she has over 100 books and novellas with multiple small presses, in science fiction and fantasy, YA, suspense, women's fiction, and sub-genres of romance.

Her official launch into publishing came with winning first place in the Writers of the Future contest in 1990. She was a finalist in the EPIC Awards competition multiple times, winning with *Lorien* in 2006 and *The Meruk Episodes, I-V*, in 2010, and was a finalist in the Realm Award competition, in conjunction with the Realm Makers convention.

Her training includes the Institute for Children's Literature; proofreading at an advertising agency; and working at a community newspaper. She is a tea snob and freelance edits for a living (MichelleLevigne@gmail.com for info/rates), but only enough to give her time to write. Her newest crime against the literary world is to be co-managing editor at Mt. Zion Ridge Press and launching the publishing co-op, Ye Olde Dragon Books. Be afraid … be very afraid.

www.Mlevigne.com
www.MichelleLevigne.blogspot.com
@MichelleLevigne

Also by Michelle L. Levigne

Guardians of the Time Stream: 4-book Steampunk series
The Match Girls: Humorous inspirational romance series starting with **A Match (Not) Made in Heaven**
Sarai's Journey: A 2-book biblical fiction series
Tabor Heights: 20-book inspirational small town romance series.
Quarry Hall: 11-book women's fiction/suspense series
For Sale: Wedding Dress. Never Used: inspirational romance
Crooked Creek: Fun Fables About Critters and Kids: Children's short stories.
Do Yourself a Favor: Tips and Quips on the Writing Life. A book of

writing advice.

Killing His Alter-Ego: contemporary romance/suspense, taking place in fandom.

The Commonwealth Universe: SF series, 25 books and growing

The Hunt: 5-book YA fantasy series

Faxinor: Fantasy series, 4 books and growing

Wildvine: Fantasy series, 14 books when all released

Neighborlee: Humorous fantasy series

Zygradon: 5-book Arthurian fantasy series

AFV Defender: SF adventure series

www.ingramcontent.com/pod-product-compliance
Lightning Source LLC
Chambersburg PA
CBHW050402190726
48284CB00007BB/2393